Making Love to a Dope Boy

Making Love to a Dope Boy

Kandie Marie

www.urbanbooks.net

Urban Books, LLC
300 Farmingdale Road, N.Y.-Route 109
Farmingdale, NY 11735

Making Love to a Dope Boy
Copyright © 2025 Kandie Marie

All rights reserved. No part of this book may be reproduced in any form or by any means without prior consent of the Publisher, except brief quotes used in reviews.

To the extent that the image or images on the cover of this book depict a person or persons, such person or persons are merely models, and are not intended to portray any character or characters featured in the book.

ISBN 13: 978-1-64556-671-7
EBOOK ISBN: 978-1-64556-675-5

First Trade Paperback Printing June 2025
Printed in the United States of America

10 9 8 7 6 5 4 3 2 1

This is a work of fiction. Any references or similarities to actual events, real people, living or dead, or to real locales are intended to give the novel a sense of reality. Any similarity in other names, characters, places, and incidents is entirely coincidental.

Distributed by Kensington Publishing Corp.
Submit Orders to:
Customer Service
400 Hahn Road
Westminster, MD 21157-4627
Phone: 1-800-733-3000
Fax: 1-800-659-2436

The authorized representative in the EU for product safety and compliance
Is eucomply OÜ, Parnu mnt 139b-14, Apt 123
Tallinn, Berlin 11317, hello@eucompliancepartner.com

Making Love to a Dope Boy

A Street Lit Romance

by

Kandie Marie

Acknowledgments

First of all, I have to thank God for allowing me to still be able to breathe life into the words that come into my mind. Allowing me to share this gift with each and every one of you.

To all of my readers, thank you for your undying patience, love, loyalty, and support over the past three years in my author career. You guys are extremely awesome, and I am so proud to be one of your authors.

To my puffs, my KSLLC fam, Racquel Williams, my sisters, and T'ann Marie and the TMP Family thank you for your constant love, motivation, and encouragement.

My children Neo and Jay thank you for allowing me to be your mommy and my motivation through life.

Last but not least, to my fav notification thank you for being a part of my world.

Chapter 1

Nahima

"Choke me, nigga! Choke me!" I begged in between moans as Isaziah pumped my body with his long, thick dick.

"This what you want? This what the fuck you want?" He gripped his hands tight around my neck, pulling me toward the wall, keeping the head of his dick inside of me.

My back was against the wall, legs wrapped around his waist as he held my thick body with all his strength. Each stroke was slow, deep, and powerful. Every time he slid in and out, he reached a different part of my pussy. With his nine-inch dick having a curve to it, he automatically hit my walls every time. Releasing his grasp from my neck, my man lowered my body gently to the bedroom floor. Positioning my body just how he wanted it, Isaziah slowly entered my booty hole as he used his index and middle fingers to penetrate my pussy.

Yeah, I said it. I loved being double penetrated by him. There was something about being filled completely in both holes that made my pussy cream. Isaziah switched up his tempo as we both knew my body was ready to explode. My body trembled as he dug deeper inside. The more my G-spot was tickled, the louder I moaned. Soon, I was squirting my juices all over our floor and him.

"I love when you make a mess. But I ain't done yet," Isaziah teased, pulling out of me to suck up the remaining extra juices.

I loved rough, nasty, downright freaky sex. But it's a completely different type of dick when it comes from a thugged-out nigga. And Isaziah Marcell Jones was the corporate thug. That was just what my pussy and my heart ordered. My man was more than just a d-boy. Isaziah went from hustling nickels and dimes to still graduating from college, stacking his bread, and creating several lucrative small businesses. But that didn't take him away from the streets. He still would live like he was middle-class, keeping himself way below the radar and never being too flashy.

Isaziah spoke like T.I., fucked like Kevin Gates, and looked like a light-skinned Haitian Idris Alba. I'm not going to lie, I hit the jackpot when getting with him. Just when I thought we were done, he was down on his knees spreading my legs and diving in headfirst. I couldn't respond before my legs were spread apart and my pussy was in his mouth. That man knew how to eat my pussy. Isaziah tongue kissed my pussy slowly, giving me a tongue-lashing that I could barely control. My pussy was singing the longer he ate me. I gripped his dreads like a harness, wrapping them around my fists, digging his head deeper into my pussy. His tongue fucked my pussy hole, and I screamed out his name as I was reaching my climax. My pussy squirted all in his mouth as I yelled and my body trembled.

Isaziah stood up and my juices dripped from his beard. Arching my back, it was my turn to return the favor. I needed to complete my man. Just as the tip of his dick hit my lips, the phone rang.

"Ignore it," I pleaded as I continued to slide his dick in my mouth.

"I can multitask." Isaziah grabbed his phone off the edge of the bed, answering it and placing it on speaker. "What up?"

"Ziah, where you at? We got an issue!" It was Marcus, my boo's right-hand man.

I started to stop, but he instructed me to keep going. "What's the issue, bro?"

"One of the stores got hit for sixty grand. Half of the supply is gone. I think it's probably them fuck-ass spics!" Marcus shouted through the phone all aggressive.

I was trying to stay focused, but Marcus's tone was throwing me off. The limper my man's dick got, my pussy started drying up. Sitting up on the bed, I patted his stomach, whispering for him to handle his business. Putting the phone on mute while Marcus continued his rant, Isaziah sat beside me, rubbing my back.

"Marcus! Marcus! Listen, calm down, it's going to be just fine. I didn't get where I am today by overreacting. I'll call up the head of the Tyshoons so we can all sit and talk. I'll make it a public meeting, so it won't get too crazy. But I'm with wifey right now, so let's link up let's say around eleven." Isaziah finally got that man to shut up.

"Oh, my bad, brah. What's up, Nahima! That's cool, man, just shoot me the location."

Without another word, Isaziah disconnected the call, pushed me back on the bed, then lay across me. Sensing his frustration, I gently ran my ombre blue and black stiletto fingernails across his chest.

"Babe, if the Tyshoons are the ones really behind this, you gotta move with them in caution. You know how Jose can be. But I thought y'all didn't have no beef."

"Exactly. Thus, if it's not them, then who could it be? Everyone else is damn near on my payroll. Most of them niggas wouldn't have half of the shit or the bitches they got if it weren't for us!"

"I've always told you to keep the circle small and be mindful of who works for us. At the end of the day, everyone around you, whether you supply them or they run your streets, you treat like family. Everyone ain't family, even blood."

Turning his head to look me in my eyes, he smiled at me. "Then what do you suppose we do to keep our empire strong, my Nubian queen?"

"Meet with the Tyshoons. You know Jose's girl gets her hair done at Bianca's shop. If you want, I can set it up with her like on some double-date stuff. That way we can make sure it doesn't come off like it's business even though it is."

"What if it was him or his peoples? I'll have to take care of him and leave his children without a father."

"If and when we get to that bridge, we'll deal with it then. But right now, I think we should go grab something to eat before you leave me."

"If I can have you for dessert first, because I wasn't done when Marcus called." Right as Isaziah was climbing on top of me, his phone rang again.

"Who is it, babe?" I questioned, praying it wasn't Marcus again.

"I don't know. It's an unknown number." Isaziah slid his finger across the screen to answer the phone, placing it on speaker.

"Ayo, if this is Z, you may wanna check on your moms. Her house looks like it's on fire," the deep male voice on the other end stated before erupting into laughter.

"Aye, who the fuck is this? And don't play with me like that! You know who the fuck I am?"

"Yeah, we heard all about the big Z. The main plug. But guess what, nigga? Your time is up. See, the Gator Boys are here now. We coming to take over. I hope you ready for a war. We gon' make you a deal right now. You and everyone you know in this city moving weight can give up your suppliers and blocks, work under us for a decent cut, and then it don't have to be no war."

While the man was on the other end flapping his gums, Isaziah and I were preparing to leave the house. No one touches our family. And sparking a house on fire, especially my soon-to-be mother-in-law's, was the wrong thing to do.

"Well, Gator Boys, if y'all still sitting around my mother's house when I get there, please make sure we talk in person. Just a little FYI—don't start a war with people you know nothing about."

"You shouldn't be unaware of who your people know or their intentions. Says a lot about your team. I'll holla at ya folk." The phone disconnected, and by that time, we were fully clothed and searching for the ammo for our guns just in case.

Isaziah's face was filled with emotion. The look of rage filled his eyes, his lips tightened, and his face scrunched up. His hands were balled into fists. Taking a moment, I whispered to him that his mother and baby sister were probably fine and hopefully out of the house in time. With a simple nod as his reply, we made our way out the door, praying for the best but expecting the worst.

Chapter 2

Isaziah

Pulling up to my mother's house, it looked like a murder scene. Her neighbors were all out front, and the fire trucks and ambulances were blocking the street. My first thoughts were if my family was okay. If they were harmed in any way or worse, God forbid, this new crew was going to see what I was made of. Plus, I needed no heat attached to me or my family. We'd lived like normal struggling middle-class niggas for the longest. There was no telling if this would trigger an investigation into my life.

My heart raced as we parked the car on the side of the street behind one of the police cars. I was glad to have the love of my life with me. Nahima had always been my strength. See, she wasn't the average girl most dope boys like me would be attracted to. We met sixteen years ago when I was walking through Times Square. It was October 2013, and I was in New York visiting my family in Brooklyn. I was a country boy in the Big Apple and truly excited. At 22, I had never been anywhere outside of Florida. Plus, I had just started pushing minor weight to help with my college tuition. I was attending Edward Waters College to gain my degree in business management and accounting. I came from a Haitian family, and my mother always instilled in us education and bettering ourselves.

When she used to tell me and my older siblings about her life there, it made me boss up at a young age. I vowed to boss up and make sure that when my money got to a certain level, I would be able to take care of my family for the rest of my life. I didn't want my mother struggling any more than she had to. When I started in the game, I was nervous. But the more I hung around the OGs, my knowledge of the game increased. That October when I took my trip to New York for family, I was also there to meet a new connect.

There was an Applebee's near Madame Tussauds where I was meeting my possible connect that evening. The restaurant was crowded almost to capacity. I was instructed to wait at the bar until further instructions, so when a seat became free, I hopped on it. While I was waiting, this beautiful milk chocolate goddess walked in dressed as Harley Quinn and caught my eye. She was country thick, just the way I like them. She had to be about 200 pounds, but her shape was everything. Her boobs sat up high, her hips were nice and wide, and when she turned around, her booty was round, poking through her neon green and black biker shorts. I knew she couldn't have been from New York built like that. But if she was, I had to at least fuck her before I left the city.

I placed my order with the bartender while still maintaining the visual of the thick cutie in the bar. As I was eating my food, I felt a soft tap on my shoulder.

"Do you mind if we sit here?" a soft female voice asked, moving to the right side of me. It was her.

"Yes, please be my guest, beautiful." I moved the barstool out for her so she could sit.

An older gentleman sat beside her, giving me a nod, acknowledging my presence. My assumption at first was that he was her pimp. I tried my best to not listen to their conversation, but I wanted a piece of her. I wasn't paying for no pussy, though. It was about an hour later when the guy walked off and I received a text from the gentleman about our new partnership.

"Excuse me?" The young lady cleared her throat before speaking to gain my attention.

"Yes, ma'am?" I responded, turning to my right slightly.

"I'm Nahima. My brother will be meeting with you shortly. But I did want to say you are very handsome."

"Wait, your brother? You are—"

"We are who you've been waiting for. I just happened to be in town for Comic Con when he informed me of y'all little meeting. I tagged along for the free food and drinks." Nahima chuckled as she lifted her straw to her juicy lips, taking a sip from her drink.

"Well, you definitely caught my eye when you came in. I caught that you're not from here. So, where do you live?"

"I attend FAMU. I'm majoring in criminal science. I'm also a Delta, and I'm on the majorette team."

"Shit, you aren't that far from me. I attend Edward Waters. I wouldn't mind taking trips to see you. That is if you don't have a man."

"Recently single as of three months ago. So, I been chilling."

"Well, if you are up to it, when your brother and I finish, maybe we can hang out the rest of the night. Hit a party or something. If that's cool?"

"Give me your phone." Nahima reached out her hands as I passed her my phone. They were so soft I didn't want to let them go.

I watched her put her number in my phone, save it, and call herself so she could have my number. We conversed for about twenty more minutes before her brother reappeared. Nahima gave me a wink as she walked off, leaving us to tend to our affairs.

"My sister had her eye on you. Seems like the feeling's mutual. Call me PT," he stated while sitting down.

"I want to thank you for this opportunity. Your sister seems cool. She was good company 'til you got here. What my numbers looking like?"

"Well, I definitely have some amazing shit this way. Tell me what you tryin'a pull off with and when. We can make it happen."

"I wanna bring someone to test it out, make sure I'm not wasting no money. Even though you came highly recommended, I still gotta make sure my clients are receiving the best."

"Understood. I'll hit yo' line with the address and shit. Make sure you got all my money as well. You looking at about seven bands for what you quoted earlier."

"Money talks, bullshit walks, right? My money is right. Hopefully this product is."

"Trust me, you'll get your money's worth." PT hopped off the barstool. "I'll talk to you soon, my mans. Look out for my call or text."

"Facts, bro. I'll holla at you."

PT disappeared into the crowd, and there Nahima came with a smile on her face. When she came back to me, she insisted that we hang out, and I was here for it. From that moment on, we were stuck to one another.

Hand in hand, we walked toward the crowd slowly. My heart was racing not knowing what to expect. My mother's house was up in flames, and the firefighters were doing their best to control the fire.

"Aye, let me through! That's my mother's house! That's my momma's house!" I shouted, trying to break through the barrier.

"Sir, we need you to calm down and wait here. Please!" an officer yelled while attempting to push me back.

"Hell no! That's my fuckin' momma's house!"

"I understand, but the best thing to do right now is to try to remain calm. Once the fire has been controlled enough, we will let you in."

"Officer, listen, my mother and sister-in-law were in that house. We just want to make sure they are all right. Please. Just think if it were your family," Nahima pleaded with the officer in a gentler tone.

"All right, come on." The officer moved the barricade just enough to let us through.

"That is why you're my better half. Thank you, baby," I whispered in her ear.

"Always, baby. Let's go find your momma."

We were walking toward the ambulance when we noticed my sister, Asia, sitting on the pavement crying as the paramedics rolled out a stretcher covered in a white sheet. Asia noticed us walking toward her when she cried out for Momma so loudly it gave me chills. It was at that moment I realized she didn't make it out of the fire in time.

Chapter 3

Nahima

The tension in Isaziah's face spoke louder than any words that could escape from his lips. My sister-in-law sitting on the cold concrete wailing her eyes out was enough to set it off. When we got to the gurney, we asked to see the body under the sheet just to confirm our worst fear. It was her. My mother-in-law was lying there almost unrecognizable from the burns all over her body. Asia stood up, embracing us as now she was just left with her siblings. She was only 16, and she still needed her mom like all of us do even when we don't want to accept it. Asia and Isaziah were consoling one another when a detective who seemed familiar came up to us.
"Isaziah Morgan, nice to see you again. Well, I'm assuming with your mother dead now it's not that nice," he chuckled.
"Nigga, my mother just died and you wanna come over here with your bullshit? I don't care how dirty they do or don't think you are. Fuck with me again and I'm gonna put my foot up your ass!" Isaziah held on to the gurney rail, clenching it tightly with his fist.
"Isaziah, you forget I don't work for your ass anymore, and my new employer is enjoying this moment. Just watch your back." The detective pretended to hug my man like he gave a shit what was going on. Then he loudly

put on a scene. "It's going to be all right, son. I promise you everything is going to be all right. May your mother rest in peace."

Isaziah shoved the man out of the way. "Aye, Oscar, thanks for the condolences. I'll definitely be in touch. I'm sure you will do your best to find out what happened to my mom. Especially after how she took you in from time to time."

As the detective walked away, I tapped Isaziah on the shoulder. "Who the hell is he? I feel like I know him from somewhere."

"You do. He used to work for us until he started stealing. We got enough cops on the payroll. He wouldn't dare try anything stupid. But if his hands are in this, I'll deal with him personally." Isaziah let go of my hand and took his sister's.

I advised for us to leave the scene, especially with all the attention we were receiving. News stations were arriving to report the house fire. I knew talking to them would only bring more attention. As we were walking to the car, I received a call from my bestie, Sharonda. I ignored the call the first time, but then when she called three more times, I figured something was wrong.

"Hello?" Sharonda screamed through the phone as I could hear a beeping sound echoing in the background.

"Hey, sis, what's up? I can't really talk right now. Can I call you back?"

"I just saw about a house fire and a person dead on the news. And it's the same street as Momma Jade."

"Yeah, let me just call you back."

"Was it her? Where's Isaziah? Sis?"

I tried to hold back my emotions, but the more she probed me, the harder it was to control. Momma Jade was not just my mother-in-law. She was like my mother. My mom died from an overdose when I was 10. My father raised me on his own, but I was left without either parent at the age of 18 when my father was killed in a hit-and-run accident. When I met Momma Jade, she embraced me with so much love it was hard not to give the love right back.

Isaziah introduced me to his mother and his other siblings after dating for a good six months. It was the end of the spring semester, and my babe asked if I would go with him to meet his family for the Fourth. Since I had the whole weekend off and Isaziah was doing well with the work my brother was supplying him, we were good to go. He booked us a nice little suite in downtown Orlando even though his mom got a beach house for their family. He claimed it was so we could fuck loudly like we did at home versus sneaking around his mom.

I'm not gonna lie, I was nervous as shit. I knew he had a slew of sisters, plus his mom! My biggest fear was that they wouldn't accept me or at least like me enough to tolerate me.

We arrived in Orlando early that Fourth of July. The rest of Isaziah's family had been there since the day before. He informed me that his family was well aware of how he made all of his money and was skeptical about him fucking with me since I was the plug's sister.

After we checked into our hotel and relaxed for a bit, Isaziah's mother called.

"Son, where ya at?" she questioned with anxiousness.

"We just checked in. We'll be on our way shortly. Has everyone else got there?"

"Yes. Just waiting on you, ya know."

"Yes, ma'am. We are coming, but we just got here."

Now Isaziah had the call on speaker, so his mom began speaking in Creole. "Ou te pote mennaj ou?"

I had no clue what she asked him, but I felt like it was about me. "What she just say? I know it was about me! Babe, what she say?"

Placing the phone on mute while his mother was going off, Isaziah responded to me, "She asked if I had my girlfriend with me. That's all."

"Wi mwen te di nou te vini. Tanpri bon. *(Yeah, I told you we were coming. Please be nice)*," he responded. "Momma, I'll see you soon. Yeah?"

"Yes. Y'all be careful. Love you."

"Love you too, Mommy." Isaziah was the epitome of a mother's boy. But against what others say about it, it truly made Isaziah into a great man.

We arrived at the beach house, and his mother was sitting on the steps shucking fresh corn to cook. Taking a deep breath, I got out of the car as he whispered that everything would be just fine. One by one, his four older sisters greeted me, and then his baby sister came out from hiding to do the same. The oldest of them all, Shereene, had a hard time warming up to me. Even with me volunteering to help cook, she gave me attitude the entire time.

The day went by, and his mother decided to take me out with her to the grocery store to grab more food for the cookout. My hesitation was seeping through when she volunteered me to go with her. I just knew it was going to scare the shit out of me. Driving the longest route ever, his mother began small talk.

"So, you met my son in New York and y'all been dating since, right?"

Damn, it's only been five fucking minutes and here we go, I thought before responding. "Yes, ma'am. Your son is a complete gentleman. Part of the reason I ended up crushing on him."

"Crushing on him? Like the Lil' Kim song?"

"No, not exactly," I said with a giggle. "I stay out of things between him and my brother. I really do like Isaziah. He has been so good to me. He's understanding, communicates well, and he's attentive, among many other things. You raised a great man."

"Well, my son is all those things and more. He took the role of being the man in the family after his father died. Did he tell you about that?"

"He did briefly. Both of my parents are gone. They've been gone for some time now. But I've gotten better dealing with the pain and moving on with my life knowing that, with every step, they're still here with me and rooting for me. Just hope I always make them proud."

"Well, you have a new momma now. I can't replace your parents, but I know that as long as you continue loving my son, you will always have a mother in me."

That intimate moment with her was the first of many. Over six years, she loved me like her own. Now to deal with her murder, it seemed so unreal. I could only imagine what Isaziah and his sisters were going to go through. The entire ride was silent. No music, no talking, not even a smack was heard. By the time we reached our apartment in downtown Tampa, all of Isaziah's sisters were in the parking lot.

"Brother, what happened? I know Momma ain't gone. You tell me right now this is a fucking cruel-ass prank!" Tanya, the second-youngest of his siblings, hollered with bloodshot, half-swollen eyes.

"Let's go inside. I don't want to talk about this out here."

"No, we talk about it now!" Shereene shouted toward him.

"What did I just say! You may be the oldest, but goddamn, you gotta listen sometimes!" Isaziah bellowed back.

"Fine, let's go! I'll follow you and your little whore in the house," Shereene murmured under her breath.

I knew it wasn't the right time, but I wasn't going to be disrespected. Turning around to face her, I politely gave her a piece of my mind. "Listen, I don't know why you don't and never have liked me. But out of respect for your brother and your mother, this is not the time! You are always welcome in my home, but you will show me the same fucking respect as I show you! Do I make myself clear?"

Shereene stood back, looking at me sideways. "Isaziah, you gon' let her talk to me like that?"

"You know what? Yeah, I am! Nahima has done nothing but try to kiss your ass over the past few years we've been together. For whatever reason you have issues with her, it sounds like it's a personal issue! So, you can either respect her and us, or get the fuck out my face! Your choice."

Shereene and the rest of his sisters stood there in utter disbelief. Then Angel came from behind Shereene to try to make peace.

"Listen. No one is going anywhere but inside the apartment. Shereene, you were definitely wrong just now. And you know Nahima loves each of us like we are her own family. Momma wouldn't want us out here like this. Let's just go inside, please."

Shereene brushed past Isaziah and me into the apartment building as the rest of us followed her. One thing about my baby, he kept his family in all the business. Each of his sisters were given certain positions in the camp. When our money became long enough to put people on payroll, his family was brought in first. I knew sitting down after his mother died, this meeting would be about protecting ourselves, our investments, and payback.

Leaving all the lights dimmed, except by the dining area, we all took a seat as we waited for big daddy to let all the information out and anything else he had to say. Isaziah seemed to be trying to regain his thoughts and provide us with the right tools to handle this situation. We had had wars with other dealers, plugs, and even gangs, but no one had ever touched family. A line was crossed that could never be undone. By the look in his eyes, Isaziah was going to kill them all.

Chapter 4

Isaziah

I was able to get my family in accord after meeting with them after the fire. Days went by, and I took my time gaining the courage I needed to give my mother the proper funeral. Since all of my siblings were making good money within their different businesses, we all pitched in to handle the funeral arrangements. We agreed that we would cremate her and take her back to Haiti to spread her ashes.

My siblings and I were close up until I got in the streets. Shereene hated the thought of me selling drugs. When she found my gym bag full of coke and weed, she ran to our mother, running her mouth.

My mom was standing in the kitchen, cleaning some goat she got from the market earlier.

"Momma!" Shereene yelled, running into the kitchen with my bag.

"Poukisa wap kriye, Shereene? Stop that!" My mom glanced up at my sister. "Kisa ki la?" When she asked why she was hollering and what was in the bag, I knew I was done for. I stood in a corner. I wasn't sure how my mother was going to react. With an old-school Haitian woman as a mother, her only son selling drugs ain't going to fly.

"Momma, Isaziah selling dope!" Shereene wanted to make a scene.

"Ziah!" My mother shouted to me. "Ziah, vin jwenn mwen!" The more she told me to come to her, my anxiety continued to flare up.

"Yes?" I finally came around the corner ready to face her.

"This yours?" My mother's eyes grew wide.

"Yes, ma'am." I swallowed my spit, skittish in not knowing what would come next.

Before my mother could start, my big sister was standing with her arms folded, smiling. Ever since our father died she did nothing but make my life a living hell. No matter what I did, Shereene always gave me her ass. My mother told her to leave, but Shereene was being a bitch about it. It wasn't until our mom threatened to beat her ass that she left us alone.

"Now, you want to sell these things and you just starting college?" My mother's tone was light with me.

"Momma, I need the money, and you need the money. Anything to help us out. It's not forever, just until I graduate or make enough where none of us struggle." I was pretty sure she didn't believe me, but it was my plan. I didn't see me in the game long once I acquired enough money to make things happen without hurting my family.

"You walk with me. Shereene, finish cooking that goat and get your sisters cleaned up. House look a goddamn mess." My mother took the bag and my hand, walking out the door.

With the door closed behind us, she turned to me. "You do what you need. I'm no stranger to this. But I'm older now, and we have a great life here. You my baby boy, and our strong soldier will continue to make us proud. Hide that shit from your sisters. Don't go to jail, and you must promise to still graduate from college!"

Stunned by her words, I just hugged her. The embrace between us was nothing but the love I needed and always felt from her. When we went back into the house, Shereene was standing there hoping my ass got handed to me. When she realized her snitching failed, she stormed off into her bedroom. Following her, I wanted to know why she treated me like she did.

"Sis, sa ki mal? What's wrong with you?" *I probed, going to sit next to her.*

"Move!"

"No, talk to me. Why have you grown to hate me so much?"

"I don't hate you."

"Then what is it?"

"Ever since Papa died, you look so much like him. Then Momma treats you like God's favorite. You are not her only child! I am the oldest, and everything is on me harder, but you the 'man of the house.' You carry nothing."

"I carry my sisters and my mother on my back. I strive to make y'all proud and get us out of this fucked-up neighborhood. We deserve better! Momma deserves better!"

Shereene looked at me with tears in her eyes. "I want better for all of us. I'm trying to do it the right way."

"Sis, you graduate in a few months, and you been offered great jobs. Take them and go. I got you always."

Knowing how my sister felt then helped me be a better brother to her and understand her more than I did before.

It had been a week since my mother was killed, and the streets were talking. Even those who rivaled me came to provide their condolences and respect. The day before the funeral, I decided to have a meeting with all gang leaders and anyone who moved weight on the streets for me or my competition. We would soon have a common threat, and that threat would have to be exterminated quickly and quietly.

The meeting location was a nice little soul food place called Food 4 the Soul Diner and Bakery. I had connections with the owners and was able to buy it out for the night after they closed up. The only outsiders who had to be around were the ones who worked at the restaurant. The Tyshoons were the first to arrive, then the Muscles, and then the Jobs. Each crew had about a good twenty members with them except the Muscles. They had about six people. Everyone important to my crew was at the meeting as well. Marcus, Shereene, my wifey, and a few of my fastest shooters sat around me.

A waitress appeared, asking if any of us wanted to order something. Everyone went around the table ordering food and drinks. Unfortunately, I had no appetite, but I still ordered something to go. When the waitress walked away to put in the large amount of orders, the meeting commenced.

"So, I wanted to get everyone here to discuss the things that may and have transpired."

"We once again want to extend our condolences in regard to your mother. We all know that's one line we agreed upon never crossing. Family never gets hurt, or killed," Alejandro stated, speaking on behalf of his crew, the Tyshoons, since Jose was running behind.

"Aye, same here. We may not always see eye to eye, but no one should lose their family members behind this shit if we can help it," Tarran, the leader of the Jobs, piggybacked on Alejandro.

"You gotta know none of us murked your moms. That can't be why you got me here with the Scarface and El Chapo wannabes!" Rome hollered across the table.

"Rome, save the disrespectful comments for someone who cares. This ain't why we here. Don't forget you're still under me. Please have enough respect for me to sit through this peacefully," I retorted.

Huffing and puffing like a big kid, Rome sat back, grabbing his glass of Sprite from the waitress as she and two of her coworkers brought us our beverages. After they went back toward the kitchen area, we continued our conversation.

"I know who killed my mother, and they are after territory. They call themselves the Gator Boys. There's no telling who they'll come for next from my crew or any of y'all's. At this point, we have to work together."

Alejandro's phone began ringing, interrupting my whole spill about these nobodies coming into our city on that dub shit.

"I don't know who keeps calling you, but you either answer it or put your phone on silent. This is a business meeting. If it ain't an emergency, you need to tell them you will talk to them later," Nahima spoke up, letting her presence be known in the subtle queen way she always did.

Alejandro was about to speak when he punched the table violently. Nahima was about to continue talking when Alejandro began shouting. We all looked around trying to figure out what happened that quickly.

"Aye, what the hell is wrong with you? If you don't calm down . . ." I uttered as I ground my teeth.

"Jose! Jose, my brother! Look!" Alejandro tossed his phone toward me and allowed me to see a text from an unsaved number that was in his phone.

It was a picture of Jose's body shot and his throat slit. I was in shock. Even though Jose and I had a complicated history and business relationship, I wouldn't want to see him go out like that. Especially not by my hands. When I zoomed in on the picture, I noticed some graffiti beside his corpse that read GTZ. It had to be the Gator Boys striking again.

"Take a look, y'all! Jose is gone and not by nobody sitting in this room! This is what I'm talkin' about! If we don't stick together, we're all gonna end up in a grave. It's either us or them! Nothin' more to be said. What y'all wanna do?" I passed Alejandro's phone around the table so everyone knew what we were up against.

"My fiancé is right. With a common threat, this isn't the time for egos or rivalries to be in play. We need to boss the fuck up and come up with a plan that secures a way for all of us to continue eating, plus stay alive," Nahima chimed in.

Rome sat up in his seat and said, "Damn, man, that's foul how they did homie. I ain't letting no sucka-ass niggas play me out my spot. They want a war, I'm with all the shits. I can make a few calls and see if anyone else know about these clown-ass niggas and where they came from."

"You do that, and we'll go see if we can find where these *puntas* are hiding. They'll pay for this and your mother! It's us or them!" Alejandro reached out to provide me and Nahima with a hug before departing the table.

Rome departed shortly after Alejandro, informing us he would be at my mother's funeral the next day. The rest of my crew and my family stayed at the restaurant, just trying to have a quiet moment in the midst of sorrow and madness.

The following morning, I was awakened by the smell of freshly brewed coffee. It was seven thirty in the morning, and I wasn't ready to face the day. Wiping the cold out of my eyes, I realized I had only received a max of three hours of sleep. I spent most of the night handling business, helping family members get into their rooms, and going down to the funeral home to say one last goodbye to my mother. We decided we would have a closed casket service due to how severe the burns on her body were. Even I could barely stomach seeing her body that way.

Funerals were never my thing. After my father's, I refused to go to another. My father's funeral was the hardest thing I had to endure. I was about 15 when it happened. We traveled back to Haiti to bury him, per our mother's wishes. Our father was gunned down on his way to the airport in Haiti. We weren't sure why he was targeted, but after fighting for two weeks, my father finally took his last breath. My mother sent for us once all the arrangements had been made. The moment I touched down in Haiti for the maybe third time in my life, I was angry to be there for that reason.

I met thousands of family members I barely remembered. When it was time for his funeral, I watched my sisters struggle to finish getting ready.

I walked over to them. Asia, being the youngest, was sobbing to the point where it was hard for her to breathe. I held her hand, escorting her to the family car.

"I'm going to clean you up, and remember, even with Dad going to be in the sky, I will always be your protector. You will never have to worry about anything."

Asia nodded her head. "You think he going to miss us?"

"He's always going to watch over us." *I kissed her forehead before entering the car. My father's death took a toll on all of us, but Asia took it the hardest.*

Now here we were doing the same thing all over again a few years later. But there was no way to back out of this. It was my mother, and just like I always needed her, now she needed me to be strong because my sisters would need me. The family cars were to arrive around ten that morning, and the service was to start at noon. We wanted to give any family or friends a wake before having the actual service for those who weren't able to stay the entire time. We agreed that as everyone was escorted to the banquet hall for the repast, my immediate family and I would escort her back to the funeral home to be cremated. For Nahima, it was as if she lost another parent with as good as my mother was to her. But I knew, throughout everything, I could depend on her to be my strength throughout the day.

Our house was starting to get full with guests moments before the family car arrived. My sisters were in no mindset to direct traffic, so my wifey handled getting everyone in the proper cars. As we drove to the funeral, my stomach was in knots while Nahima held me in her arms. My sisters were holding hands as they held their tears. This moment felt so surreal to us all. Never in a million years at 28 would I think I would be burying my mother from something as horrific as this. To be honest, it felt like it was all my fault. If I weren't in this life, she would still be here with me and all of us. *There's no more phone calls or family dinners on Sundays with her famous mac and cheese. When I have my children, they won't have the pleasure of having either of their grandparents around.*

For our own safety and privacy, I made sure the funeral was at an undisclosed location. This was one day I didn't want to have any unwelcome or unwarranted guests. But security was in place, and all of us came strapped just in case. *With these nuts on the loose, there's no telling what they may do.* My mother's casket was lavender purple traced in gold. I had planned on marrying Nahima in the fall, and my mother was helping me plan our surprise wedding. *Now who's gonna help me or be there?*

Our driver opened our doors, and as my sisters stepped out one by one, my heart sank deeper and deeper into the pit of my stomach. I had been holding my composure for a week, but slowly I was losing my grip on reality. The moment I touched her casket to help usher her in with my two uncles and Marcus, my knees were giving out on me. My cousin Jacob came up behind me, holding my waist.

"I got you, cuz. Come on," he whispered as he helped me hold the casket up to walk toward the pulpit.

Seeing me break down only set the reality in my sisters as well. Shit was killing me. *I promised to take care of her and my sisters for life, and this is what happens?* I hated myself, and I couldn't get it together. As the funeral proceeded, my sisters and I were distraught. By the time everyone was ushered to the repast location at a Masonry banquet hall nearby, we had to do our best to make our way to the funeral home to have my mother cremated. We were at the funeral home picking the urn for our mother when Marcus called, alerting me my home was just broken into. Could be no one but those fuck-ass Gator Boys. I informed him to take care of everything quietly while I spent the day remembering my mother and her legacy.

Chapter 5

Nahima

Two weeks had passed, and Isaziah had been a different person. I could feel him becoming a different man than he was prior to these chumps coming in and turning our lives upside down. I was sitting in the trap house awaiting Marcus when Isaziah called me. Our trap house was nothing like what you would see in movies. We upgraded from our last one. This one was on the east side. The exterior looked like a normal house. Beautiful bricks, front lawn trimmed with a rosebush sitting toward the left of the white rails that complemented the brick steps. One you walked in, there was one television in the living area, one couch, the kitchen was set up with all-black curtains, about four pots on the stove, the dining room table was set up with black tablecloths, a box of plastic gloves, and laundry baskets. The laundry baskets were for everyone's clothes for breaking down the weight. Needed no mishaps or missing products.

"Where you at?" he asked in an uptight tone.

"Babe, I'm waiting on Marcus still. He hasn't gotten here yet."

"What the fuck you mean? He was supposed to be there thirty minutes ago with the drop."

"Look, I'm waiting just like you asked. I could be doing other shit."

"Other shit like what? You fuckin' another nigga now?"

"Yo, you tripping right now. I've never stepped out on you once and I'm not now."

"You been acting funny and shit lately. Matter of fact, FaceTime me so I can make sure you where you supposed to be."

"Fine."

While Isaziah went off on a rant, I could tell he sounded a tad bit intoxicated. That was another thing that changed about him. Isaziah barely got drunk. A social drink here and there, but never to the point where it altered his mood or thinking. He always liked to stay in tune with his surroundings. But since his mother's passing, the break-in, and the constant attacks on us and the other crews, he began drinking more. When FaceTime connected, his eyes were barely open, and he had a bottle of D'Ussé in his hands.

"You drinking again?"

"Don't question me! That look like the spot. Walk through and turn the camera around so I can see."

"Babe, is that really necessary? Since when don't you trust me?"

"Bitch!"

"Bitch? You know what, Isaziah, I'm gonna handle this for you, but after this, until you can limit your drinking, stop being disrespectful, and remember who the fuck I am, I'm out. We can do things from a distance. Honestly, I get that you're mourning, and with everything going on, it's really a lot to handle. But you don't have to handle it by drinking alone. We're supposed to be a team, but instead, you treating me like an enemy!"

"An enemy? You wanna fucking leave me? That's what you saying?"

"No, I'll never leave you. But you gotta get it together. Right now, you're acting like a weak-ass bitch instead of the man I know and love. That's who you need to be to seek revenge for your mother and to teach those Gator Boys a lesson."

"Yo, hold on! Don't hang up. Someone's at my door!" I could see him struggling to get up from our brown leather sofa and wobbling to the front door.

When he opened it, there stood his sister Tanya and Marcus. That didn't sit right with him nor me.

"Nahima, bring yo' ass home! I'm gonna deal with this fool in front of me who can't follow simple directions." Isaziah disconnected our FaceTime call.

I left, and as soon as I got into my car, Teyana Taylor's "Issues/Hold On" echoed through the stereo. The lyrics ran through my soul. I couldn't let go of my love for him, but this wasn't the man I knew. There was a reality check that needed to take place. The only ones who could help me with him were his sisters. Even though me and Shereene could never see eye to eye about anything else, her brother was the one neutral thing or person we could agree upon.

First, I thought I should just pull up on her, but knowing how she really felt about me, texting may be the best option first. I pulled over at Popeye's and took a minute to text her before grabbing something to eat.

Nahima: Hey, Shereene. I know we aren't the closest, but we need to talk about Isaziah.

Shereene: What about him?

Nahima: Listen, he is grieving and angry, but the drinking and disrespect is out of hand. His judgment is cloudy. We can't have no shit like that, especially when we have someone gunning for us.

Shereene: He seems like he's just coping with the loss of our mother. Your mother and father weren't killed, so you have no idea how he or any of us feel.

Nahima: You don't know anything about me or my parents! This ain't about me. It's about Isaziah. If he doesn't get right, we're all gonna possibly end up hurt or dead. Maybe it was my mistake to reach out to you.

Disappointed in how she responded to my concerns, I placed her text on DND and went on about my day. As I walked into Popeye's, Alejandro bumped into me.

"Hey, Nahima. Tell yo' mans I may have a lead. We'll talk," he whispered into my ear while he gave me a friendly hug.

I just nodded, moving past him and heading inside. I could feel eyes on me as I made my order. Peeping over my shoulder, I noticed this short dark chocolate guy with huge eyes, dreads down to his waist, and these dusty-looking clothes staring straight at me. Beside him was a taller roughneck-looking nigga. He had to be a good six feet tall, bald head. He was kind of chubby for his height. The taller fellow seemed to have a cut on his upper right cheek and a tattoo on his forehead with the letters GBZ.

Putting two and two together, I skipped out of line and went back to my car rapidly. Just as I got into the car, the two of them stood behind my car like they wanted me to hit them. With no second thoughts, I pushed my start button and hit reverse. Either they would get out of my way or get run over. My foot hit the gas and I kept going. Before I could hit them, they jumped out of the way. I made sure I took the longest, most confusing way home in case I was followed. No chances could be taken with our lives on the line.

I was approaching the house when I sent Isaziah a message asking him to grab whatever we may need because we had to go. If those men were part of the Gator

Boys, they knew who all of us were. *They may know our cars, our addresses, and where all of our businesses are.* We had to be at a safer location. Our lives were being turned upside down, but I knew we could make it right again.

Chapter 6

Isaziah

Why the fuck is she texting me and not just coming in the house? I thought as I grabbed my bottle of Patrón out of the freezer. I walked toward the front door to see where Nahima was when a silver Jeep pulled up slowly to my house as two guys hung out the back with their guns pulled out. Next thing I knew, shots were ringing out left and right. Tossing my drink out on the front lawn, I reached under my white T-shirt to grab my pistol. Nahima was coming from my left, aim on point as one of the shooters fell backward into the car.

"Babe, get in the house!" I shouted, moving toward her while shooting at the car as it sped off.

"Are you hit?" Nahima questioned, meeting me in the driveway.

"Nah, I'm good. Are you all right?" I took her into my arms, grateful for her presence.

"Yeah, we gotta get out of here. These niggas saw me at Popeye's, and I almost ran them over. I made sure I wasn't followed but . . . but . . ." Nahima broke down into tears.

"Shhhh. Look, we can go buy some clothes. I just wanted us to meet at Momma's house because I thought this would be safer, but obviously not. We got to switch up cars and everything. With them possibly having police or a detective on their team, they can track our license plates or anything. We use nothing but cash from here on out. Send the emergency text to everyone."

Nahima and I rushed inside, hoping that those niggas wouldn't be back. I made the decision to stay at my mother's until things cleared up, but it wasn't a safe place either. We needed to handle business in the city but not stay here. Maybe Nahima was right. I was off my game. Spending most of my time drinking and not working on the issues in front of us wasn't helping. I'd been the worst boyfriend, boss, brother, and friend to everyone. It was time to shake all this off, deal with my grief, and channel my anger into finding my mother's killers. My revenge would be sweet, but only if I got my mind right.

I wanted to wait until nightfall to disappear. My sisters were on standby, waiting for their next move. I had Marcus pick up a hooptie from a mom-and-pop dealership, plus some burner phones so we could move without being traced if possible. A little after midnight, everyone had arrived at the house. It felt like we were fugitives on the run. I sent word to the other dealers in the area, letting them know to move carefully because we were all being hunted.

"All right, family. We all stay together. These Gator Boys have help knowing not only who we are, but our locations, cars, and more. We need to be on our toes. You all were searched, and phones were taken before entering this house. Right now, we can't be too cautious as to locations and traitors. You all will follow Nahima and me. Let's get to our location as fast as possible but without causing alert to any state troopers who may be out."

"Isaziah, how long are we going to be gone? What about our businesses? How we supposed to make money if we aren't here?" Asia seemed a little puzzled by everything going on.

"Money is the least of our worries. Most of you have businesses online that can generate revenue wherever you are. The rest, I hope you been smart on these blocks. We will stay gone as long as it's needed. Any other questions?"

"No questions, but I feel we all need to be smart. These niggas seem to always have one up on us, and we're running away! This is our territory! This belongs to us! You're acting like a pussy!" Marcus screamed in frustration.

Bumping his way past my sisters, Marcus got up in my face like he was going to fight me.

"Don't buck up, nigga, if you ain't gon' do shit! We move as one unit. Whatever decisions I make, it's made for everyone's safety! Do you understand me? So, either fall in line or get left. Do you understand me?" I barked out.

Marcus relaxed his chest as he took a few steps back. Nodding and acknowledging his position, he fell back. I looked around the room, and everyone understood their positions, and forward we went. Bags in hand, we headed out to our cars parked in the back of the house as my security watched the front entrance. Nahima and I stood at the back door to my mother's home as we watched everyone get into their cars safely. We were the last to hop in our car. One by one, with us leading the way to our temporary destination, Nahima held my hand, keeping me calm.

We arrived in Atlanta around five in the morning at the Hyatt House Hotel downtown. I went in and paid for everyone's room for two weeks. The Hyatt House downtown was cool. The front desk was over to the right, and to the left of me was a little bar. When I say little, I mean it was the same size as the reception desk. Once you got past the main lobby, there was a meeting area to the right and an outside garden area for the smokers or those who like to sit outside. But who goes to sit outside when they at a hotel? While I got on the elevator, my mind wandered. *Is this it for me? Am I going to make it out of this war alive? Should I send Nahima away for her own safety?* I couldn't fathom the thought of losing her or anyone else close to me. Because of me my mom was dead, and I didn't know if I could ever forgive myself for that.

I was hoping that I could get back to Tampa within that timeframe, cease all of this madness, and get back to life. Grabbing the hotel keys from the clerk, I met everyone in the parking area to provide their room keys. Once we parked and got settled into our rooms, I decided to run my baby girl a hot bubble bath. It would be different if I took the time to deal with things differently, but I just drank everything away and almost lost everything important to me that was left in this world. Nahima didn't deserve half of the things I said or did over the past few weeks. Instead of her leaving me in my drunken sorrows, she stayed with me.

"Babe, how about you put the laptop down and come take a bath to relax? I ran your water for you. Then I can give you a massage when you're done." I watched her perfect, thick chocolate body lying across the bed with her round booty cheeks poking up in the air. She was such a goddess that just watching her made my dick hard as a rock.

"Babe, you take it. I'm tryin'a see what all I can find out about these boys. I'll take a shower after you finish," Nahima responded, keeping her eyes locked on the computer screen.

Walking to the bed, I closed her computer, then grabbed her by the hand to stand her straight up so I could undress her. "After the day you had, let's just enjoy our night and leave our cares outside this room for just a little while. Let me focus on you."

Nahima obliged, allowing me to strip her down then guide her to the tub. With some nineties R&B playing in the background, I washed my queen's body slowly. The aroma of her honey bubble bath mixed with the light scents of lavender from the candles she lit earlier was setting the tone for an amazing night. After drying her body off slowly, Nahima dropped to her knees, pulling my sweatpants down, revealing my long black dick to her. With a smirk and my dick in her hands, she spit on the tip, then stroked me slowly.

"Tell me what you want me to do, daddy," she said seductively.

"Suck this damn dick then." Cocking my head to the side, I watched her open her mouth wide, slowly taking my cock inside of her wet mouth.

Releasing a soft moan, I tossed my head back while I gripped her shoulders. "Move your hands, baby. No hands. Suck this dick like you love it. Like you love me."

Nahima went straight to work, swallowing my dick like a porn star. The only time she gagged was when she went too deep. I would move her back just so she could get some air. I loved the sound of her choking on my dick. If my dick weren't hard before, seeing her all teary-eyed and hearing that sound always put the icing on the cake. It wasn't long before I made her get up from her knees. That sweet pussy of hers was calling me. Lifting her and twisting her body upside down, I held on to her as I sucked that sweet pussy and asshole of hers 'til she screamed out my name. Even then, every cry she let out only made me dig my tongue deeper into both of her holes. From the front to the back, I sucked every bit of juice out of her 'til her body shook from her orgasmic release. Keeping her in my arms, I walked slowly to the hotel bed and laid her body there so I could get more than just a taste.

"You haven't had enough?" Nahima teased, trying to scurry to the headboard.

"Where you think you going? Daddy's got a lot more for you. Bring me my pussy."

Nahima crawled slowly toward the edge of the bed while I stroked my dick, keeping myself ready. It had been a few weeks since we had sex, and this nut for both of us was going to be worth the delayed gratification. Her eyes were filled with lust as she eyed my body, biting on her bottom lip. Grabbing hold of her ankles, I yanked her body down for her to be flat on her back.

"You holding my legs. You gonna fuck me or just look at me?" she teased.

"Don't start talking that shit," I advised.

"Nigga, let me go. You ain't fucked me in weeks. So again, either fuck me or let me go," Nahima stated, sounding really sexy.

I loved when she talked shit to me. Everything my woman did turned me on. After seeing her come out with the gat shooting the previous day, it literally had me ready to make love to her right then and there.

"A'ight, bet."

She wasn't going to say nothing else. Tossing her legs on my shoulders, I spat on her pussy while sliding inside of her. One hand was on her ankle guiding her left foot to my mouth so I could suck on her toes, and my other hand gripped her neck tightly as my dick filled her pussy. I wanted to punish her. Not because she was bad but because something needed to get my frustrations out. And Nahima was going to be my dick's punching bag.

Chapter 7

Nahima

"Isaziiiiahhhhhhhh!" I screamed out as he fucked me hard and fast.

God, his dick was hitting places it never had before. Maybe us not fucking in weeks put us in a better place. Up on my knees, arching my back just right, I propped this ass up so he could fuck me from behind. I was anticipating his thickness, and not knowing what hole he was going to enter first had my pussy wetter than the ocean. He turned me into the biggest freak ever. I'd had sex with other guys before, but none of them took me to the level Isaziah did. This nigga gripped my hips tightly, tracing my spine with his tongue, making my body shiver.

Isaziah took his time teasing me, knowing I was ready to cum again. He rammed his dick into my ass with no warning. His dick sat in my ass while he yanked my head back, instructing me not to cum until he told me to. His hands still pulling on my hair while I threw my ass back, he filled me with every inch of his dick.

The harder he fucked my ass, the louder my moans came. "You bet' not cum, bitch! You fuckin' hear me? Don't you fuckin' cum!" Isaziah instructed as he yanked his dick from my ass, repositioning me on my side and lying beside me so he could fuck me. That first stroke with just the tip of his dick made me bite my bottom lip.

"Don't hold that shit in. Tell daddy how good his dick feels inside of you." Isaziah slowly dug into my pussy with my right leg dangling from around his neck.

I was ready to cum, but he still wouldn't allow me to. The more I tried to withhold it, the more my pussy purred. Soon, Isaziah was moaning in sync with me. He finally granted me permission. As I came, so did he, releasing every last drop of his seeds inside of my pussy while I squirted all over the hotel sheets. Without pulling out, he cradled me within his arms.

"That was amazing," I whispered.

"Every time I'm with and inside of you, it's amazing. I'm sorry for everything. I haven't been dealing with my mother's death in a healthy way, and it's been affecting everyone and everything. That drive-by put a lot in perspective. I almost lost my life and yours. I can't have that." Isaziah traced his fingertips along my spine slowly.

"Listen, you have to learn how to deal with your mother's passing in your own way. But don't ever forget you're not alone. I'm here for you and will always be."

Isaziah sat up on the bed with tears in his eyes. "Nahima, listen to me. I want to be everything for you and more. You are my world. I know the timing isn't right, but I want them to not just say 'wifey' when referencing you. I want them to say that you are my wife. You are my wife. The timing isn't perfect, but will you marry me?"

Reaching down into one of our suitcases, Isaziah pulled out a small black box. He stood in front of me, and down on one knee he went. "I bought this ring the day before Mom was killed. We actually went to pick it out together. She was so excited to officially have you be a part of the family."

"She still will have me as her family. She will be here in spirit and with us through every step. There is no need to ask. My answer will be and always will be yes." I gave him my hand and allowed him to slide the ring on my finger.

The ring was beautiful. Sixteen carats, square-shaped diamond with a rose gold band. It was way more than anything I could have imagined receiving. I pulled him toward me and kissed his lips. Isaziah never ceased to amaze me. I was beyond thrilled and ready to share the news, but the time would present itself.

"Let's formally announce it to everyone once we avenge Momma," I stated, holding on to his hands.

"Whatever you wanna do, baby."

"Well, right now I want to make love to my fiancé and sleep in his arms."

"Your request is my command. We need to do a breakfast meeting later so we can go over some things."

"Yeah. I think I found some information about them. But we'll do that later. First come here." I pulled Isaziah up on the bed with me, wrapping my legs around him, allowing his dick to slide inside of me. We made love until the sunset glistened through our hotel window.

The following morning, I woke up to an empty space beside me. I grabbed one of the burner phones Isaziah left charging on the nightstand to check the time. It was almost one in the afternoon, and I was still in bed. I used the hotel phone to call his cell to see if he took the SIM card out. The phone just rang straight to voicemail. Since all our rooms were on the same floor, I grabbed some clothes to toss on to see if anyone knew where he could be. Just as I was opening the door, Isaziah walked in, drenched in sweat.

"Where the hell have you been?" I questioned, looking over his clothing and body.

"I went to the gym downstairs with Marcus. What's wrong?" Isaziah gave me a little peck on the cheek before he stripped his clothing off at the door.

"Nothing, I just didn't hear you leave or see a note or something. With everything going on, I just was a little nervous," I responded. "Nigga, you stink! I hope you taking a shower."

"Shut yo' short ass up, wobble-head-looking ass. I'm taking a shower, and you're coming with me." Isaziah started tickling me before he lifted me up in his arms, carrying me to the shower with him.

After we showered and dried one another off, we cracked the balcony windows so we could smoke. As we lay in bed, I reached over his bare body, grabbing my laptop. Before our sexcapade last night, I was able to find some people from Tallahassee who had mingled with the Gator Boys and were looking for them. They called themselves TaynoSayes. The crew members were made up of different nationalities and seemed like a family based on the pictures I saw on Facebook. I didn't want to friend them, but since their pages were public, I took my time to snoop. Isaziah turned over and snuggled up under me, asking me what I was looking at. Turning my computer slightly, I showed him the two main leaders of the group and provided him with the details of what I found.

"These fellas run a crew called the TaynoSayes. I'm not sure if they sell weight, but they definitely have beef with the Gator Boys. I was thinking about inboxing them and seeing what info they could provide me in detail. But take a look at these posts." I passed the laptop to him as he sat up in bed, placing the pillows behind his back.

Isaziah's face became stern as he went through the pages. These two crews had been beefing for a while from what we could see. Every now and then, you would see a member from the Gator Boys comment on their posts calling them pussies, bitch niggas, and throwing threats left and right. One of their leaders was named Justin "Jay Boogie." He was murdered by one of the Gator Boys.

"We needed information and allies. They are perfect. If anyone can help us get to them or get rid of these assholes, it'll be them." I expressed my opinion, hoping he would take heed.

"Well, if anyone reaches out to them first, it'll be Marcus and I. 'Cause if they say anything out of the way to you, there will be no allies or help from them. Shoot them the message and get a number, and we'll do the rest. Understand?" Isaziah hopped out of the hotel bed and walked to the restroom.

"I gotcha, babe." With his permission, I sent one of the main members, Tyshawn, a message, hoping he would bite. It wasn't even a minute later when he responded.

Nahima: Hey, what's up?

Tyshawn: What's good, gorgeous?

Nahima: Nothing much. I see we have something, well, someone, in common.

Tyshawn: Word, what's that, sexy?

Nahima: The Gator Boys. A common problem we can eliminate together if you're interested.

Tyshawn: Is that right? How I know you ain't one of they l'il hoes tryin'a set me and my crew up?

Nahima: Those sons of bitches killed my mother-in-law and are threatening my family, so you tell me if that sounds like anyone who wants to set you up.

Tyshawn: A'ight, shawty. I'll hear you out.

Nahima: Shoot me your number, and my fiancé and I will call you soon.

With a little pressure, Tyshawn gave me his number. These little boys fucked with too many families. The universe always makes things just, and Tyshawn was a part of that key of making things whole.

Chapter 8

Isaziah

Wifey was the ultimate Inspector Gadget. There's not much that she couldn't find out. Nahima blessed us by looking up anyone who may have had beef with the Gator Boys. After she got the number to the guy named Tyshawn, I initiated a team meeting with everyone. Since we had missed lunch and breakfast, I decided we would just all go out for dinner. I called each room, instructing everyone to meet in the lobby at four so we could eat and discuss everything. Now I knew that our rooms were paid up for at least a week, but I already made up my mind to keep everyone here versus everyone traveling back and forth with me. Nahima, and my sisters especially, needed to be as far away from the bullshit as possible.

Their safety was all that mattered to me. We were all I had left, and no one could take them from me. I wouldn't allow it. The time had approached, and mostly everyone who was a part of the crew—Marcus, Asia, and Shereene—were downstairs in the lobby when Nahima and I emerged from the elevator. I couldn't say hey to everyone before my sister Shereene asked where we were all about to go. I decided soul food was the best place to go, and I'd heard of Mary Mac's Tea Room, which wasn't too far from us on Ponce de León Avenue. Good food always brought people together, according to my momma.

Without giving too much of an explanation, I directed everyone behind me and said I would lead the way.

It took us ten minutes to get to the restaurant. I honestly felt as if we should've taken an Uber. Atlanta traffic was crazy. After we waited a good ten minutes, they were able to seat all of us. While waiting for our waitress, it was the proper time to start releasing information. First, everyone needed to hear the best news that could be stated.

"All right, y'all, I'm hungry like y'all niggas. But until our waiter or waitress gets here, I have news. Nahima and I have news." I stood up, holding her hand.

"Well, what is it that you have to tell us?" Shereene snickered boldly.

"Well, sister, since you're not in a mood for an introduction or anything, I'll cut to the chase." I cleared my throat as I glanced at my beautiful wife-to-be. "Nahima and I are getting married." I held her hand out to the crew, and everyone congratulated us but my sister.

"Why would you do something like this now? Momma ain't been dead two weeks and you come with this shit? Let's not forget the niggas after us all because of you!" Shereene yelled.

Disappointed in my sister's reaction, I shook my head and sat down. I wanted to cuss her ass the fuck out, but I knew that Momma would not like that. A conversation would be had with my older sister in private. I just never understood why she hated Nahima so much from the start. Changing the subject, I moved on to the main topic. Nahima grabbed her laptop from her bag, opening it for everyone. The great thing about laptops is you're able to take screenshots of things as well. Since the burners weren't nothing but old-ass Androids and flip phones, there was only so much we could do.

"So, this guy y'all are looking at knows about the Gator Boys," I started my statement, but the waitress came with our drinks and to take our food orders. Once she finished, I continued. "The guy's name is Tyshawn. He belongs to a group called the TaynoSayes. They apparently have beef with the Gator Boys. Wifey here was able to find him after snooping around the internet for a while."

"She did, huh? What else is she good for?" Shereene whined, cutting her eyes.

"You know what? I'm so tired of you and your smart-ass comments. I swear to God sometimes I feel as if you only hate me because I'm dating—well, now going to marry—your brother! I have done nothing but attempt to love you and bond with you over the years. Every time you have given me nothing but your ass to kiss. I am tired of it and you! I will only talk to you for business. I don't want you in my home when we return, and I don't want you at my wedding! You are an evil, selfish bitch! If it weren't for Isaziah, I would've whooped your ass a long time ago!" Nahima shouted as she pounded her fist on the table.

"Nahima, chill out. We can deal with this privately." I attempted to sit her back in the chair, but she shoved me away.

"Nah, Isaziah. If she wants to jump over the table, let her, but she's a dead woman if she touches me! You need to control your little pet better than this," Shereene laughed while folding her arms across her chest.

"That's enough from both of you. We are not at home, and we are in a place of business. Stop fucking causing a scene!" I yelled sternly.

My sister and Nahima both kept their attitudes but sat down quietly without saying another word. Redirecting our focus back to the main issue at hand, I went on explaining about the TaynoSayes. In the midst of me going over the details thus far, Shereene got up from the table.

"You know what? I would rather not deal with this. If they come for me, they come for me. I'm out. By the time you get back to the hotel, I'll be on my way home to Florida." My sister walked out of the restaurant. I couldn't just let her leave like that.

Chasing behind her, my other sisters and I went to stop her from leaving. Not only did I want her safe, but Shereene was one of the toughest ones on my crew. She was never afraid to fight, stab, or shoot a nigga. My sis was never afraid to get dirty. If we were gonna avenge Momma and take our home back, I needed her by my side.

"Sis, what is wrong with you?" I probed, grabbing her arm.

"I love you, but you be making decisions without consulting all of us first. Like what the fuck? Why does she even need to be here?"

"Are you kidding me? She is your family just as much as I am. If you love me, then you will love Nahima just the same. She has never done wrong to you or anyone in this family. So, whatever your nonexistent issues are, you deal with them! We need to take out those motherfuckas before they take us out. You either stand with all of us or none of us. I don't wanna lose you too."

"I love you but . . ." Shereene stuttered, unable to look me in the eyes.

"But what? You don't love your brother enough to stand with me as we've always done?"

My sister was hurting, and I needed to be strong for her. I held her in my arms, and Shereene melted as she sobbed loudly. My sister wasn't as evil or hard as she seemed. I wanted her to understand she would always be my heart, but there was room for me to love others outside of family. After I consoled her for several minutes, Nahima poked her head out the door of the patio area where we were all standing.

I motioned for her to come out with us so the two of them could talk. Leaving Shereene and Nahima outside to talk things out, I prayed that they could finally have some type of communication. Hopefully, they could have some peace. Nahima wasn't my sister's enemy, and regardless of how Shereene felt, Nahima never did anything toward her. Hopefully, they could be all right. Leaving the two of them alone, I allowed my sisters to watch the door while I went back to our table to finish discussing the issues at hand.

"Now let's finish business. Oh, shit, the food is here! It looks good as hell." My plate was full of collards, cornbread, baked chicken, a side of gizzards, rice and gravy, and I had a dessert. It looked and smelled amazing. I was ready to eat. "Wait, y'all. Let me get them in here to see this goodness!"

I was like a fat kid in a bakery. Doing my happy dance all the way to the patio, I noticed Nahima was holding her belly and Shereene was being held by the rest of our sisters. Storming out into the area, Nahima had blood covering her hands, and my sister was holding a small hunting knife in her right hand.

"Shereene, what did you do?" I screamed right as she broke free, running out of the restaurant.

"Baby, I . . . I don't know if I can stop the bleeding," Nahima whimpered as I picked her up in my arms.

Asia grabbed Nahima's phone. "Isaziah, I'm sorry. It all happened so fast."

"All of you let this happen to her! Move the fuck out of my way!" I kicked the door open, walking past the table. My sisters went over to the table to inform the others of what was happening.

"Nahima, just hold on, baby. I'm going to the nearest hospital. Just hold on, okay?" Gently sitting her in my passenger seat, I set the GPS for the nearest hospital, which was Grady, and prayed that we would get there in enough time to make sure she wasn't hurt severely.

Chapter 9

Nahima

When we got to the emergency room at Grady Hospital, two nurses grabbed me, rushing me onto a gurney. I was completely shocked by Shereene actually stabbing me. I thought things were taking a turn for the better when she pulled out the knife. As I was taken into an operating room, I reminisced on our brief conversation.

"Listen, I'm not sure why you don't like me or what I could have done to ever make you feel the way that you do, but I honestly just want your acceptance and to work past it all," I expressed while sitting on one of the patio chairs.

"Well, listen, things can get better." Shereene sat beside me, kind of close enough to touch.

"Tell me how? I just want us to bond and be like friends or sisters. Isaziah and I are getting married. I want you there. Regardless of what he said earlier, we both know he would want you there. So, tell me how things can get better. I'm willing to work on it." I was willing to get right and bury the hatchet.

Shereene laughed at me. "You know why I don't like nor trust yo' ugly ass? How you go from being his plug's sister then y'all damn near making just as much as your brother? The thing is, it's not all about you. There's a lot that you nor my brother don't know, especially about *our family! I don't want nothing from you. I don't want you to be my friend, my sister, nothing at all. I want you out of our lives forever!"*

A knife appeared in her right hand. A short, subtle hunting knife. Deep inside, I knew she wasn't about to stab me. I really didn't think she was going to harm me, but I was wrong. In a quick instant, she leaned over as if to hug me, stabbing me in my abdomen and twisting it. I felt every inch of that knife and every ridge on it.

"You are in the way of all of our happiness. Now you won't be. I was going to let someone else take care of you for me. This was the perfect opportunity. I hope you rest well in hell with your bastard-ass parents." Shereene pulled away from me, slowly removing the knife.

Holding my side, I watched Asia and the rest of their sisters come to my aid.

This was not what I envisioned with Isaziah trying to make peace between us. Now here we were. I was sedated due to the pain I was having, and every time they even touched me, I would scream out. The medication had set in, and I drifted away gradually.

Once I woke up, Isaziah, Marcus, Asia, the rest of the sisters, and the crew were all by my side. My first thought was, *where the fuck is Shereene? That bitch attempted to kill me. For what? For fucking what?* It seemed like the enemy list was starting to grow longer. I hated to say it, but my thoughts were running rampant with theories of what her motives may have been. Was she secretly in love with her own brother? Was she jealous of me in some way? Or worse, was she working with the Gator Boys? There was so much running across my brain, causing my blood pressure to increase.

"Babe, hey, how are you feeling?" Isaziah came over to my hospital bed, running his hands through my hair.

"Where is she? Isaziah, where is she?" I shouted, rising up from the bed.

"Listen, we can talk about that later."

"No, Isaziah, where the fuck is your sister?"

"Listen, Nahima, there's something more important that we need to go over first." Isaziah looked over the room, and everyone slowly got up from their seats and went out.

"Where is everyone going? Isaziah, what the fuck is happening?"

Once everyone had left, Isaziah's face filled with regret and gloom. He forced a smile onto his face assuming I wouldn't know that something was wrong.

"Listen, I haven't said anything to anyone but Marcus. When Shereene stabbed you, she didn't injure just you. She punctured something within you, killing our seed." Isaziah's half smile disappeared quickly.

"What are you talking about? What seed? I wasn't pregnant!"

"Apparently you were. I guess you didn't know because I didn't."

"Isaziah, you think I would hide a pregnancy from you? I would love nothing more than to have your fucking child! What the fuck are you thinking?"

"I wasn't saying it like that. I'm just saying you were still drinking and shit like normal. So, I know you wouldn't do that if you knew. That's all I'm saying."

"Where's your sister? 'Cause she has a lot of blood on her hands now! Literally!"

"When I came outside and noticed that you were bleeding, she ran out of the restaurant. Marcus is trying to get his police connects to trace the license plate linked to her rental. She may be heading straight back to the county. But who knows? She did check out of her room though."

"Well, get my clothes from that chair and let's go find her! What if she's the reason those niggas are after us?"

"Nahima, I understand she wasn't thinking clearly when she came after you. But Shereene setting me up? Her only brother? She loves me more than anything. She would never hurt me."

"How sure are you about that? Huh? Look at what she did to me. Shit, before she stabbed me, she was saying things about family secrets and other things—"

"What family secrets? What are you talking about? I'm not understanding where this is coming from. It's one thing for you to be upset, but don't lie on her."

"Isaziah, are you fucking serious? Your sister tries to fucking kill me, kills our seed that was brewing in my womb, and you sitting here in my motherfucking face trying to take up for her? Have you lost your fucking mind?"

I was dumbfounded at Isaziah during that moment. I knew his mind must be going crazy, but taking up for his psychotic sister was not the way. Unbeknownst to us all, I was pregnant. That was the perfect time to find out. It felt like God was punishing us. I didn't understand why.

The nurse walked into my hospital room in the midst of our argument. She was so skinny and young I figured she may have just finished nursing school.

"Hey, Ms. Nahima Thompson, correct?" She walked toward my bed, reaching for my IV to check the fluids.

"Yes, that's correct."

"Can you verify your birthday for me?"

"It's September 12, 1989."

"Perfect. So, the doctor will be in to see you in a few. But right now, I just want to make sure you're comfortable and receiving enough fluids. Do you need anything? We're waiting to see if you can eat real food or if they just want you on a liquid diet until you're discharged.

I'm going to check some vitals really quick, and then I will be out of your hair." The nurse began gathering her equipment to check me out.

Just as she placed the thermometer in my mouth, a knock came, and then two police officers walked in. Isaziah's eyes grew as he turned to look at me. The last thing we needed was any type of case or police action, especially in a different state.

"Hey, folks, good afternoon. We just wanted to ask the victim here a few questions about what happened today," the chunky white police officer said, scratching his fat-ass stomach. He looked to be two doughnuts away from being on *My 600-lb Life*.

"Officers, if you can, just let me finish checking her vitals. If her blood pressure seems to be good, then I will come out and inform you that you can come in. How does that sound?" The nurse kept her warm hazel-brown eyes on me with a welcoming smile.

"Yes, ma'am. No problem," the taller, skinnier dark chocolate officer stated, nodding at me before they walked out of the room.

Isaziah and I knew this wasn't going to be good. Damage control needed to be done as quickly as possible. Shereene was lucky she was family. The only way to handle her would be personally. Everyone at this point had to understand my issue with Shereene was going to be personal and the Gator Boys was personal as well. Everyone was going to catch the wrath. If you got in the way, you were going to be handled.

Chapter 10

Isaziah

How did we get here? Shereen stabbing Nahima, and these Gator Boys coming for me. How can these two things be happening at once? Then to top things off, I could've had a child out here. This is the hardest pill to swallow. My world was crashing down right in front of me, and I had no clue how to stop it. While Nahima was with the nurse, I decided to speak to the officers. Shereene had to be handled by our family. If the police got to her, she would be locked up.

The two officers were standing right beside her door when I walked out. Instead of ignoring them, I decided to have a conversation with them. I was always taught to treat them like a frenemy. Stay on their good side so they never have anything to suspect.

"Hey, Officers. I want to thank you all for coming to follow up with the incident. You know my fiancée and I just had a rough few hours. We suffered a miscarriage today as well."

"Certainly, I'm sorry to hear that. You know, my wife suffered one about a year ago, and now we have a six-month-old baby girl. I know what you both are feeling. It'll take time. Are you able to tell us what happened today?" the black officer stated while his partner stuffed his face with hot Cheetos.

"Yeah, my condolences as well about your baby. I'm sure your fiancée is needing time to cope with everything. That's a lot to deal with, you know? Being stabbed and losing a baby at the same time. The lady who stabbed her, how well did y'all know one another?" his partner asked, wiping his hands off with a napkin he pulled out of his pocket.

"We knew her. She was always a friend of the family. I'm not sure what made the stabbing take place. She could've been trying to harm herself, and Nahima tried to help her. I wasn't out of there with the two of them. There's not much that I can tell you on that end. I haven't been able to reach her since the young lady's phone was off. We had come out here for a little family vacation." I hoped they wouldn't attempt to poke holes in any story given.

"Well, it seems like that vacation isn't going as planned, huh?" A chuckle echoed from the white officer's belly.

"What the hell is wrong with you, Jeffery? Come on, we're going back to the station. Sir . . . I'm sorry, you didn't tell us your name." The black officer extended his hand toward mine.

"I'm Isaziah Jones-Roberts."

"Mr. Roberts, I'm going to let you continue with your day. If we need to ask any more questions, we will be in touch. When your fiancée is awake, here's my card. Have her reach out to me or someone at the station. I'm Lieutenant Roscoe. If you need anything, please let us know, and I apologize for my partner. Y'all enjoy your day."

I watched them walk off while everyone sat around watching and whispering. Before I reentered the room, my phone vibrated in my pocket. Looking down, I was receiving a call from an unknown number. It could've been anyone. Ignoring the call the first time, I hollered for Marcus. When he approached me, my phone went off again. Passing it to Marcus, I voiced that I wanted him to find out who was calling and why.

The door to Nahima's hospital room was only cracked when Marcus tapped me on the back, indicating he wanted me to hear who was on the phone.

Peeking in to check on Nahima, I saw she seemed to be nodding off. The medication would help with her pain and make it easier to sleep through it. Closing the door, I followed Marcus into a hallway as he held the phone on speaker and asked someone to hold on. We found an unlocked broom closet to sneak into so the conversation could continue.

"A'ight, hello?" Marcus said.

"Where's my brother? I want to talk to Ziah. Where is he?"

I shook my head and told Marcus I wanted to say nothing. Marcus was continuing the conversation. "He's with Nahima right now. Where are you?"

"It's not important. Tell Isaziah that I love him, and I'm sorry. It's never going to be okay! There is so much that I did. I've done something wrong. I just don't know how to fix this." Shereene was hysterical as she blubbered her words through the phone.

"Listen, Shereene, just talk to me. I'm not Ziah, but I'm still your brother. Why don't you talk to me? You sound like you've been crying. Talk to me, and tell me what's going on. At least where you are going. Talk to me," Marcus inquired for more information from my sister, but she wasn't biting.

Shereene stayed crying through the phone and dancing over every question asked. My frustration with her was at an all-time high, and I was done with the avoidance.

I grabbed the phone from Marcus so I could get the answers myself. "Shereene, what the hell is wrong with you?

First you stab and try to kill Nahima. We lost our fucking child because of you and your fucked-up ass emotional impulse for no fucking reason! You tell me, you fucking tell me right now, where the fuck are you?"

"I can't tell you that. I'm just sorry. I'm sorry, Isaziah!" Shots rang out in the background, and the phone went silent.

"Shereene! Shereene. Can you hear me? Shereene!"

Shereene never responded. Soon after the silence, the phone call disconnected. What if she was killed by someone? Was my sister dead? As I came out of the broom closet, my palms were sweaty, heart racing and head pounding. What happened to her possibly was enough to make me lose my mind. From my mother, to my fiancée, my unborn child, and now Shereene, my whole life was crumbling piece by piece.

"Are you able to trace this number? I need to find where she is now. Do you understand? Take everyone back to the rooms. I'll be in touch." After providing the instructions to Marcus, I went back to Nahima.

Nahima slept mostly. Time lingered, and I checked in with Marcus throughout the day for updates. Knowing Nahima, I knew she may not truly feel any sympathy for Shereene if she was dead. I loved every woman in my life. Without my mothers or my sisters, Nahima wouldn't have the man she did today. Nahima was awakening from her sleep. Knowing how she was about recognizing my mannerisms, I knew she was bound to know something was wrong.

"You stayed?" Nahima stretched her body slightly as her right hand landed on her side over the bandages.

"I would never leave your side. I know you wouldn't leave mine. Even when you should've kicked my ass, you were still here and taking my shit." Lowering the volume on the television, I leaned back in the recliner chair, tossing my head to the side and glancing at her.

"Did I miss anything while I was knocked out? I really want something to eat and to get out of this bed. How much longer do I have to be here? This room is horrible."

"Babe, we can go as soon as the doctor clears you."

"Why do you sound like that?" Nahima side-eyed me after realizing my tone was way off.

"Sound like what, babe? I may just be tired. Today was really long mentally and emotionally. A lot happened today."

"Outside of me, what happened? Where did everyone else go?"

"They at the rooms, I guess. But let's just focus on you. How are you feeling?"

"I'm fine outside of being ready to leave. I want you to tell me why you're so big on not telling me what else has transpired. I hate when you lie to me."

With a deep breath, I turned to my side and told Nahima what happened. "Shereene called from an unknown number. And while we were trying to find out where she was, shots were fired in the background. The phone went quiet and then it disconnected. I think she may be dead."

Chapter 11

Nahima

Hearing the news about Shereene wasn't gratifying in any way. Her possibly being dead wouldn't fix the pain she caused me or avenge my seed from being taken from me before I had the chance to even know about it. My love was hurting in ways I would never know. I could only imagine the pain he was feeling after losing his mother and his oldest sister within weeks. It wasn't time for me to be selfish. We needed to be strong for one another. My heart was hurt from the pain of losing my seed, but I knew God had a better plan. And with the beefs, there was no need to be pregnant and deal with that, too.

I was released from the hospital after two days, and I was ready to get back to Florida. Hiding out in a hotel wasn't going to solve our issues any faster. The pace of resolution needed to speed up. Not knowing if Shereene was alive or dead was even worse. But we couldn't go back to the city without some type of game plan. Lots of people would be hurt or killed once we touched back down. Our connects with the police needed to be in place. *The more organization we have, the easier we can execute our plans.*

In the words of the late and great Michael Jackson, they were about to be "hit by a smooth criminal." Isaziah helped me into bed while Asia let herself in, bringing me some flowers and a bag of food from Church's Chicken.

"People still eat Church's?" I joked as the smell of the fresh chicken filled my nostrils.

"I do sometimes. Shit, I like their corn and their shrimp." Asia lay beside me in bed with her bag of food, grabbing the remote to scroll through the channels.

Isaziah was in his own world, pacing the floor, phone in hand like he was waiting for something.

"Hey, babe, if we're going to stay out here a little longer, you may want to think about having Tyshawn come out here so we can meet with him and see how he can help eliminate this problem."

"Nah, we need to find Shereene first."

"But what if they have her? Listen, I know you wanna find her and know if she's dead, but if we can at least get in the minds of the Gator Boys, it may lead us to her and be able to avenge your mother. Have you heard from anyone in the city?"

"Nah, trying to keep contact with them at a minimum, remember? If they watching them or tracing lines, they could find us here. Is that what you want, my nigga?"

"First of all, my nigga, you know what the fuck I mean. There's a way to be smart about everything. Right now is not the time to let your emotions cloud your judgment. You are the leader of this family and organization. Act like it, or you'll lose everyone and everything."

"Nahima! Shereene may be dead, and you wanna talk about the Gator Boys?"

"Yes! Yes, nigga! I want you to understand because you forgot how we handle niggas who cross us! Either we can handle them together, or I can do it alone!" I stood up in front of the bed with my arms folded.

Isaziah had to get with it or get lost. We were wasting time going back and forth about Shereene when we could've been ten steps ahead of everyone by now. I could be home resting in my bed, but instead, here I was in a hotel hundreds of miles away from home. If he could just get out of his feelings for one second, we could come up with a plan that would help all of us.

"You gonna fix this shit yourself?" Isaziah asked nonchalantly.

"If I have to 'cause my fiancé won't. One of us has to have enough balls to do something. Apparently, the one with them isn't acting like it. Again, we can either work together like we always do, or if and when I need your assistance, I'll pull you in." I got in Isaziah's face, not backing down.

"Asia, go back to your room. I need to talk to Nahima alone." Isaziah contorted his body just enough to catch a glimpse of his sister in his peripheral vision.

Asia got up from the bed quickly, gathering her food and any other belongings, then headed straight to her hotel room. Isaziah's chest was all swollen. I was anticipating an out-of-this-world argument, but I wasn't backing down from him or anyone else.

With the room door shutting behind Asia, he went off. "Who the fuck are you talking to?"

"Nigga, I was talking to you. You need to get your shit together. I'm only saying something 'cause I love you and I want to do this with you. But our family and business can't be at risk 'cause you're not thinking the right way. Either get your shit right or you'll wake up to me gone as well and being ten steps ahead."

His hard breathing through his Mario-sized nostrils was felt against my cheek the closer he got to me. I waited for him to make a move. His eyes were burning, and I thought for a second that this may be the first time he ever swung at me. Isaziah grabbed my neck, pulled me close to his lips, and kissed me passionately.

Pushing him away, I stared straight into his eyes. It was as if we were both consumed with fire. The more he gazed over my body while biting on his bottom lip had me aroused like never before. I knew I was having some bleeding from the miscarriage, but it wasn't about to matter at this moment.

"Down on your fucking knees," he instructed aggressively while stripping his pants off.

"I decide what I want and what I'm going to do. Maybe I want you on your knees." I was still sore from the stabbing. I was feeling self-conscious about my stitches.

"You don't wanna listen, huh?" Isaziah was so angry with me, it was all in his stance, but surely, he was gonna let it out.

"Fuck you gonna do? You know I'm nowhere near scared of you."

Sinisterly, Isaziah released a slight chuckle before walking up on me and taking my clothes off piece by piece. "I don't give a fuck about no blood or no wounds. You wanna boss up on me, so I'ma boss up on you. Since I ain't got no balls, right?"

Tossing me onto the bed, he pulled my underwear to the hotel room floor with one hand as he jacked his dick with the other. He slid inside of me with my right leg wrapped around his neck and his left hand holding my leg back as far as it could go. His stroke was forceful, deep, and a bit brutal. This was some new dick he was tossing in my guts. Even though it ached a tad bit, I was so enjoying it. Coming onto the bed, Isaziah slammed every inch of his dick inside of me and made a circular motion with his hips, hitting every piece of my walls. My nails were digging in his back as he dug into this pussy. He was killing my pussy softly and I was enjoying every moment. Isaziah flipped me over, ramming his dick in my ass.

"Who the fuck is the head of this family, huh?"

"Fuck you, nigga!" I shouted as he slid in and out of my asshole.

"You still wanna talk that shit, huh?" Isaziah yanked my hair, pulling me into a doggie position with his dick still in my ass.

He pumped into me hard and fast. My body shivered as Isaziah rubbed my clit while he continued to fill my asshole with every inch of his dick. He wanted to prove a point, and it was definitely made. While he stimulated my clit, my orgasm was peaking.

"You better nut for me. You fucking hear me? Don't hold that shit in, fuckin' cum!" Isaziah's right hand released my hair, making its way around my neck, choking me slightly.

He pulled out of my ass and lay on the bed, grabbing me, pulling me to his face. My pussy was sucked until I squirted all over his face and the sheets. It was like a shower. I had squirted plenty of times but never like that before. As I came for him, Isaziah was jacking his dick. When he was ready to cum, Isaziah pushed me off of his face and shoved his dick in my mouth. I sucked him to completion, swallowing every drop of his sweet cum.

After we came, it didn't make a difference in my decision. Hopefully, that and our little spat would make Isaziah get his shit together.

"So, now that your head is clear, you ready to get this shit done or am I alone in this?" I asked, holding his hands.

"You never do anything alone. I got you just like you got me. You not meeting up with no nigga alone. If you really want to get him here, I will allow you and Marcus to contact him and schedule everything. While you pump him for the required information, I'll work on another lead on the Gator Boys and Shereene. But we're always a team." Isaziah kissed my hand before dozing off. Isaziah was always crafty with finding out information, but I wondered if he would be able to find any additional details that could help us.

That's the thing—sometimes you can't be soft with your man. Sometimes you have to be the bitch, be that bitch, and make them get on their shit. Isaziah was sleeping peacefully while I reached out to Tyshawn. It was time for all of this to end.

Chapter 12

Isaziah

Nahima hated being in Atlanta. She was ready to go home, and living in the hotel for the past two weeks wasn't the best. She grew tired of constantly eating out and no actual home-cooked meals. Atlanta was a nice city, but it wasn't our home. Since Shereene went missing, it had been hard on me because I felt like I failed. I vowed to my mother at an early age to always protect this family. Now my mother and possibly my sister were gone, and I didn't save them like I should've.

When we started getting more and more money, at one point, Nahima did make the suggestion to have another residence somewhere else. I couldn't understand why she was so pressed about it at that time. We had made our first million, and Nahima was big on flipping and keeping all the money clean.

"We made a million really quick. Is it always gonna be coming in like this?" Nahima asked me after we made love on top of the money.

"Well, I hope so, beautiful. Anything is possible. I hope you know this happened because of us. We better than Bonnie and Clyde."

"I truly love you. You know that?"

"I know you're the best thing that's happened to me outside of my momma and crazy sisters."

Rolling over, I grabbed her, pulling her into my grasp. Nahima gave me a simple wink and said, "We got to be smart if we're gonna make money like this. It can't just be in a shoebox or something. Let's open some businesses, little by little, nothing alarming. Get the proper business licenses, bank accounts, and all. It's the best way to do what we want and stay under the radar."

"You're always thinking outside the norm. You watch too many movies and shit. Real life ain't like that."

"How do you know? We haven't even tried it yet and there you go shooting the shit down. Sometimes you gotta listen to your queen to make sure you succeed." Nahima glanced at me then at the $100 bills stuck to my leg.

"You got money on your ass, so don't say nothin' to me," I teased, smacking her ass gently as the $20 and $10 bills jiggled on her booty.

There was something about how she handled us reaching our first goal like it was just regular money we were touching. She wasn't impressed. If anything, she was hungry for more.

"I'm serious. Listen, if we don't invest all this money now and just blow it on ridiculous shit, then what are we really working for? We both are about to graduate and have our own degrees. We can make money to not only pay off our loans but set our future children up for life. There's so much more we can do with this money. Let's be smart and frugal. It's the only way we can sit above the rest. We also need to look into another house, but not here."

"Why we gotta move?"

"Not saying move for good, but just something for the summer or something. We can rent it out during the times we aren't there."

"Let's talk about that later. Right now, I wanna work on dinner."

That conversation was what got me in the right mindset so that we could build up on our street hustle. We went from knocking off the corners, to building our own team to help with the work, to becoming our street's plug. From different businesses like a nail salon, a boutique, a barbershop, T-shirt shop, and more, everyone was set up. The money was beyond good.

Even though I wasn't going to the meeting with Nahima and Tyshawn, I was nervous. We knew nothing about him outside of the stuff we saw on Facebook and the minimal conversations we had with him. She wasn't going alone. I made sure of that. Marcus and one of our henchmen were going to accompany her to the meeting.

Marcus's dispatch connect was able to trace Shereene's license plate to a little town outside of Tampa. Apparently, she had the police dispatched there, but there were no signs of a shooting, blood, or a missing person. There wasn't even a phone left in the car. I made the decision to head to the coordinates to see if I could locate some evidence as to where she could be.

Nahima hated the thought of me making myself vulnerable. Driving alone with a target on my head could only make me crazy or fearless. It was a mixture of both. I had people in the city needing product, and it was gonna be harder to move around without the streets talking. We kept all communication down to a minimum with the others back home just to be on the safe side. With some officers working with the Gator Boys, we couldn't be seen out front like normal. I kept myself under the radar with having high-ranked officers and councilmen on my team. With them in my pocket, I was able to find out some of the newer officers were paid off by these fake-ass gangsters. It wouldn't matter in the end, because they were all going to meet their Maker.

Getting to my destination, I had Alejandro from the Jobs meet me there as well for apparent backup and to make a business exchange. Reaching for one of the burners, I sent him a text to see how far he was from me. Shereene's rental was on the side of this deserted road. With nothing but sticks surrounding us, she could be anywhere. Her body could be in the woods adjacent to our cars or anything. Walking the distance, it would probably take her three days to walk home from this area. I pulled behind the rental to inspect the car. Placing my gloves on, I got out of the car, mentally prepping myself for the worst.

The car had no bullet holes, no broken glass, no signs of any type of force. So, what in the world happened? Did she escape the car before the shots rang out? This was mindboggling to say the least. I kept hearing her screams and the shots on the other end of the phone, and tears fell from my eyes as I wondered if I failed to save her. Tugging on the car doors, I found that none but the back passenger-side door opened. I opened the door to nothing. The car was empty. It had nothing but empty bags from McDonald's and two gas station receipts from her trip. Reaching in between the seats, I pulled the latch to unlock the front passenger door.

There had to be more in the car that wasn't looked at or that I hadn't come across yet. Anything I could find at that time might provide me a trail of some sort. Alejandro sent me a text saying he was about twenty minutes out from the location while I still searched my sister's car. The worst thing I could do was leave my sister without any help or a chance at survival. Getting into the passenger seat, I searched her glove compartment, finding a Kahr CW9, a torn manila envelope with a stack of money inside of it, and a short note with a list of names, most of them scratched out except for mine and a few others. Going over the list about five times, I couldn't understand the chicken scratches, and it only added to my frustrations.

What the fuck was my sister up to? This didn't seem like her, but there could be things I didn't know about her. There had to be an explanation for all of this, and I was going to find out. Since the rental she got was a little older, it had a latch to pop the trunk from the driver's side. Releasing the lock from the trunk, I closed all the doors to the car and checked her trunk for anything. All of her luggage was still how she left it.

Turning my head and checking my surroundings, I noticed a navy blue Dodge truck pulling up behind me. As I closed the trunk behind me, the car flashed its lights at me before Alejandro popped his head out the window.

"What's up, homes?" he shouted, exiting the car.

"I can't call it, my dude. Thanks for meeting me here." I slid my gloves off, placing them in my back pocket.

"You sure this the best place to handle any business? A cop or something could pop up."

"Why would you think that? Have I ever handled business in a hot spot? Come correct!"

"Aye, no need for all of that. Just was asking. Let's get this shit out of the way."

"Why you so damn jumpy? Fuck is goin' on?" I was opening my trunk to reveal four large duffle bags when I noticed how jumpy he was.

"Listen, you need to leave now. I fucked up, but they had my daughter, man. I don't want her to die 'cause of our lifestyle. I told the Gator Boys I was meeting you today. They'll be here soon. I want you to get those sons of bitches. They may kill me and my little girl. If they do, tell everyone I loved them."

I thought he was playing with me, but the terror in his eyes informed me he was telling the truth.

"What the fuck?" I shouted, shutting my trunk.

"I have two hundred thousand in my back seat that belongs to you, and I got some pictures of these guys and some info on who they're working with. We got about six more minutes before they be here. Let's do this, and you get the hell on. If I make it out alive, I'll be in touch." Alejandro wasted no time. He scurried to the back of his car, grabbing all the bags at once and tossing them in my back seat as I grabbed the envelopes on the floor.

"Alejandro, listen—" I wanted to speak my piece as I got into my car.

"We can do that at another time. Those niggas are grimy as fuck. I hope you kill them all. Now go! And shoot me in the arm."

I understood what needed to be done at that moment as an attempt to keep his daughter alive.

As I swung around, a black Cadillac was approaching. With no second thought, I pulled out my Ruger, firing off four shots at Alejandro. I didn't wait to see what happened. I sped off down the highway, checking behind me every few moments to see if I was being followed. Alejandro spared my life when he didn't have to. For that, I was forever grateful. I just prayed he and his baby girl were going to survive.

Chapter 13

Nahima

I wished I could split myself and Isaziah in half. Just as much as he wanted to be in my meeting, I wanted to be with him to meet with Alejandro. All things happen for a reason though. Isaziah truly didn't trust that Tyshawn would come with intentions of working on getting back at the Gator Boys. Everyone always got at least one chance with me. Either they were smart and we continued our relationship, whatever that may have consisted of, or they fucked up, burning a bridge that could've worked for us all. It made me no never mind either way. I was still going to live and make the best of my life.

Tyshawn arrived at the Hartsfield-Jackson Atlanta International Airport around one that afternoon. Marcus and I picked him up in front of the Jet Blue terminal entrance. He was shorter in person than he seemed in his pictures. He had to be a little taller than a midget, about four foot seven. He was stocky up top with a nice muscular frame. His skin was brown like almonds, and his hair looked matted. He was in desperate need of a retwist or to just cut them off and start over.

Blowing the horn twice to gain his attention, I rolled my window down, yelling out his name. Tyshawn made his way to the car, and Marcus met him out front.

"No disrespect, my man, but I gotta search you first," Marcus informed Tyshawn, blocking the back seat.

"Nah, I understand you gotta do what you gotta do." Tyshawn cooperated and set his bags on the ground while getting searched by Marcus.

Once Marcus cleared him, they got into the car, and we headed to our destination. I got him a room at the Westin downtown so he wouldn't be too far from me. I wanted Tyshawn and Isaziah to meet after he returned from Florida. Until then, I needed to accumulate as much information as I could prior to my fiancé's return.

"Hey, so here's your room key. I'll be back within an hour to pick you up, and then we're gonna grab some food and go over this vital information and how we can help one another. Cool?" I passed Tyshawn the room key with a warm smile.

"Okay, cool. I would like to take care of everything if possible for dinner. You have done enough. Out of good faith, and since we will be business partners, I'd love to treat you to our business dinner." Tyshawn flashed his teeth at me. Surprisingly, they were all there and clean.

"We can arrange that. Stay by your phone." Once he closed the door, I nodded and sped out of the parking lot.

I went back to my hotel room to take a power nap but not before helping Asia with taking her braids out. She approached me from the right, looking shook as if she saw a ghost.

"Asia, what the hell is wrong with you?" I inquired.

"I saw her. Shereene . . . I saw her!" she blurted out hysterically.

"What do you mean? She called you or something? Tell me, how did you see her?" Tapping the hotel door with my key, I ushered her inside my room with Marcus following and our henchman, Torry, guarding the door. Even though I could hold my own, Isaziah felt better knowing that I had an extra set of eyes on me and his sisters.

Asia was crying to the point where she could barely breathe. I got her to take deep breaths, and Asia got to a decent headspace to start telling me what triggered her outburst.

"So, are you ready to talk? Where's the rest of your sisters? Everyone's been so distant since Shereene left. Maybe we could all go out after my meeting." I rubbed her back gently, keeping her calm.

"Rahea and Anne are out at the mall. Tanya found some little boy toy, so she went to get some. I'm here looking like a fuzzball." Asia chuckled.

"Well, at least someone is getting some dick out here."

"You and my brother seemed to be doing enough of that for everyone. But I have to show you this." Asia passed me her phone after unlocking it.

Shaken by what was appearing right before my eyes, I saw that Shereene's body was laid out across the front porch of their mother's home. Her hair seemed tangled and matted, her face had a few bruises, and both of her wrists were slit. Under the picture, there was a caption that read: We will kill everyone you love until we get what we want from you. Don't make us keep doing this.

"Has anyone else seen this?"

"No, I received it right before I saw you. What do we do?"

"We have time to figure that out. But I need you not to say anything to anyone, especially Isaziah. When he gets back tonight, we will have a family meeting. I got thirty minutes before Tyshawn and I meet. I'm gonna take your hair out. Forward me that picture, too, and sit on this floor. Let's get started."

Asia sat on the floor, separating her hair from the remaining box braids. As I took the rest of her braids out,

Asia sat on the floor quietly. I knew she was zoned out. Receiving a picture like that had to be hard on anyone. It took me longer than I expected to take her hair out, which put me behind on my dinner meeting. Asia requested to go with me, but I felt safer with her in the room.

Leaving Asia in my room with strict instructions not to leave the hotel, Marcus and I drove back to the Westin, where Tyshawn was waiting out front smoking a Black & Mild. Our dinner meeting commenced at South City Kitchen Buckhead. As much as Tyshawn wanted to choose the restaurant, I felt better making the decision. He was still gonna pay for the meal if his pockets were right. Our first round of drinks was ordered before going over why he was in Atlanta with us.

"I wanna thank you again for taking care of the travel expenses for this meeting."

"No problem. My fiancé and I figured it would only be right since we weren't able to come your way."

Tyshawn received his drink from the waitress and leaned back. "Well, again, it's appreciated. So, tell me, what do you wanna know?"

There was no need to be really civil. "I wanna know everything you can tell me about the fuck niggas, the Gator Boys. They killed two of my family members and one of my crew members. I don't just want them out of my territory. I want them dead. You're gonna tell me how to kill them," I stated in a hushed tone aggressively.

"You don't seem like the killer type," Tyshawn said, sucking his teeth.

"What does a killer look like?" I took my steak knife, lifting it to my mouth as my tongue licked on the tip of it.

"Guess you never know until someone is pushed. If I knew how to kill them, I would've killed them myself."

"Well, you tell me what you know, and I can make sure you and anyone affected by these clowns will get a chance to watch them go under twelve feet."

"You mean six feet?"

"No, you heard me right." Using the knife, I stabbed it into the table as hard as possible to get my point across. "Don't ever think that because I'm a woman I can't hold my own. You may watch shit like that on TV, but everything we do, we live by this shit."

"Respect, queen. I understand. Well, I can tell you that the two main leaders of the organization are best friends. One is called Shorty G. I assume they call him that due to his height. The other dude, his name was Ron. Not sure if that's his real name, but that's his name or whatever. Word is they come from a small town, and they didn't have many customers for what they were tryin'a do. They were spending more money on product than they were regaining income-wise. They hit my city like visitors, and I took them around me and my crew. I should've known they were too friendly for some street niggas. My brother thought maybe they were on some fruity shit, but it was just them tryin'a find a way to get in my organization and take it over."

"So, how did y'all exactly meet?" I was intrigued to know how they got in. "These niggas were able to infiltrate your people like that?"

"I met them through one of my partners. They claim they knew them niggas from school and had been friends for a while. My partna's name was Philly. He was so cool. Philly was never a snake, so I trusted his judgment. He told me that Shorty G was new to the game and wanted to learn. He wanted product. I supplied them for a few months. Philly was in charge of working with them and making sure all the money was good. Then things got funny. Money was coming up short, and Philly wasn't coming around as much. Soon after that, we got hit. Most of our product was taken. My main soldiers were taken from me." Tyshawn sat forward, his eyes watery.

"Philly let them in? Where's he now?"

"Dead. I did what needed to be done. The Gator Boys have a track record of getting in good with someone in your team and having them flip on you. If they came after you and anyone working or related to you, they got to someone in your crew. Find the bad apple and kill it."

Chapter 14

Isaziah

I was halfway back to Atlanta when I realized I needed a new burner and a new rental. If them niggas was smart, someone would've caught my license plate info. Regardless, I needed to get rid of anything that could tie me to Alejandro and my sister's car. I tossed my current phone out the window as I noticed a Metro PCS store near the airport. Swinging in there, I could just purchase a phone outright without linking any of my actual personal information to the phone line. I purchased six phones, just enough for those who needed them.

After grabbing the phones, my next stop was the airport. I had a few fake IDs on me, so if my license was run, no hits would come back for the rental. The current little car we had wasn't fast enough. I wanted a car that was common but could still switch to sports mode in case of an emergency. It took me about an hour to get the car and paperwork, but my new little Subaru WRX was going to be the perfect fit. See, what was wrong with a lot of dealers and connects, they wanted to live like superstars or like them niggas off of *Belly* or *Paid in Full*. But flashiness always comes with a price and the wrong attention. This car was something that a white person would probably buy before a nigga would.

Exiting the parking lot, I sent Nahima a text with the following instructions:

Isaziah: I need you to listen to me closely. Do not ask questions. We don't have the time for that. Tell everyone we are checking out. We are switching to a different hotel out near the Camp Creek area. I need everyone at the hotel. I'm going to send you the address in thirty minutes. That nigga Tyshawn too. Until otherwise, his safety is our concern. I'll send the address in a few.

Nahima: Okay.

It was simple and taken care of just like that. Knowing how everyone but Shereene respected any call my fiancée would make, it made things easier to delegate knowing it would be completed. Sad part was, we were on the run like fugitives, but none of us had ever been convicted of anything. On the way to the hotel, I made a call to Alejandro's sister, Vanessa. She was always true to the streets. No one crossed her simply because she was one of the only friends Nahima really had, but she was also hell on wheels.

"Say it straight," Vanessa stated through the speaker loudly.

"Where's Dro? Has he made it back?" My concern for him and his daughter's safety was at an all-time high.

"*Uno momento por favor, señor.*" Someone she didn't want in her conversation must have been around.

I was fluent in a few languages, so if we needed to switch it up on them, then I would. A few seconds went by, and then she came back to the line.

"What's up? I don't have long."

"Where's Dro?"

"He just walked in. He's really banged up. He made a deal with the devil for his daughter. He got her back. But he was told if he and the other girl working together don't deliver you soon, they'll both die."

"Vanessa, did they mention anything to you about the girl they were working with, or do you know anything?" I inquired, as answers were needed to know in what direction we needed to go.

"No, I don't know shit but this: I won't lose him or anyone else. You fix this!"

"I'm going to take care of this."

"You better. If he dies, I'm holding you accountable."

"Vanessa, I promise, they will die before any of us or before they take anyone else we all love."

"Where's Nahima?"

"Safe. Handling things on her side. You know how she is."

"True. We will be in touch."

Vanessa didn't leave room for me to say much more before disconnecting the call. I walked into the hotel shortly after getting everyone's rooms. Soon, everyone would be arriving. There was a lot on my mind, and I just wanted to relax and figure all this shit out. There was a lot Vanessa said without saying it. I was able to book all of our rooms for at least two weeks. My car had enough work and money in the trunk to put a nigga behind bars for a lengthy amount of time.

The hotel clerk didn't ask too many questions. She just smiled bashfully at me the entire time. When I finished signing the paperwork, she asked me how long I was in town. After I replied that my fiancée and family were on the way to meet me, her bashfulness turned into an attitude.

"You act like a bitch wanted to fuck you or something." She popped her big soup cooler lips at me while rolling her neck.

"I'm not saying anything, ma'am. I just responded to your question. My fiancée and family will be here for two weeks. It was just a simple response." *She must be used to a different type of nigga.*

"Well, my bad then. I thought you were saying that to be funny. I apologize. But you are cute though. You really got a girl? Does she like girls? If so, I get off at twelve. I can always sneak up." The young lady popped her spearmint gum as she passed me the first few keys that were programmed.

"I'll talk to wifey and see what she says. Right now, I am truly exhausted and just want to unwind. It was a long trip."

"Yeah, I feel you. Well, let me finish these keys so you can get some rest. You may need it for later." With a wink, she finished the other ten keys before providing them to me.

As I was receiving the last key, Nahima and the crew walked in. The nigga Tyshawn was right behind her like he was her bodyguard. My vibe was off with this nigga. Maybe it was because of how close he was to my girl, or just maybe it was a hunch he was in with them niggas the Gator Boys too. At this point, we couldn't trust nobody.

"Hey, babe. Glad to see you made it safely." Nahima greeted me warmly with a kiss on my lips.

"I'll always find my way back to you." With my arm wrapped around her waist, I could see the clerk eyeing us with a devilish smile. "Ma'am, are we all done?"

"Yes, sir. You have all your keys. You have any problems, let us know." The clerk smiled back at Nahima and me before I passed everyone their keys.

This time we were separated between two different floors. I looked down at one of the keys. On the back of the envelope, the name Tish was written with a heart. Considering she was tryin'a smash, I knew that had to be the key to Nahima's and my room. Instead of taking that room, I passed it over to Marcus just in case the clerk tried to use a master key to slide in my room.

We settled into our room, and Nahima wanted to dive into everything. My headspace wasn't there. We communicated pretty effectively, but after the day I had, peace of mind without any of the extra was needed. While she talked and talked, I went on to the shower, allowing the water to wash me of the shitty day.

"So, you're not gonna listen to me? You just gon' get in the shower? Nigga, I'm talking to you! And what the fuck was that with the little clerk? She suck your dick while you were waitin' on us?" Nahima yelled at me, yanking the shower curtain back.

"Bitch, you done lost your mind. You don't know what the fuck I went through today! The last thing I want to do is argue with anyone, especially you!"

I was trying to close the shower curtain, but Nahima refused to let go of it, staring me dead in the face. "That's gonna be the last time you call me a bitch. You wanna be alone, then be alone. I may come back, I may not." Nahima stormed off, leaving the steaming hot water hitting my body and the bathroom floor.

"Nahima! Nahima!" I called out for her, but all I could hear was the hotel door shutting.

"Damn it!" I shouted to myself. I fucked up by calling her a bitch. *Damn, sometimes women have to understand that when we need time to just give us our space. But I shouldn't have taken my anger and frustration out on her.* Turning off the shower, I grabbed one of the Egyptian cotton robes so I could try to catch her before she got too far. By the time I got to the lobby, she was pulling out of the parking lot.

Chapter 15

Nahima

Isaziah had to have lost his damn mind at that moment. Especially for calling me out my name. He was going to get more than cussed out. Obviously, he forgot who had always been there for him. Rough days happen, and right now we were being tested. Falling apart at that moment wouldn't be good for anyone. I was sure he was going to follow me, but I wasn't stopping. Isaziah never had shit hit the fan like this before, but he had to do better with his emotions. A lot needed to be sorted out. I was sure something unimaginable happened while he was on his trip, but I wasn't here for him acting like a toddler.

I could see Isaziah in his robe standing at the entrance of the hotel as I left the hotel. Needing time to just clear my head and everything, I decided to take a drive through the city and see where I would end up. I knew nothing about Atlanta, where to go or not to go. I didn't want to hang downtown, so I traveled out to the west side. There had been a lot of foot traffic as I rode near the campuses of Morehouse, Spelman, and Clark Atlanta. Even though it had been a little min since I was in undergrad, I truly enjoyed being in the midst of energetic, young black folks. It was a vibe you can't get nowhere else. I needed that good energy in my presence. Looking at them, it made me think back to a much simpler time in my life.

The money was easy, and classes were tough, but I kicked ass making the dean's list, and Isaziah and I were more in love than ever. It was so simple.

I kept going past them with a smile and thoughts of how effortless our lives were. I got to the outskirts of Bankhead, pulling up to Blue Fame. The parking lot was lit. You could tell there were really some hood niggas in there with some money by the types of cars in the parking lot. Parking my car toward the front of the club, I went in with just twenty bands in my purse and decided to have a little stress relief of my own.

I probably went a little far by accusing Isaziah of sleeping with or getting head from that chick at the front desk, but he pissed me off. I was trying to tell him that we were possibly set up according to Tyshawn, and Asia received that picture of Shereene's dead body on their mother's doorstep. Even when you want to be someone's peace or rider, you need time apart. That was what I was giving the both of us at that moment.

Walking into the strip club, I saw it was packed with nothing but a bunch of D boys, and most of the strippers were really pretty plus thick as fuck. Now they may have had some work done, but they were looking bad as hell. I found a seat near the stage and made myself comfortable.

This stripper named CoCo Delight hit the pole just as I ordered my drink and food. She was beautifully toned, her body was super curvy, tits about a good, full C-cup, her brown skin was covered in tats, and her booty was just the right plump size for her shape. The way she moved her body on that pole turned me on in a way I thought would never happen. Now don't get me wrong, I believe all women are beautiful, but I'd never been sexually attracted to a woman until now. The way she climbed that pole as her top fell to the stage and then she dropped down into a split perfectly, I was in lust. CoCo Delight crawled over to me real sexy like, then lay on her back, using her abdominal area to push herself up into a headstand with her legs wide open. I never ate pussy before, but maybe I needed to try tonight. It wouldn't be cheating if Isaziah was in the room.

I always found a way to get payback when he pissed me off. This would be perfect. He wouldn't have a clue. He would just sit there and watch 'til I knew he was hard enough to drill through a brick wall, then I'd make her watch. I knew I threw a good $100 or $400 at her, knowing I couldn't show off like we normally would. All our money needed to be used sparingly. CoCo was working extra hard for this cash. Her set ended quickly. As she was grabbing all her money from the stage, I leaned over the edge, motioning for her to come close to me.

"What's up, baby?" she hollered over the music.

"I wanted to know what all you're into." I slid a $100 bill in between her ass cheeks.

"I'll be down to see you in a second," she said, blowing me a kiss. I took her response and went back to my seat with my food and drink waiting on me.

I was enjoying my entertainment as Isaziah repeatedly called my phone. He knew if I left angry, it was best to just let me have my space for the time being. I was gonna be home sooner rather than later. There was no reason for him to be so pressed. If it were a true emergency, I would have received a text, but since I didn't, I ordered another drink as I was approached by this guy blinged out like he was a superstar.

"Aye, shorty, I got a section back here if you don't wanna sit alone." His breath reeked of alcohol.

"I appreciate it, but I'm sitting here," I gracefully declined, flashing my engagement ring slightly.

"Well, congrats, Miss Lady. At least let me get you a drink or something on me. You are extremely beautiful.

Don't turn me down on that please." The tequila I had was starting to creep up on me, but he was starting to resemble Trey Songz.

"Well, I mean, I guess I shouldn't turn down a drink or a dance, right?" I stood up to look him in his eyes.

Just as he went to reach toward me to pull me closer, my new eye candy, Co Co Delight, intervened. "She's in good hands, Shane. How 'bout you go back to your little crew?"

"Damn, shorty. Why you being like that? I was just asking if she may want a drink or something. I can't be friendly?"

"If you don't get your nasty dragon-breath ass away from her and me, I will have all y'all escorted out of here."

"CoCo, don't be like that, baby. You weren't this mean to me when I was busting that pussy open every night."

"Shane, you weren't busting shit open. Every orgasm you thought I had was faked. Again, nigga, move or I'll get security to move you all." CoCo was shoving the Shane guy away from me.

"Hey, what's up with him?" I was nosy and drunk.

"He's bad business. He kinda pulled some snake shit. That's the only reason he's on top like he is. The rest of them niggas just scared of him," CoCo responded.

"What you mean?" She had my attention in different ways.

"He hooked up with some lame niggas from some part of Florida and they pulled together to off his mans. Then ratted on them niggas, and a few of that crew went to prison for his murder. But not him. Not too many people know that. If they did, he'd be dead right now his damn self."

"You say a crew from Florida?"

"Yeah. But what did you wanna talk to me about? I'm sure it wasn't this."

"Yeah, we can get there. But what was the crew's name? Do you remember?"

"Gator something. Why?"

"You sure?" Either I was drunk or she really said that the name was Gator something.

"Yeah, what's wrong? Your whole mood just changed."

"Can you give me your number? I gotta go. I do want to see you later though if you're into something like that."

"Yeah. You from outta town or something, ain't you?"

"Yeah, how you know?"

"You talk different from us. Let me put my number in your phone." CoCo placed her number in my phone, and I jetted out of the club.

Atlanta was big but not that big. Isaziah needed to know about this as soon as possible.

Chapter 16

Isaziah

Nahima popped back in the hotel around one in the morning. I wanted to argue, but she had this look of terror in her eyes. All I wanted to do was embrace her without the extra back and forth. Nahima shut the door behind her as she began stripping down to her beautiful skin.

"You wanna talk?" I asked in a whisper. "I wanna apologize for calling you out of your name in that manner. It won't happen again."

"It's fine. We can talk in a moment. I just want to shower." Nahima stumbled her way into the shower.

I lay on the bed watching *Goodfellas* as it was showing on HBO. When she emerged from the bathroom, she seemed a tad bit more sober than before. With her bath sheet wrapped around her wet body, she lay beside me, not saying a word. Nahima must have been truly pissed with me, and that I didn't like. The silent treatment is a killer more than anything else. Turning over to look in her eyes, I offered to finish drying her body off and oil her up like she enjoyed.

"Babe," Nahima moaned out while I massaged her shoulders. "I'll tell you what happened if you finally tell me what happened." I figured that was coming. She had her way of making someone talk, especially me.

"I get to my destination, and I see Shereene's rental, but there's no bullet hole, no blood, nothing left behind. Then Alejandro popped up like he was supposed to for the drop, but he seemed super off. Come to find out, them dusty-ass clowns kidnapped his daughter, forcing that man's hand. He told me about the supposed plan after I contacted him about making the exchange. Then next thing you know, he's rushing me away. Now I got all the fucking work and money in my trunk."

Nahima popped her head up, looking astounded at the words that just came out of my mouth. "What the fuck? Alejandro? Why you ain't off that nigga?"

"Did you not hear me? If it weren't for him, you wouldn't be looking at me right now!"

"So, where is he now? What else happened?"

"He's home with Vanessa. He was beat up pretty bad according to her, and his daughter is alive. But he and whoever else they got working with them got until a certain time to get me back home, or they killin' everyone."

"Well, Tyshawn said to me that someone in their organization linked up with the Gator Boys and that's how he fell. They killed his right-hand man and all. So, the question is, who is the rat in our shit?"

Nahima had a point. Who was the rat? Was it a female? Was it one of the guys? Who would want me or my family out of the way this bad? My thoughts ran rampant with different ideas of who could be behind all of this. Nahima sat all the way up with her titties dangling in my face.

"There's more that I need to inform you about." Nahima tossed her head back with a heavy sigh.

"What's on your mind?" I kneeled down to the edge of the bed to suck on her toes.

"Mmmm, baby, wait. This is serious," she moaned out as I licked the soles of her feet.

"I'm listening, baby, talk to daddy."

"Asia got a text from a random number, and it was a picture of Shereene with her wrists slit. I'm so sorry, baby. I'm so sorry."

I dropped her feet from my mouth, not knowing what to say or feel. My eyes crowded with the tears I was trying to hold in. Nahima reached over, taking me into her arms.

"Let it out, babe. It's okay, just let it out." Nahima nurtured me in her arms as I bellowed until I couldn't anymore.

How in a matter of weeks do I lose not just my mother, but my big sister too? This was a double blow that I know my family wasn't prepared for. Shit, we were barely dealing with having Momma gone, but to lose Shereene too? It was way more than anyone could handle. My sadness turned into rage at that point. It wasn't going to be simple to erase the situation. I planned on providing a massacre when I touched down in Florida. *The Gator Boys better say their prayers and kiss they mommas.*

It took me a while to regain my composure. Time slowly drifted, and when I looked up, Nahima was asleep, mouth wide open and snoring louder than the bears in the woods. Even with her loud-ass snoring, she looked extremely beautiful. I was reminded of some of the beautiful things and people I still had in my life who had to be protected. Without her, I would be incomplete, and our legacy was not to be taken for granted. Each day, at that moment, was more of a precious gift than it had ever been for me before. Letting Nahima sleep, I kissed her on the forehead before I took a little stroll.

Since I had everyone provide me and Nahima their room numbers, something told me to go meet with this Tyshawn nigga face-to-face. It was mad early in the morning, but there was something about him that didn't sit right with me. He had to be up to something. I just couldn't put my finger on it. I took the elevator up to floor seven, praying that my intuition was wrong about that nigga. I knocked on door 762 twice, and then he opened the door.

"Hey, man, what's up? It's mad late, everything good?" Tyshawn asked, cracking the door open.

"Yeah, just want to have a little chat. You gon' let me in?"

"Well, I mean, I ain't really dressed to be around some niggas right now."

"Then get dressed and let me in. We need to talk."

Tyshawn yawned in my face, and I could smell his hot-ass breath. It took that man ten minutes to come back to the door and allow me into the hotel room. I came with no weapon or anything. Couldn't have any dead bodies in hotel rooms, especially when the rooms were under my alias name. Walking into the room, I found that it smelled like weed and ass. The worst combination to smell. Holding my breath, I took one of the chairs at the desk and sat down.

"What's up that couldn't wait 'til later today?"

"I understand the meeting with my wife went well. But I still wanted to meet you. I know what you told her, but I want to hear from you myself." I didn't know about the full conversation, just enough to get him to talk to me openly if he was truly interested in working with us.

"Same shit, man. Niggas came in wit' one of the homies wanting to buy product and go from there. But my nigga betrayed me, making a deal with them niggas. Killed my partner and tried to kill me. They took almost everything I worked for and loved. Trust me when I say I know and feel what y'all going through." Tyshawn lay back on his bed, propping up just a tad.

"So, you didn't know them before that moment? There was no connection between the two of y'all or nothing?"

"You trying to hint on something, brah?" Tyshawn became a little hostile with me, harshening his tone.

"I ain't hinting on shit. I suggest you change your tone with me, too, or shit can get really ugly, my dude."

"Shit can get ugly then. I ain't scared of you or that bitch you got. Keep fuckin' wit' me. I'll fuck yo' wife in front of you and make you watch me slit her throat and let her bleed to death. I don't give a fuck about you or her! She so sweet. I'd hate to do her like that 'cause her old man can't hold his shit together." Tyshawn threw out a threat I couldn't forget about.

"You gon' regret those words coming out yo' mouth, but you got it, my dude. I just wanted to get to know who my wife was letting in our circle. She believes your little bullshit-ass story. If you ask me, you probably set your people up and now feel sorry for it."

"If I did? You have no clue what I go through every day! I want them niggas dead just as much as you do!"

At that point, Tyshawn and I were face-to-face in the middle of the hotel floor. With all my energy, I shoved him out of my face and exited his room. Whatever this man's issues were were no longer my concern. If he could throw a threat out like that, there was no telling what he may do to any of us. I had to eliminate the threats one by one until everything was wholesome again.

Chapter 17

Nahima

Waking out of my sleep, I received a call from Tyshawn. It was only about four in the morning. He was irate and screaming about Isaziah cussing him out and trying to tell him how he was lying about the things he told me. I wasn't sure what was going on inside my fiancé's little brain, but he was gonna shoot us in the foot before we even got the chance to get started.

This was unusual for Isaziah's behavior. But these few weeks had shown me nothing was impossible with him or his family. I searched for Isaziah through the hotel, but he was nowhere to be found. I called Marcus and received no answer. Then I called Asia. She answered but hadn't heard from or seen Isaziah since we checked in. Either he was hiding somewhere in the hotel trying to get his emotions in check or he had dipped out. I was getting ready to attempt to call him when I received a call on the room phone.

"Hello?"

"Come out to the front. We need to take a ride."

"Isaziah, what the fuck is going on? Why the fuck are you going to people's rooms threatening them early in the fucking morning?"

"Nahima, just fucking listen, goddamn! Please, just come on. Don't say shit to no one. We need to head out for a bit."

"Fine, let me throw something on."

"I'll be waiting."

The call disconnected, and I scurried to find something to toss on. Something about Isaziah's voice over the phone rubbed me the wrong way. He sounded a tad aggravated but shook. Eyeing my black biker shorts, I tossed them on with my white crop-top hoodie and Nike slides. Grabbing the hotel key and my purse, I rushed out to meet Isaziah, who was parked in the front blocking the entrance.

"Come on, get in!" Isaziah shouted as he opened the door for me from inside the car.

Isaziah had Jeezy's "And Then What" blasting through the car's stereo. We rode in silence for about thirty minutes before we pulled up to a McDonald's.

Isaziah parked the car and turned the music down just enough so we would be able to hear one another talk. "We gotta talk about a few things."

"Damn right! Why the fuck did Tyshawn call me all upset saying you threatened him and accused him of playing both sides? Why would you do that?"

"That ain't what happened. Nigga got uptight when I started asking him about the Gator Boys and shit. He gave me a different version of what he told you. Nahima, why would I threaten someone who's not a threat to us? The man said he would rape you in front of me then kill you while I watched! Why wouldn't I threaten him back?"

"He said what?"

"You heard me! Why would I have to lie to you about that or anything? You gon' trust a stranger over your man?"

"I wouldn't go that far, Ziah."

"Obviously you were thinkin' something out of the way 'cause you were ready to jump down my throat over this nigga."

For a moment there, he was right. My mindset wasn't on him or what may have triggered Isaziah to go off. I knew my man better than that, but with everything that had happened, who was to say his judgment wasn't at least a little clouded?

"I just know you been struggling with things since your mom passed and there's something going on in your mind that you won't let out. Now knowing that Shereene is truly gone, I can only imagine how you're feeling. I just wanted to be there with you through this, through it all, but you got to let me in, babe. You haven't been as transparent as I need you to be. You want to protect us, but I want to protect you." I placed my hand on top of his gently.

"Babe, I know. It's just hard to deal with everything. Sometimes I'm just sitting filled with so much hurt but more so anger. And now it's as if I'm responsible for Shereene's death. If I had gone after her or anyone, she would be still here."

"Listen to me. You can't blame yourself for what happened to her or to any one of us. You didn't force her to leave. You didn't tell her to walk out of your life. None of this is your fault. You have always done right by all of us in this crew and this family. If anyone says any different, then fuck 'em. But you're my handsome, sexy-as-fuck fiancé. You are so amazing, and no matter how hard you are in these streets, your heart is a pot of gold." I looked into his eyes and could feel all his pain.

"Are we gonna make it through this?"

"When don't we make it through anything? This is just a harder test than most. But I got you. I love you so much."

"How do you stay so strong for us?"

"I gain my strength when you aren't strong enough. Just like I know you do for me. I love you."

"Not as much as I love you. But we gotta get rid of that nigga, Tyshawn. I had some research done myself in between time. Some of what you heard was true, but his people died because of him, not the other way around."

"How do you know? Is that where you been?"

"After he had his little tantrum, I left the room. The room key gave me access to the office room. Using those computers, I searched up his full name and saw a few things that made me a little disturbed."

Isaziah passed me some papers that included a copy of Tyshawn's arrest records and a copy of some messages sent to Isaziah from this guy who was a family member of the friend Tyshawn had referenced to me earlier. The family member stated that Tyshawn had not been paying his friend since some new people came into town. Then one day they were arguing at a club, and his friend was shot twelve times and found in the alley of the club. He knew it was Tyshawn who either pulled the trigger or set it up.

What I was reading was astounding to say the least. Here I was feeling sorry for that snake-ass nigga. He didn't deserve prison time. He deserved to be under the ground. Maybe my man had every right to feel the way he did. *We can never show anyone our hand. That's how you become vulnerable in this game. You get fucked up.*

"So, what do you wanna do, babe?"

"We have him help us get to the Gator Boys. He can either comply or die. Those are his only options."

"That's fine with me. Hopefully he chooses option A instead of forcing our hand."

"Wanna get some breakfast? I'm ready to eat something. You would be perfect to eat, but I need actual food, too."

"You can eat that, too," I said with a chuckle. "But I could go for some Waffle House, not no McDonald's."

"You got it."

Making our way to Waffle House, we rode through the city streets of Atlanta, seeing what kind of places we could possibly set ourselves up for work.

"Hey, babe?"

"What's up, momma?"

"We need to build a team out here. That way the product and shit we got can move."

"How are we gonna find a place or someone to do that with? We don't have no one here we trust who could get our shit off and we still get our money."

He was right. Isaziah had his hand on my thigh while I leaned my seat back some more. As I pondered on his statement, a light bulb went off inside my head.

"I know who we can test out. We can talk about it while we eat."

"A'ight. My wifey, Nahima, with the plan."

"As always."

I had the perfect person in mind. Not only would she be good at moving weight for us, but the bitch she knew who fucked with the Gator Boys could be used. Like my hubby said, them niggas ain't gon' have a choice but to cooperate if they wanted to see a new day after we were done.

Chapter 18

Isaziah

After having breakfast, Nahima and I traveled toward Bankhead. She took me to this little strip club called Blue Flame. In my mind, I was like, *oh, yeah, this the joint I heard about in songs and stuff.*

"Why are we here?" I wondered as I parked behind this blue Challenger.

"I want you to meet someone. Hopefully, they're here already." Nahima got out of the car, slowly grabbing her pocketbook.

"Nahima, we can't just bring anyone in! We don't know nobody out here like that."

"We gotta start somewhere. You trust me, right?"

"You know I do. It's everyone else I don't trust."

Nahima laughed at me as she stood on the side of the driver's door waiting for me to get out of the car. Hand in hand, we walked into the club. It felt like all eyes were on us. We walked through the front doors, past the check-in area, and Nahima and I were arm in arm walking through the club. The bottle girls were making their way through the crowd toward one of the VIP areas. When I looked toward the bar, one of the strippers winked at me while still focusing on throwing ass on the customer behind her. The tables that surrounded the main stage had been about halfway occupied. With half of the ten tables about full, the dancer on the stage was climbing the pole, but not enough money was being thrown. The other dancers on the floor were sitting around on their phones. Nahima tapped my shoulder, motioning me to follow her.

"Hey there, pretty lady." Nahima tapped this chocolate thick, big-booty female.

The young woman was bent over in her G-string, grabbing some ones off of the floor when she noticed us behind her. She immediately hugged Nahima with a slight ass grab before extending her hand to mine.

"CoCo, this is my fiancé, Isaziah. Isaziah, this is my new buddy, CoCo."

"It's nice to meet you, CoCo." I shook her hand quickly while admiring her body. She was undeniably a chocolate goddess. There was something about her that made my dick jump.

"Likewise," she replied, keeping her eyes on Nahima. "What you doing here? I never got a text back or anything. You left here so fast the other night, and now I know why." CoCo chuckled with a menacing grin.

"Whatever, girl. Are you on your shift, or do you have a moment to take a little break really quick? We wanna talk to you about something."

"I got time for you, babe. Let me get my phone out of the back. I'll meet y'all out front."

As she walked away, Nahima caught me watching CoCo's ass switch from left to right.

"I know, her ass is nice as hell, right?" Nahima teased before grabbing my hand.

"It's not better than yours."

"Yeah, well, your dick is starting to show through your sweats. Get it right." With a pat on my dick, Nahima walked in front of me, switching her phat little booty.

While waiting outside, I sparked up my spliff, leaning against the car. CoCo showed up about ten minutes later in some sweats and her little purple bra she had on. She approached the car with a smile and seemed like she was pretty easygoing.

"What's going on, y'all? What made you take a trip all the way to see little ole me?"

"We have a proposition for you. My fiancé and I have some merchandise we need help selling. We are willing to give you fifty percent of all sales made. But I need you to lead us to that nigga who was in my face when I was here the other night." Nahima took the blunt from my hand so she could take a hit or two.

"Fifty percent of whatever we make together? That's a little generous. I don't know anyone moving like that. Whose decision was that? Yours? The hubby? Or a collective agreement?"

"What my wifey says is law. I don't double cross her or vice versa. If that's what she wants to give you, I'm all here for it. But we will need whatever she asks you."

"I can get down with that. And the two of you. We can work that out. I'm all about a check. This my stomping grounds anyway. When do you wanna get started?"

"Take us to meet ole boy from that night, and we will go from there. I take it you can get in touch with him quickly."

"Yeah, I'll call him now." CoCo placed her phone on speaker as she chose the number for Shane.

The phone rang a few times before a deep Darth Vader voice answered. "What's up, little momma? I was waiting on this call. You finally want some more of this good-ass dick?"

"Nah, nigga, I got some work for you. I wanna bring my new little shorty over there and talk numbers. You wit' it?" CoCo put on a front just enough to bait him.

"We can do that, shawty. But I wanna get some of that pussy. What's up, though?"

"Depends on how other things go. I'll consider letting you slide in again. What time can we slide through?"

"Shitttt, give me 'til 'bout nine. We can link up then."

"That's cool. We will see you then."

"Bet." Shane hung up sounding a tad bit more excited than he did when he first answered.

Since everything seemed set up, I wanted to get my hands on Tyshawn until we had to link up with this other nigga. We needed to make sure that if we murked his ass, no trail would lead back to us. I left Nahima talking with CoCo while I walked off to make a call to my main man Marcus.

"What up, boy? You and sis straight?" Marcus answered the phone quickly, sounding out of breath.

"Yeah, we good, nigga, but are you okay? Breathing all heavy in a nigga ear and shit. You wanna call me back or something?"

"Fuck your skinny David Ruffin–lookin' ass." We both belted out laughter before Marcus could finish his statement. "I'm straight though. What you need?"

"That dude, man. That Tyshawn nigga. I think he been lying to us. He either tryin'a set us up or he wants to make things right that he fucked up. Either way, I'm good on him. Find out exactly if anyone knows where, when, and why. Find out where we can get rid of shit and all. We need nothing to lead back to us."

"That's a huge ten four. I don't know much about Atlanta like that. I'll do some research on it all. By the time you get ready, I'll have something for you."

"I love you, my dude. Thank you. Keep me updated. Have Rich keep an eye on him. If he moves out of that room, Rich moves. Understood?"

"Got it, boss. No worries."

"Cool. I'll catch up with you."

When I walked back over to the two of them, I could see CoCo reaching around Nahima's waist. I was low-key shocked at what I was seeing. Nahima wasn't pushing her away. If anything, she allowed CoCo to cop a few feels on her. I cleared my throat so they could acknowledge my presence.

"Everything good, babe?" Nahima and CoCo were locked arm in arm.

"Yeah, just starting the process on something we discussed earlier. But what's this? Why y'all so cuddly?"

"I was thinking since we had some time to kill, CoCo here could hang out with us, show us around the city. Maybe show me how to do some of her tricks or whatever, unless you had something else in mind."

"Well, I think that if you would like to have her company for a little before we handle business, why not? CoCo, we'll follow you to your crib."

CoCo stood back looking a little more scared than anything. "Why my house?"

"Because we are visitors. We wouldn't do business with you if you ain't seem trustworthy. Go ahead now, cute self. Me and the hubby will be behind you."

CoCo was hesitant at first and just stood there. Then she walked off, getting into her little red Corvette, pulling the top back and blasting some Future. I had no clue what the two of them had on their minds, but I was soon going to find out and was with whatever.

Chapter 19

Nahima

CoCo allowed us into her home, and it was a nice little one-bedroom apartment near East Point. Inside, she told us to make ourselves comfortable while she took a shower. Isaziah, being on edge like he was, asked if he could hold on to her cell and Apple watch until she returned. I thought it was a little much, but still, we didn't know her or if she would double-cross us. Anything was surely possible at this point. As CoCo got herself together, Isaziah and I decided to roll up and smoke at least half of the spliff before she got out.

Now one thing about letting myself get high, I tended to get horny fast as hell. When the weed started to hit, my pussy started to throb and was getting moister by the second.

"Wanna put it out?" he asked me while leaning back on her black leather sofa.

"You can keep smoking if you want. I wanna do something else instead." Tracing my fingertips on his chest down to his pants, I reached under his sweats, caressing his dick, which was semi-hard.

"Shouldn't we wait until we get in the car or back to the room?' Isaziah eyed me seductively. His mouth was asking me one thing, but his eyes and his dick were telling me something different.

I didn't respond with words. I kicked my sneakers off, propping myself up on the couch with my ass in the air, and began sucking his beautiful dick. I started off slow with just the tip. Sucking on the head of his dick, I felt Isaziah grabbing on my ass cheeks tightly. Then going down to his shaft, I opened my mouth wider, clenching my fist as I learned in a deep throating tutorial video to help pinch the nerve so I wouldn't gag on it. The deeper his dick went down my throat, the more it grew.

Isaziah took his fingers, shoving them in my pussy. Stroking my pussy, this nigga had me super wet. My nipples were getting harder and both of us were moaning so loud, I was sure CoCo would be able to hear us, but I didn't care. His dick tasted so good, and the more he played in my pussy, shoving his fingers deeper inside of me, I was about to cum for the first time.

"You can't cum yet, bitch." The intensity in his voice turned me on more.

Letting his dick slowly out of my mouth, I sat up to take my shirt and bra off. Isaziah grabbed my hardened nipples, pinching them roughly as I slid my pants off onto the floor. His hands still on my breasts, he lowered my body, laying me on my back on her sofa. Just as he was about to slide in, CoCo came into the living room.

"Damn, you know this isn't y'all house or nothing? Like, where the fuck are y'all manners?" CoCo shouted from the corner of the living room, standing there in nothing but her towel.

"I'm sorry. You're right. We got a little carried away," I stated, sitting back up and reaching for my clothing.

"Don't get dressed. It's rude not to ask me to join and you're in my home. Come sit that pussy on my face." CoCo dropped her towel and walked toward us, sitting right behind me.

I arched my back as if I were going to fuck doggie-style so I could suck Isaziah off a bit more since he went a little limp. CoCo sucked on my pussy so fucking good. She was really the first female I interacted with, and she was making me feel like I should've fucked one before now. Her tongue felt amazing around my clit. The moans from CoCo and me must have turned Isaziah on more than I thought.

He pushed me down, instructing CoCo to sit on my face. I was nervous until she told me she would guide me. As we did as big daddy told us, Isaziah lifted my legs on his shoulders while sliding inside of me. CoCo rode my face slowly while massaging my clit as Isaziah slowly stroked my wet kitty. The curve to his dick felt so amazing every time he hit one of my walls. As his pace picked up, the harder his strokes hit.

"Her pussy taste good, bitch? How that fuckin' taste?" Isaziah probed, fucking me harder.

I could barely answer him. My body trembled as I felt myself about to cum.

"That's it, babe. Cum for us. Keep eating this pussy though, don't stop," CoCo moaned out as her pussy juices filled my mouth.

Isaziah kept telling me not to cum, but I couldn't hold it. The urge to pee took over my body, and my climax was peaking like never before.

"You think I should let her cum, sexy?" Isaziah asked CoCo before stuffing my toes in his mouth.

"Yeah, she ready." CoCo stimulated my clit faster until my pussy exploded, and I squirted all over Isaziah and CoCo's couch.

"Fuck yeah, turn that ass over, baby." Isaziah wanted CoCo off of me.

He wasn't done with me yet, and I knew I was in for a hell of a ride. We never had a threesome before. The excitement from it was enticing us, and we were enjoying ourselves. CoCo suggested we get more comfortable and go to her bedroom. Once inside her black and purple bedroom, I laid my body across her dark purple comforter, spreading my legs wide to play with my pussy. Isaziah stood at the edge of the bed jacking his dick while CoCo made her way onto the bed with me.

Propping up on the bed with my knees embedded into the comforter, I helped my man jack himself, getting him back ready to slide inside. With a slap to my ass, Isaziah turned my body, positioning me doggie-style in front of him. CoCo propped her body under mine so my pussy could be in her face and hers in mine. Isaziah slid into my pussy with his right thumb in my booty hole. Feeling the double penetration from him while CoCo sucked my clit like a pacifier filled me with so much pleasure.

After cumming several times thanks to the two of them, my body tapped out from the countless orgasms. CoCo and Isaziah came in my mouth at separate times, and it was an amazing taste to swallow her cum right before Isaziah's. Time went by as we recuperated. The smoke and the sex made us all lazy at that point. Time drew nearer for us to meet with Shane, and CoCo started acting nervous.

"What's wrong, shawty? Having second thoughts?" Isaziah was getting dressed while CoCo twitched her leg and bit her nails.

"Yeah. Everything's good. I just wanna get this done, that's all. Are y'all gonna kill him?" CoCo eyed Isaziah then me anxiously.

"Nah, we ain't killing nobody. That's not what we do. But we do need his help with something. What's wrong, boo? You're mad tense for no reason. Everything was just good." I rubbed my hands across CoCo's back just to help attempt to calm her down.

"Listen to her. She wouldn't lie to you, especially after what we just did. If we wanted to kill either of you, it would've been very clear." Isaziah smiled at the two of us, then asked if we were ready to go.

Isaziah kept CoCo's phone on the way to meet with Shane. He provided her his location, and we met up near Old National Highway near the Red Roof Inn. The parking lot we met him at was deserted, and it looked like nothing but $5 hoes met up there.

"You want to get out of the car and talk to him first? Or you scared or something?" Isaziah was becoming a little more hostile with CoCo than before.

"Nah, I ain't scared, nigga. I just . . . I just don't feel right. But whatever." CoCo got out of the back seat, slamming the door behind her.

We allowed them to talk outside without us. He was taller than I remembered and not as cute. His face had a bunch of bumps all over it, a distinct cut was on the left side of his face, and his hair was in an Afro. When she finally gave us the okay to get out, Isaziah tapped the glove compartment as an indication to grab our guns out of it. Something was setting him off, and I was feeling the same. We got out of the car and waited to see what they were going to say or do.

"Now!" CoCo let out before we could say anything. Shots rang out, and we dodged behind the right side of the car.

With every few glances, we would take a shot. I had no clue that Isaziah had sent Marcus our location throughout the day. We were running out of bullets when Marcus, Sean, Asia, Lauren, and Tyrone pulled up, taking out everyone we couldn't get to. I caught CoCo in hiding with the guy Shane and took that as my opportunity to take care of them personally.

Rushing behind her, I grabbed her tracks, dragging her to the middle of the parking lot as she hollered for me to let her go. Isaziah was right behind me with Shane as the crew surrounded us.

"You set us up, stupid little bitch! We were really gonna break some real bread with you, but we don't do snakes. Your presence is no longer needed or appreciated. Thanks for the nut, too." No jam in the gun, I cocked it, then fired three rounds into her chest and one toward her dome.

CoCo was left bleeding on the ground while Isaziah held Shane. He must've realized that this was going to be his fate if he didn't cooperate.

Chapter 20

Isaziah

You can call it kidnapping, but I called it a guarantee. After shooting CoCo in that parking lot, we gave Shane a similar gun with the same bullets, making him shoot her one more time before Marcus placed him in cuffs and in the car with him. For the past two days, we kept him locked up in the room with Marcus until we figured out how to use him and Tyshawn to our advantage. To be honest, we had no intention of killing little shawty until she switched up on us. She switched up before any work could even be done. That was her fuck-up, and God hopefully understood that we did what was necessary.

Nahima and the remainder of my sisters took the day to hit the city and do some shopping and working. When I say working, y'all should know what I mean. Our work had to be distributed so we could continue making our main source of income. Our online stores were still doing their thing, which was cool, but the weight had to be moved quickly. While my lovely ladies were hitting the ho stroll and shit, looking for new clientele, Marcus and I decided to take Tyshawn out for a bit. Sometimes when you're going through a lot, your judgment can be clouded. In retrospect, I wanted to give Tyshawn at least one more chance to get it right.

Marcus went to grab Tyshawn from his room while I headed to the garage to grab one of the rentals. For his sake, I hoped he would change my mind about him during our little day trip. There were some people we were going to link up with later, so this trip had to be as unproblematic as possible. Nahima sent me a text while I awaited their arrival.

Nahima: Hey, babe. Just seeing how things are going on your end.

Isaziah: Haven't started yet really. But it should be cool. If not, you know the rest.

Nahima: LOL. You right, I do. Be safe and keep me posted.

Isaziah: Always. I love you, Nahi.

Nahima: I love you too, big baby.

Marcus and Tyshawn had gotten into the car as I wrapped up the text from Nahima. These niggas got in the car with a full-blown attitude. All I could wonder about was what happened between them. I needed shit to not be so tense before we could get started.

"What the fuck wrong with y'all asses?" I asked while pulling out of the garage.

"Yo' boy was trippin' and tried to fight me. I won't let him punk me!" Tyshawn spat out with an attitude.

"Nah, this nigga said he wouldn't go nowhere with either of us, so I made sure he brought his ass. I don't want no more bodies coming up missing. Then he got up and came on."

"Well, the two of you better hold it together. We gotta take this ride." Turning my iPhone on to Car Play, I allowed my Apple Music to play my nineties mix playlist as we hit the road.

The two of them talked about my music choice, and the ride was cooler than we thought it would be. We got to a pit stop on the way to our destination to grab food when

Asia called me, telling me that they were able to get about 80 percent of the product out of the way. I was pleased to hear how they were handling things without any of the men being there.

Placing our order at the Burger King drive-through, I received a text with information with regard to our final stop. Everything was in motion, and for Tyshawn, this was going to be his chance to set the record straight. The food was super fresh, and my burger was looking like a steak. I hadn't eaten since the day before, and my stomach was starting to sound like the plant from *Little Shop of Horrors*. "Feed me, Isaziah," was what my stomach called out.

I didn't want to waste time sitting in the parking lot letting niggas eat, as we were on a time schedule. Nahima and I had plans to deal with Shane later that evening, so all timing had to be on point. Tyshawn started fidgeting in the back seat as if he knew what was up.

"Aye, man, are we still in Atlanta? This don't look like we still in Georgia."

"You been asleep off and on most of the ride, so how would you know?" I responded as we pulled into the driveway of a bando.

"Y'all going to kill me? Look, man, I got kids and family who need me, my nigga. Please don't kill me! I was just joking 'bout what I said I would do to your girl, bro. Just chill for real." That man was pleading for his life, and I wasn't even touching him.

I laughed at him while parking the car. "Nah, nigga. You said you were here to help us, so that's what this is. Everyone out of the car."

Marcus held on to Tyshawn as we walked up the squeaky wooden stairs. Once inside, we saw that the walls were bare, and a soft sound of The Isley Brothers singing "Between the Sheets" played in the background.

My instructions were to meet everyone in the main dining hall at the back of the house near the kitchen. Marcus and Tyshawn followed me, passing by a few older people sitting and smoking their shit. We went into the dining hall, and there they all sat. Tyshawn walked in behind me and noticed the faces in the chairs.

"What the hell are y'all doing here? What's going on?"

"Like I said, you wanted to help, and they are here to help as well." Smiling at everyone around the table, I took a seat and waited for things to begin.

The older woman who resembled Viola Davis sat with her arms crossed as her salt-and-pepper dreads dangled from her head. The man sitting next to her looked pissed just to see Tyshawn's face. His eyes were reading out hatred, and the vibes were colder than ice. There was one last woman sitting toward the end of the table. She barely looked up at him, and when she did, her eyes filled with tears, her lips trembled, and her hands shook a tad.

"I want to thank you all for having us this afternoon. Glad we could be on time," I started the conversation off.

"Glad we could help you all out. Especially on short notice. It's nice to see you again, Tyshawn," the older woman stated, keeping her arms crossed and her eyes locked on me.

"Hey, Miss Jesp." Tyshawn had his head held down like he was ashamed.

"Can you tell us how we can help? I am Majesty, and it's nice to meet the two of you in person." Majesty, the younger woman at the end of the row, pointed to me and Marcus.

"The pleasure is ours. You all know Tyshawn, correct?" I asked, already knowing the answer to the question.

"We sure do." The gentleman leaned over the table, turning his attention to Tyshawn. "Don't we all know one another? Rat-ass bitch."

"PJ, look, I know you're mad at me, but you have to understand it wasn't my choice."

"What wasn't your choice, Tyshawn? There's something we all know, that's true, which is that the Gator Boys and we all know what happened. Well, I know based on what you told my fiancée." I thought I would let things get on out of the way.

"What did he tell you about those Gator Boys exactly?" the older woman asked as she leaned back in the wooden chair.

"Tyshawn, you want to tell them, or should I?" When I looked at him, he seemed petrified. When he didn't respond, I decided I would let the story out. "Apparently, the Gator Boys, who are responsible for my mother's and older sister's deaths, infiltrated his organization. But they didn't just come in and attempt to take over like they're trying to do me and my crew. They came in using someone in his. I think he said the guy's name was Polly or something like that."

"Nah, you mean Philly?" the gentleman asked.

"Yeah, that's it, Philly. Philly introduced them to one another, and then Philly the whole time was gunning for his spot. Teamed up with the Gator Boys and tried to kill my mans over there. Tyshawn told us that's why he had to kill him." I took a cigarette out of my pocket, looking at everyone's reaction.

The three of them were astounded by what I just said. Majesty shook her head and said, "No," over and over again until she screamed out, "Liar!"

Tyshawn looked up finally as he sobbed quietly. "Majesty, please listen." Tyshawn pushed his chair back as if he was going to stand up.

"You fucking liar! Philly loved you like a fucking brother! You killed him because you were jealous! Them niggas met you online, and you hooked up with them faggot-ass niggas. You let one of their niggas fuck you in the ass so you could be in with them. Philly found out after they sent him the video. When he asked you about it, you got upset. He went to meet with you, and that's where things went left. I was in the car, asshole, but none of y'all knew. I stayed quiet and low, but I could hear it all. You killed him because you wanted to be the head. With him gone, you did just that. You lied to everyone and gave them that bullshit-ass story. You ain't nothing but a punk bitch, and I hope my man haunts you every night when you sleep. Philly ain't deserve to die, especially not by your hand. You wouldn't have half the shit you got if it weren't for him!"

Majesty, the older woman, and the gentleman stood up, pulling out their guns, pointing them straight at Tyshawn.

"Please, you gotta listen to me. It wasn't like that. I didn't want to kill him. I promise I didn't. I loved him. He was my brother. Shit been fuckin' with me since. I had to follow orders. It was either him or me. Them niggas was offering more percentage, and I needed it for my kids. Please don't do this. Majesty, think of your godchildren. Please!"

"Yeah, you ain't think of them or my kids when you pulled that trigger." With tears streaming from her eyes, she fired her gun, and the two other people followed.

Majesty shot her gun until her clip was empty. The older guy had to hold her hand to take the gun from her. The room grew quiet, and Marcus got up to grab the gloves. Tyshawn's little lie unfolded quickly, and then he got served justice, and not by his own hand at that.

Chapter 21

Nahima

I wasn't too shocked when Isaziah called me informing me of the not-so-tragic ending to Tyshawn's life. Even hearing what was said about him and what he did gave me peace that the universe had served Tyshawn the karma he was meant to receive. Sadly, he wouldn't be able to help us like we thought. He was all out for himself, and who knew? He could've flipped on us at any moment. Now we had to use Shane, and I wasn't so sure how that would play out. We needed leverage, and I was going to take my time to see what or who we could use before Isaziah returned.

I was lying in the hotel room waiting for my pizza to be delivered when I caught the five o'clock news.

"Breaking news: the body of a dead woman who has yet to be named was found on Fulton Industrial Boulevard early this morning. There seem to be no witnesses, but investigators are trying to see if the security cameras around the building were on during the time of her murder. If you or anyone you know has information about this young woman's death, please call Fulton County Crime Stoppers at 404-555-5668," the reporter stated.

My stomach dropped. We had no idea there were cameras at that location. As much traffic the hoes out there got while sucking and fucking for $40 or for their next fix, you wouldn't imagine it being a place so secured like that. Damage control again. I was getting tired of that shit. We never worked sloppy, and all ins and outs were to be known before going to that location. My first thought was to call Isaziah, but I knew he was about forty-five minutes away, so waiting for him to come and talk in person would have been the best choice. Everything we did was a dangerous game. Trying to get a head start on things, I reached out to Marcus and Terry to have them do some digging in a group chat with Isaziah.

Nahima: Hey, we have a problem. I know Isaziah isn't back yet, but I need y'all at my room in ten minutes.

Marcus: What's going on? I was trying to get a nap in.

Terry: I'll be right there, boss lady.

Marcus: Aye, sis, I'm coming, just let me finish my nap. LOL. Y'all don't ever let a nigga get enough sleep.

Babe: We can go on a real vacation after we settle this shit. I'm not far from y'all either, so wait 'til I get there. Nahima, I'll call you when I'm pulling up.

Nahima: That's fine. I still want everyone who's in this group chat here as soon as possible. No excuses. Since Marcus needs a nap, I'll give you guys an additional thirty minutes. So, thirty minutes from now, I need to see everyone. Understood?

Marcus: Thanks, sis! I'll see you in a minute.

Terry: Yes, ma'am, I'll be there shortly as well.

Babe: I'll be pulling up soon, babe. Stay by your phone.

Nahima: Okay.

As the conversation came to an end, there was a knock on my hotel door. I hoped it was the food because ya girl was hungry as hell. I looked through the peephole, and the pizza guy had his head down, bobbing back and forth. They must have had their earbuds in. When I opened the door with the cash in my hand, I was bum-rushed by two people in black masks. Without my thinking twice, my reflexes kicked in, allowing me to swing at one, and I tried to head out of the door when I heard a familiar voice call out my name. The other attempted to swing but missed, allowing me to land a jab right to the left cheek.

"Nahima, I don't want to kill you. Just come with us," the female voice said to me through her mask.

"I know that voice. I know you, don't I?" I turned slightly to see if she would reveal herself to me.

"I love you, I do, but this is just business. Thank Shereene." She slowly pulled up her mask, and it was Asia with a few tears coming down her face.

I looked at her, then eyed my phone and keys on the table near the door. I couldn't believe what I was seeing. Of all people . . . Asia? I knew once Isaziah heard this he wouldn't believe me. Why would he? It's his little sister we were talking about, you know. Before I made a clear run for it, the other masked person attempted to hit me from behind. Lucky for me, I could see them creeping in the mirror, allowing me to block their advances and knock them out by hitting them on the head with the vase sitting on the table.

I wasn't sure if Asia would shoot me, but I took a chance. Moving rapidly, I snatched the keys and phone off the table and began running down the hall. As I ran, I heard three shots go off. I wanted to turn back, but if I did, who knew what would happen to me?

Isaziah

"Babe, I'm 'bout to pull up, what's up? Your food never came or something?" I answered the phone after two rings when I heard Nahima's ringtone go off.

"No! Turn around! I'm about to pull out. We got to go now! And I mean now!" Nahima sounded hysterical on the other end of the phone.

"What are you talking about? Nahima, I need you to calm down and talk to me. Where are you right now?" I was concerned, and she needed to be calm enough to let me know what had taken place.

"I just pulled out of the parking garage. Isaziah, I know you won't believe me, but someone was with Asia, and they came into the room when the delivery guy was there. They both had ski masks on at first, and then Asia lifted hers, saying she didn't want to kill me. I grabbed my shit while she was unsure whether to shoot me, and I ran down the hall. When I got to the elevator, I heard gunshots. I left her there, and I don't know if she's alive. But whoever she was with wanted me or you. Or maybe both of us! But we can't go back to the room. Isaziah, we have to go back home and end this," Nahima blubbered out as I could hear her sobbing loudly.

"Okay, tell me where you wanna go. Is that you right to the left of me?" I flashed my lights at the car that resembled hers.

"That you, babe? I see your lights. I'm going to follow you." Nahima flashed her lights back at me.

"Okay, let's just get you away from here first. But you gotta stay calm enough to drive, you hear me?" I hollered not to scare her but to get Nahima to hold it together.

Pulling out in front of her, I drove as fast and far away from the hotel as possible. I figured it would be best if she ditched her car at a restaurant or something before we continued our ride. I saw a graveyard, and I flashed my lights at Nahima so she would follow me in there. Soon, I got the text asking me why we were in a graveyard at night. Keeping my car running, I hopped out when I saw her getting out of the car.

"What are we doing here?" she asked, coming up to me.

"We need to leave your car here. Report it stolen and shit. We aren't going home or back to the city. We need to find a safe area."

"Isaziah, look around. It's just us! Even though Asia's hand seemed to be forced, she was with someone trying to attack me! We don't know who we can trust anymore!"

"You know Asia wouldn't harm you. How do you think you're here right now?"

"I wouldn't be barely here if she weren't trying to kill me! Isaziah, our family and organization have been compromised! I know you have to see that by now! If you don't, it's only because you choose not to!"

As much as I hated the idea of her being right, Nahima had a point. The bond Asia and Nahima shared was crazy close, so there would be no reason for Nahima to lie about it.

"So, where do we go from here?"

"We need to figure out where Asia is or if she is still alive."

"Nahima, you didn't want me to go inside!"

"Because they could have hurt or killed you. Then what would you want me to fucking do? Huh, Isaziah, what the fuck do you want me to do?"

While Nahima was screaming at me, my phone rang, and it showed up as Asia. Even on the burner cells I saved everyone's number so we could stay in constant communication.

"Hello?" I placed the phone on speaker so we both could hear.

"Isaziah, I'm so sorry. Tell Nahima I'm sorry. Please come get me. I need you to come get me."

"Asia? Asia, is that you?"

"Isaziah, please! I need help! They're gonna kill me. I let her go, and then the person I was with tried to shoot me, but she missed, and then I shot back. She's lying on the floor dead, I think. Please, I'm your sister!"

Nahima shook her head no. The trust she had for my sisters was shattered. That one moment changed a whole history. But she was still my sister, and I had to know why.

"Send me an address. I'll meet you." I hung up the phone without having any more conversation.

Nahima stepped away from me, still shaking her head. "Isaziah, this could be a trap."

"She won't get to you or me. I promise." Gradually moving in closer, I grabbed her hand.

"I don't feel good about this."

"Yeah, neither do I. I'm 'bout to hit up Marcus and have him set things up so we can have a leg up in case she's playing us."

"We shouldn't kill her though. Asia needs to be somewhere other than a grave."

"I'm not going to kill my sister unless I have to. Come on, let's go."

Nahima and I got into my car, going straight to our destination.

Chapter 22

Isaziah

I couldn't believe where we were in our lives right now. If someone had told me six months ago that my sister would be betraying me, one sister dead by her own hand, and my mother murdered, I would've thought they were high on that shit. Even with Nahima still saying we shouldn't meet with Asia, it was my duty as her brother to figure out why she felt compelled to try to kill us. She had to have known that if I was in there, they would have attacked me and Nahima. Or maybe that was the plan all along?

It was told to us that someone within the crew had to be the mole. It seemed as if she played her position just enough to get to this moment. Maybe things were all my fault. Maybe this could have all been prevented. I had gotten comfortable in my position and where Nahima and I were planning to go. Shereene should not have felt the need to commit suicide, and Asia should not be working with the enemy.

I had to fix this somehow, and if talking to Asia in person would help lead down that path, I was willing to risk it. Marcus gave me a call after figuring out the info on the location Asia sent me. He told me it was an abandoned mall, and nothing but the Popeye's across the street from it was open. The next few stores or anything were about five minutes down the road driving. I thanked him for the info, and he said he would be nearby. I could tell he wanted more information as to what was going on.

"Babe, maybe we should send Shane in there or not go at all. My spirit doesn't sit well with any of this. Two of your sisters attempted to kill me, and one almost did. Let's just really weigh all this out."

"I already made up my mind. No matter what happens tonight, you don't come in there, and you don't try to save me, understand?"

"Babe, I'm not leaving you alone anywhere! You know that where you go, I go. I ain't leaving you 'cause you wouldn't leave me. If Asia wants to kill you, she has to kill me too. Real shit."

"If we make it through tonight, let's aim to get you another baby in that belly."

"We can try now. A little quickie never hurt nobody."

"You tryin'a have a nigga weak and all discombobulated when walking in there? You know I need recovery time to get my mind right." I laughed a little bit as I cocked my head to the side to look at Nahima. "You are so amazing, you know that?"

"You are my everything, you know that?"

"I do."

"We should file for a marriage certificate and get married in the morning. Don't tell a soul." Nahima took the blunt and sparked it as it hit her lips.

"You being funny?"

"No. When—not if, but when—we make it out of that meeting with Asia tonight all alive and healthy, we get married and tie up loose ends here in Georgia. They had CoCo's body on the news earlier trying to get her identified. We should have someone check that area for anything that may possibly lead back to the rentals or us. Check for the security cameras before the police get hip to anything."

"Goddamn it! If it ain't one thing, it's another motherfucking thing! This is bullshit!" I hit my steering wheel out of frustration.

"It's just the damage control. See if Marcus or Terry can swing by there just to check things out," Nahima suggested as her fingertips traced the back of my neck.

"Yeah, I'll call Terry now." Unlocking my other temporary phone, I chose to call Terry instead of Marcus because Marcus needed to have his head on straight for meeting up with Asia.

Terry answered the call quickly. "Mr. Jones, what can I do for you today?"

"Terry, there may be a little hiccup with the girl we were last with. We planted a different set of fingerprints on the gun, but the area may have had cameras."

"Say no more. Send me the address and I'll check it out. If the tapes were on, I'll make sure they are erased and out of the police's hands."

"Thanks. I'll have your payment for you when we are at the new spot. Get everyone else in order when you finish. We will be switching locations one last time before heading back to Florida."

"Yes, sir. Anything else you or Mrs. Jones need at this moment?"

"No, we are fine, Terry, thank you. Keep me updated."

"Yes, sir."

Our call ended, and Nahima seemed a bit less stressed than before. I gave her a reassuring smile, hoping that would help her feel better. Nahima and I took a ride near the destination where Asia said she would be. Asia was sending text after text wondering where I was or what time I was coming. She was pressed but for reasons unknown. I wasn't sure if she was in any real danger or if she was trying to set me up at this moment.

"Are you going to respond to her?" Nahima asked, looking out her passenger window.

"Nah, I ain't got nothin' to say. But when Marcus gets there, I will have a lot to say."

"Wait, what? What you mean?" Nahima cocked her head to the side all confused.

"Just wait, babe, you will see," I instructed. I had a plan in motion that I didn't say out loud, but I figured it would work.

Chapter 23

Nahima

Isaziah was hiding some vital information from me, and I wasn't having it. First of all, finding out Asia was one of the reasons these niggas were coming for us was a hard pill to swallow. I did believe there was more to the story, but without hearing it from her directly, what were we to believe? I knew Isaziah wasn't thinking about leaving me alone and trying to handle his sister himself. Sometimes he forgot that we were a team. *There is never an I in team, so he'd better get his mind right.*

I was sitting in the car when Marcus called via FaceTime. Isaziah sat up and turned the lights on inside the car so Marcus could see his face.

"You in position, boss man?" Marcus asked as I could hear rustling through some bushes or something.

"Yeah, everything good on this end. Any sign of Asia?"

"Nah, not yet. I set the traps up in the bushes first before heading to the front door. She knows I'm coming?"

"No, I told her it would be me. The goal is to get her to talk as much as possible. Only kill anyone if you have to. If you have to shoot, I hate to say it, but shoot to kill."

"Everybody, boss?"

"At this point, everybody. No hesitation." Isaziah's spirit was heavy. I could feel it through my bones.

"Say less. I'll take it from here."

"Call me when you see her so we can hear everything."

"Bet. I'll hit your line." Marcus hung up the phone, and that was it.

Isaziah sat in silence, and I was stuck trying to piece together what his little plan was. After sitting quietly for a few moments and running different scenarios through my head, I finally broke the ice.

"So, what the fuck was that about?" I was going to get an answer one way or the other.

"Nahima, I wanna make sure the first part of the plan goes right first."

"No, nigga! You're going to tell me now! I deserve to know as your fiancée and your business partner. Tell me what the hell the plan is."

"Nahima!"

"Isaziah!" I snapped back. *He should know saying my name in any tone don't do shit to me but possibly make my pussy wet.*

As he sucked his teeth, he rolled his eyes before expressing his thoughts. "I had Marcus set up some bear traps along the side of the building after seeing a picture of it on Google Maps. That's what I been doing on my phone in between the calls and shit. I don't believe Asia would have done this on her own. Shit, we both know that. It may be easier for her to release to Marcus than to one of us. I'm sure she believes we both hate her at this present time."

"I don't hate her. How could I? But I am confused and concerned. If she wasn't doing it out of free will, then who put her up to it? And why?"

"That's what Marcus is gonna find out and FaceTime us once he has her alone."

"You really think she's gonna fall for that? She is your sister."

"She is the most gullible of them all at that. I want to see how she's going to react to him."

"For our sakes, I hope she answers his questions truthfully. What were you saying about shooting?"

"Marcus has no backup but us. But for him to be a big-ass nigga, he moves real fast. The only thing not guarded on his body is his head or legs. I need my wingman to make it out. He has been loyal to us from the start, Nahi. His safety should be a concern to us like ours is to him. We gotta have his back. But if he has to shoot everyone in there, he needs to shoot them all. Even if that means killing Asia too."

"Are you okay to deal with that if that happens?"

"I won't have any other choice, will I? Don't let anyone see you. I'm going to pop the trunk, and you grab the guns out of the back."

"Right now?"

"Nah. Wait 'til Marcus calls back. But look at this. Terry took care of our little possible headache. That's all good."

Isaziah passed me his phone, showing me where Terry had found out all the cameras were down during that time except one. The one that was on, there was no footage from the parking lot area we were in. It felt like one piece of the weight was taken off my shoulders and Isaziah's. We just needed to get the rest of the fucked-up puzzle out of the way.

"I just want you to keep your head on straight and not overthink. It's going to work out fine. I promise."

"Isaziah, you say that, but sometimes overthinking can help."

"Babe, just trust me. That's all I'm asking, damn."

I couldn't respond before his phone went off with a call from Marcus. Marcus had his Airpods in so no one would suspect that he was on the phone with us. We could hear him knocking on the door but couldn't hear anything.

What was crazy was that she sent us to a bando in fucking Cobb County. From what I heard, Cobb wasn't like that, but maybe I heard wrong. Isaziah placed his phone on mute, then told me to make sure I texted Marcus any questions or instructions we had.

"I'm looking for Asia," Marcus said as the door opened.

"She's upstairs to the left," a male voice responded, letting him inside.

We could hear Marcus moving through the house and then a loud whimpering sound. Then he said, "Asia?"

"What are you doing here? Isaziah was supposed to show up. Where is he?"

"He's on his way. He's running behind. But come on, we can go meet him."

"No, you don't understand. Isaziah has to be the one to get me, not you."

"Asia, your brother is on his way. Why can't you just leave with me?"

"Because if he's not here, they're going to really kill me."

"Asia, we won't let anyone do shit to you. Let's go, come on."

Marcus continued to plead with Asia to leave with him, but she constantly refused. I was ready to go in and get her myself. I was irritated with her acting like she was being held hostage. It was clear from her statements she was not trying to get help. I was ranting to Isaziah as he kept trying to keep me quiet.

"Nahima, shut up and just listen!" Isaziah shouted.

"Nigga, she was going to set you up and you're gonna leave Marcus in there?"

"Babe, he's still trying to pump her for information. Just shut up before we miss something vital."

I was over it, but maybe he had a point. We had shit to do, and Asia was a major key. Instead of getting upset any further, I just lay back and waited to hear more.

"Asia, listen to me. Whatever is going on, we can figure it out as a family. Come on, let's go." We could hear the two of them tussling back and forth.

"I said no! Listen, go now! Please tell Isaziah to just come on, and I'll leave then."

"Asia, he ain't coming 'til I get you out of here!"

Marcus and Asia got real quiet. Then we heard shots ring out, and everything went quiet. Isaziah and I looked up and could see people struggling and flashes from the gunshots. Isaziah was about to open his car door when I grabbed his hand.

"Babe, we need to wait. We run up in there and we could be ambushed. Let's get Terry, Phil, and the rest of your sisters here. If everyone's still inside, we shoot everything moving down to a roach if we see it, grab Marcus and Asia, and get the hell out of there."

"Nahima, we just can't leave him in there! Why just sit here idle? We're supposed to be his backup!"

"Isaziah, please just wait! Listen to me, please. I can't lose you. Most importantly, we can't lose anyone else."

"I hope you come right behind me. You're the eyes I need. I can't see everything." Isaziah looked at me, grabbing my hand.

I was against going in there without the others being there, but I knew that if I didn't follow him, he would be more vulnerable.

Cocking my gun, then grabbing some extra clips for both of us, I nodded before I followed Isaziah out of the car.

Chapter 24

Isaziah

Nahima wasn't feeling going in there, but I couldn't leave Marcus in there alone to fend for himself. He would never do me like that. What would a real nigga do? This real nigga went by the code and loyalty. As soon as I opened my car door, I peeped three niggas coming from the side of the house. I closed the door quietly and texted Nahima to slide out of the car quietly so we wouldn't draw any attention to our car. Since we parked down the street but not too far from the house, I didn't want them to see us. Nahima met me at the trunk of the car, stuffing her phone in her bra.

"What you see?" she asked in a whisper.

"There's about two or three niggas on the side of the house. I'm waiting to see how they gon' get around to the door."

"I thought the traps were down there. They would've been caught by now, right?"

"Shhh, I hear something." I held my hand over her mouth so she wouldn't get loud.

I heard a crackling sound as if someone was coming up from a different direction in the gravel.

"Fuck! Help! My leg! My fucking leg!" a male voice screamed out loudly.

I whispered in Nahima's ear, lowering my hand from her mouth. "It sounds like someone got hold of the trap."

"That's one down. There may be two or three more people over there," she responded.

"We move in slow and quiet. You hear me? Just like that robbery we pulled on them niggas who robbed Shereene a few years ago." Three years ago, we took a hit from a rival gang. They stole about half of our product and over $100,000 in cash. I was livid. I wanted to burn everything down to the ground. Nahima was the one who was able to bring me back to a calmer place. She set up a plan after narrowing down who had our stolen goods. We located them on the south side in a little townhouse apartment. When we got to the apartment complex we had Marcus with us. Just with the three of us, we tackled the mission. Nahima took the niggas out in the front, covering Marcus and me while we broke down the door, giving no mercy.

"Okay, babe. I got your back. I sent out the location to the rest of the crew. They should be here soon too for backup."

"Your phone on silent?"

"Yeah, I did that before I got out of the car." Nahima gave me a quick kiss. "I love you. If we don't make it through this—"

"We will make it out of here together and alive. Ain't no if's. I got you, babe."

"And I got you." Nahima's palms were sweaty as I went to grab hold of her hand.

She was nervous about the outcome, but I needed her to trust me. We moved slowly from behind the trunk of the car toward the left side of the house. We watched for the traps before going anywhere. Since it was dark out, we weren't sure exactly where the traps were. We just had to feel through the tall grass. The guy who was screaming from being caught in the trap was still on the ground, and his partner was still trying to get his leg out of the trap.

"If we kill them, we can take their guns, and if they got masks, toss them on."

"Is your silencer on your gun?"

"Nah, I didn't grab it. You got yours?"

"No, shit!" I kicked the grass out of frustration.

"We just get up close and shoot them first before they can make a sound or anything. Come on." Nahima tapped my shoulder as she moved ahead of me, headed to the back of the house.

I followed her, and we moved around the house, where we could see the two men still on the ground caught in the traps. With a little sign language about which direction we were going in, we crept up behind them slowly. I was able to get behind the nigga on the ground, and Nahima got behind the one stuck in the bear trap. At the same time, our shots went off in back of their domes. Two simple shots to the head. Even if they survived it, they would be veggies.

Only one had a ski mask on. We snatched it off, and that nigga looked to be in his early twenties, just starting his life. I lowered his eyelids before I motioned for us to move forward. Nahima was my number one soldier. She would take a bullet for me if she had to, but I was going to head inside first. We were about to make our way to the front door when we heard the door open.

"Aye, Jasper! Roc! Y'all niggas still out here?" someone shouted. "Please, y'all, it ain't funny. I got shot, man! Y'all gotta call the bosses, man. This shit ain't work the way it was supposed to."

I peeked around the corner to see who was talking. It was a tall, lanky nigga who looked like Jimmie from *Good Times*. He was coughing and pleading for help. I could see him holding his belly, and when he coughed, little drops of blood trickled around the corner of his mouth.

"I know you niggas hear me! Help me!" the man shouted again. "No, please don't kill me. Don't kill me!"

Four shots went off, and then it was silent. When I noticed Nahima moving behind me, her chest was lighting up. She dug in her bra, pulling out her phone. Nahima's eyes grew bigger as she looked at the screen.

"Who is it?" I whispered, trying to understand why she looked so shocked.

"It says Asia." Nahima showed me her phone, and I turned my head to see where the man was at the door.

"Marcus?" I noticed Marcus standing at the top of the steps, holding his side.

"What?"

"Marcus is at the door." I pulled her closer to me. That way, Nahima could see that Marcus was still alive.

"I'm not gonna go up there until everyone else gets here. It wouldn't be smart. We don't know what is on the other side of the door."

"Man, look at him! Marcus could be hurt. You stay here and wait for Terry and them. I'm going to make sure he's okay." I blew her a kiss and went up to the steps.

Nahima was calling out my name, but I was already in front of the house. Marcus was laid out in the middle of the floor, his hand covering the right side of his abdomen.

"Marcus! Brother, get your ass up! Come on, let's go!" I attempted to pick him up, but he was way too heavy for me.

"Bro, you gotta get out of here. Asia set you up. There's someone on their way to kill you or something. Asia said she was working for someone, and she was so scared. She was scared. Before she would tell me more, she was shot by one of the guys in the house."

"Where is she now?" I hollered as Marcus attempted to sit up.

"I don't know." Marcus opened his windbreaker, revealing his bulletproof vest. "Check upstairs."

"I'll be right back. I promise." I hopped up and ran up the stairs, hoping my baby sister was holding her own and still alive.

I turned to the left of me, opening the first door, and the room was empty. The following room was the same. I got to the third door to the left, and it was jammed.

"Isaziah, if that's you, go! Go! I'm so sorry!" Asia screamed behind the closed door.

"Asia! Asiaaaaa! I'm not leaving without you! Open this fucking door!" I shouted while attempting to break the door down.

I took two steps back, and just before I lunged toward the door, everything went dark.

Chapter 25

Nahima

The longer I waited outside, the more nervous I became. I checked my Apple watch every second it felt like, and still there was no sign of Isaziah. He told me to wait, and like any good fiancée, I did. But now his time to do whatever he wanted was up. I had started creeping around the corner when I got a text from Terry saying that they were about to pull up.

"I lost my phone. Where the fuck is my phone?" I could hear Marcus asking himself in between grunts.

When I looked around the corner, Marcus was stumbling down the steps, searching for his phone. Standing up and moving out to meet him, I saw Terry pull up and open the car door.

"Marcus, come on, get in! Where's Isaziah?" I noticed he was nowhere near him.

"Nahima, he went looking for Asia when I told him not to." Marcus hung his head.

"So, you fucking leave him? He went in there for the two of you and you fucking left him?" I shouted, punching his chest.

"I'm not leaving him, you are! Our orders were to make sure you were safe at all costs. Once we get you out of here, then we will go back and get him."

Marcus tried pushing me in the car, but I pushed him back, trying to escape his grasp.

"Marcus, move! Get the fuck out of my way! I'm not leaving him!" I shouted.

No matter how hard I struggled to break free, Marcus was ten times stronger than me. Terry was yelling at both of us to get in the car when we saw lights approach.

"Y'all can go back and forth, or we can get in the car before whoever that is rushes up on us!" Terry shouted.

I turned my head to see the lights on the car getting brighter and brighter. "Nah, whoever it is gonna get they shit knocked in. I pay y'all motherfuckas just like Ziah does. So, either you're with me or against me! I'm going to get Isaziah, and y'all take care of whoever that is. Ya hear me?"

Terry and Marcus looked at me then back at one another. Marcus stepped back, pulling out his gun. "I'm with you, sis. I'm ready to go home."

Terry put the car in park, leaving the engine running. "Damn right. Let's end this bullshit."

Terry reached in the back seat, grabbing his duffle bag, opening it to reveal heavy machinery. I grabbed my Magnum gold tiger-striped Desert Eagle Mark XIX pistol and the AK-47. Terry, Marcus, and I loaded our guns.

"If I don't return in ten minutes with or without Isaziah, you leave me, do you understand?"

"Boss lady . . ." Terry stood there looking in my eyes, concerned for me.

"I mean it, fellas. No matter what happens, thank you for your loyalty. Take care of our family." I ran away from the car, going inside the house with my pistol cocked and ready.

Every door was opened, and every room got searched. I noticed a door in the kitchen that was locked, but I couldn't find the key nearby. I knew if Isaziah and Asia were being held anywhere, it was going to be in that room. I went through every drawer in the kitchen and had no luck finding the key. My frustrations were at an all-time high. I had to take a moment to breathe so I could think clearly.

When I leaned up against the kitchen counter, I noticed someone crawling on the floor in all black. I ran up to them, gun aimed, and told him to get up.

"Please don't shoot. I'll give you whatever." He was trailing blood down the hall.

"I need the key to that door in the kitchen! You get me in that door, I'll make sure you get help and live. Okay?"

"You promise?"

"I promise. Just help me please. My sister may be trapped here." I put the puppy-dog eyes on him, pretending to be upset.

"Anything . . . I'll do my best. Tell you whatever you want to know, anything you want."

He was so sincere, and he was in no position to play with me. That nigga fell for my sweet, nonthreatening tone. He hobbled into the kitchen, grabbing the wooden chair for leverage so he could stand up. His knees were buckling as soon as he got straight up.

"Where's the key for this door?" I asked, standing beside the door.

"I don't know this door. I only had a key to this back door to get in earlier. When I came in, niggas was shooting, and I was ambushed by my own team. Ever since the boss and his new girl started fucking around, they been on some other shit. She been trying to make all the calls. Like she been trying to prove herself or something."

"Who is the new girlfriend? What's her name? Tell me who she is. Is she here right now?"

"No, they went out of the back right before you saw me with boss man, some guy who was knocked out cold and a girl screaming for help."

"What did the guy look like? Who are you working for? Who shot you?"

"I got shot by his ole lady. I wanted to help the girl asking for help. I'm only down to make money. I don't want to be doing no crazy shit like this! I wanted to help them both, but that girl looked so scared. She kept asking them to stop and let her go."

"Did she know them? Was she working for them like you?"

"She didn't seem like it. All I know is that tonight was the first time I saw or heard of her. They called her Asia or something."

I was confused. If Asia wasn't working for or with these niggas, then how did she get caught up with them niggas? What would cause her to possibly be around them niggas unless it was someone she knew?

"Can you tell me anything else?"

"They heading back to Florida. They told us that they would provide locations to meet up when they got settled. They even have a nigga from out here who's supposed to be coming out of there to work between the two states for them."

"Can you give me names? I want or need names to help me find my people."

"The only names I know are Shack Shane, Tee, and Jay Boogie. The girl making calls and shit, she the one fucking with Jay. But she never told us her name."

"That's all you can tell me?"

"Yes. That's all I know for real."

I nodded my head, thanking the young man. His head was hung low, and he was not paying me any attention. When his eyes locked with mine, my pistol was out, pointing straight at his chest. With a final thank-you, I fired two shots: one in his chest and the other in his throat.

His body hit the floor as I ran toward the stairs to see if maybe they pretended to leave but were hiding out.

Every door upstairs was wide open, and no one was in sight. I spun in a circle. I was helpless and had no idea where to go or what to do. Where was my fiancé and my baby sister-in-law? I stood in the middle of the hall and screamed out my frustrations.

"Nahima, you may wanna see this." Marcus and Terry came up the stairs, holding out my phone.

"What is it?"

"Press play." Terry handed me my phone without even looking me in the eye.

I hit play, and Asia appeared with Isaziah. They recorded beating them up in some yard or something. Asia was pleading for them to stop as blood trickled from her mouth, and her eye was starting to get swollen from the punches. Isaziah was in the background yelling for them to stop. The more he yelled, the more they tortured the two of them. Then things took a turn for the worse when a gun was pulled out. A person emerged from the corner and their voice was masked when they demanded $100,000 to return them to me alive. Then the video was over.

"Nahima?" Marcus called out as my hands trembled.

"You show no one else this video. We do what they say only to get them back. Once they're both safe, we kill everyone! I want them and everyone associated with them dead. No fucking mercy! The nigga I killed in the kitchen, take his phone. He'll be receiving instructions soon on where to go, and we can use that." I stormed off, heading back to the car. This wasn't over by a long shot.

Isaziah

Hearing my sister scream the way she did ran venom through my veins. The more I tried to break free, the angrier I became.

"Who are you? Why can't you let my sister go? You wanted me, you got me!" I shouted.

"You wanna know who we are? Babe, it's all good. We can show them now," the male voice instructed.

"Bitch-ass nigga, you got a female helping you? You some type of pussy?"

The nigga punched me in my jaw.

"You hit like a bitch."

"Oh, yeah, motherfucka?" The male who seemed to be the head of everything punched me again and again until he saw blood.

The blood that dripped from my mouth, I spat on his shoes. He stepped away from me with a giggle. When he removed his mask, I didn't know who he was by name, but I was sure he was a part of the Gator Boys.

"Let me introduce myself. My name is Justin. My crew and everyone who fears me like you should call me Jay Boogie. I don't get down on the dance floor. I get down and boogie in these streets. I am the head of the Gator Boys." Justin aka Jay Boogie walked over, grabbing the other person's hand like it was his girl. "Show them who you are, babe."

Slowly, the other mask came off, and standing in front of me and Asia was my sister.

"Shereene?" I asked. I was in total disarray.

Chapter 26

Shereene

Yeah, I guess I'm the bad guy. Why would I turn on my brother? Why would I attempt to kill Nahima? It's all so simple. There were things my brother had never known and would never know unless it was forced to come out. It may sound weird to you, but I always loved my brother. Not just in a sisterly way. I never understood why I felt that way, but I had been like that since I was 16. Isaziah and I were not that far from each other in age. The first time I realized that my love for him was different than a normal sibling's was when I masturbated for the first time ever in life.

Isaziah had just come home from football practice when I caught a glimpse of him undressing through the crack in his bedroom door. Momma had gone to work and left us in the house alone. My other sisters had gone out doing their own thing. I was the only one still home because I was supposed to go out to the movies with this cute little guy from school named Terrance. Isaziah's body was so amazing at 15. He was starting to get muscles and all. I was so turned on. I had no idea that could happen to me.

My pussy was throbbing like it never had before. My pussy was wet and that had never happened to me before either. I wasn't sure what was going on with my body. When I slipped my hand in my panties, I touched myself for the first time, and it felt amazing. I thought he caught me when I released a sigh filled with ecstasy. I scurried into my room and hopped on my computer to look for some type of porn. I had been watching it every now and then, but I never got turned on or touched myself to it. I pulled up Xnxx.com and searched for black porn. This light-skinned, big-booty girl with pink hair popped up first. I plugged my headphones in and clicked on the porn.

I watched the star in the movie rub on her clit, and I followed her motion. I watched the video and imagined the two people were Isaziah and me. That was the first time I had an orgasm. I didn't know how loud I was until a knock came on my bedroom door.

"Aye, sis, you all right in there?" Isaziah shouted through the door.

"Yeah . . . yeah, I'm okay. Mind yo' fucking business. Get the fuck away from my door!"

"Damn, mean ass. You were in there sounding all crazy. I ain't know what the fuck was going on."

"Leave me alone!" I shouted while moving my hand from my pussy.

My fingers were sticky and wet. I assumed that meant that I came, and I was so ashamed. I thought something was wrong with me, and I couldn't talk to my mom as to what or who turned me on. My mother was easy to talk to, but I never thought I would have to converse with her about sex. That was the first time I realized I was turned on by my brother. Some people may think that it's sick, but I thought it was love. When he brought that bitch Nahima around, I didn't like her just 'cause she was trying to take my soulmate away, and I couldn't have that.

It had been at least two days since me and Jay Boogie kidnapped Isaziah and Asia. I was sure these fools were trying to figure out a way to get them without paying us, but I wasn't falling for any of that shit. These Gator Boys were just a pawn in my game. Jay Boogie was about to see how it really felt to be hustled.

Asia was just collateral. I knew she had a deep love for Nahima, but her family would always come first. I brought her in to help me get rid of Nahima. But she got too scared to shoot her in the hotel when we tried to grab her ass. Instead, she let her go, and that was why she was stuck. I was disappointed at how she got conflicted that fast. Asia needed to be taught a lesson. We decided not to stay in Georgia, so we went back to Tampa and settled into an apartment on the west side just to stay out of the way. Jay Boogie did whatever I said when I said it. For him to have his own organization, he sure didn't have the balls to lead it like Isaziah did us.

Jay Boogie walked into the house with a big bag of food from McDonald's.

"Babe. I'm back. I got everything. Do you think you can grab the drinks out of the car for me please?"

"That's the least I could do."

I went out to his car to grab the drinks, checking around us to see if I noticed any discrepancies with the cars surrounding the house. I carried the drinks inside and found Jay Boogie in the kitchen, feet up on the table, a burger in one hand and his phone in the other.

"You couldn't wait until I got back in to eat together?" I asked, placing the drinks on the table.

"You wanted me to wait? You should have said something. I won't eat the rest until you're ready."

I just rolled my eyes and grabbed the remainder of the food to take down into the area where Asia and Isaziah were being held. On two separate sides of the room, we gave them each a twin-size mattress.

"My family, I brought you something to eat," I stated as I got to the middle of the room.

"What is it, poison?" Isaziah belted out without even looking at me.

"You're funny. It's McDonald's. Either eat this or don't eat at all." I stood there with the bag of food in my hands, waiting to see if they would grab it.

"I would like to eat please, sister." Asia walked over to me, her eye still slightly swollen from the beating Jay Boogie provided her.

"What about you, Isaziah? You want to eat?" I turned and looked at him with a devilish grin.

"Leave it, Shereene."

"I'm sorry, what did you say?"

"Just leave the fucking food and us alone!" he shouted, sending shivers down my spine.

"As you wish. Until your little wife-to-be becomes useful, y'all are here to do as me and Jay Boogie wish."

"Fuck you. When I make it out of this, I plan to spit on your fucking corpse!" Isaziah shouted at me as I placed the bag of food in the middle of the floor.

"I'll be back with your drinks. There will be someone here in the morning to clean out your shit buckets."

I turned, going back up the stairs. The whole time I was thinking about Isaziah's anger and how turned on I was. Jay Boogie was left still in the spot. My siblings would get their drinks after I released. I tapped Jay on his back to gain his attention, he looked up at me, and I tossed my shirt to the ground.

"Take my fucking pussy right fucking now." I looked at him with lustful eyes.

"Shit, okay, babe."

Jay Boogie grabbed me, tossing me over his left shoulder to carry me into the bedroom. I planned on fucking that man the way I would have fucked Isaziah if I had the chance.

Chapter 27

Isaziah

"Asia, we need to find a way out of here," I expressed after my sister, Shereene, disappeared back into the snake hole she crawled out of.

"Isaziah, if we don't listen to her, we could die. I don't want to die," Asia whispered to me.

"We're dead as long as we sit here. Please just do what I say. I only want Shereene dead. I won't let anyone or anything harm you. I never have and I won't start now." I searched around the dimly lit basement we were in. The wooden steps creaked horribly, the rail was loose, and it smelled like something or someone had died in there and was never cleaned up. When we made it down the steps, there were some boxes and a few old bookshelves.

"There's only one way out, which is that door? We can't just get out any other type of way?"

"Asia, just trust me. We will get through this alive." I gave her a warm smile so she would feel calmer.

"I hope you are right. I just hope you're right." Asia sat back on her bed, holding her legs between her arms.

My baby sister was scared to death, and to be honest, I was scared too, shit. I didn't know what to think or believe. We could be waiting for Nahima to come up with a plan and they may have killed her. Anything could be a setup at this point. I sat up, watching Asia until she went to sleep. After she fell asleep, I took my time to get up and search the room once more. It was hard to see in there once the light started to flicker. Trying to be as quiet as possible, I saw two small windows in the left upper corner.

I wanted to see if there was a way to get out from one. Since both of our frames were decent in size, I figured we would both be able to fit into it. A ladder was adjacent to the window along with a top shelf with different paint cans and little tools. The slightest sound while we were down there would trigger them to come down to check us out. It was dark when we got here, and we only saw light through that window or when the door opened. There could be one to fifteen niggas out there guarding the house.

We needed a way to get out of the house. I had to devise an escape plan that wouldn't get us killed. After checking through the basement quietly, I could hear someone approaching the door. I went back to my corner and pretended to be asleep. A creaking sound escaped into the dark, cold basement with every step they took coming down the steps.

"Wake up, bitch!" I heard a male voice shout toward my sister.

"Please, I don't wanna go," I heard Asia beg.

I heard him cock his gun. "Get yo' ass up or I'll shoot you right here."

"Jay Boogie, please, I don't wanna do this. I promise I won't say anything about before to anyone, I promise. Please don't do this." Asia was pleading to this man, and I couldn't make out exactly what she didn't want to do.

"Your brother asleep?" Jay Boogie asked Asia.

"I don't know. I guess so."

"Good."

I turned my head to see if I could catch a glimpse of what was going on in her corner.

"Please, Jay, please don't do this to me!" Asia screamed out.

"Shut the fuck up!" I sat up and I could hear the two of them tussling. He was trying to force the barrel of his gun inside of my sister's mouth.

I know I wasn't about to watch nor hear my baby sister get raped. If he killed me, I would be saving her for a moment. Asia's cries were subtle with the gun in her mouth. As I watched Jay Boogie attempt to get his dick out of his pants, I snuck up behind him, grabbing him by the neck.

"You a fucking perv! Take the gun out of her mouth. Do what I say right now!" I said in a harsh whisper.

I wasn't trying to alarm anyone else, just like he thought he wasn't going to alarm me while raping my sister. I squeezed on his neck tighter and tighter until his voice grew faint. Jay Boogie finally removed the gun from my sister's mouth, placing it down beside his right leg.

"Asia, take the gun."

"What?" she asked, trying to regain her composure.

"This is our chance! Take the fucking gun!"

Asia grabbed the gun and pressed the barrel into his dome. "I ought to shoot you right now."

"You're gonna get us out of this house, and I want everything you have, starting with your car keys. We are not to be followed by any of your henchmen, and there will be no money given to you all. Let's start with you getting us upstairs. Give your keys to my sister right now." I squeezed my arm tighter around his neck until Jay Boogie was barely able to speak.

"I can't breathe," he muttered breathlessly.

"Good. Just do what I say and I may let you live another day. At least for the time being."

Jay Boogie reached into his pocket, grabbing his car keys. Asia snatched them from him before we walked toward the middle of the basement floor.

"Asia, stay close to me and stay aware of your surroundings."

"Okay. Okay, I got you," Asia responded, sounding more confident and aggressive than ever before.

My sis finally got that gutta spirit in her to awaken. Holding on to Jay Boogie, we crept up the stairs one step at a time, trying not to alarm anyone. Asia walked right behind us. Once at the top of the steps, we entered the kitchen area. We made it through the living room and kitchen until we reached the front door.

"Where are y'all going?" Shereene's voice emerged through the dark stairwell.

"Asia, don't get weak at this moment. She is no longer your sister. She is the enemy," I hollered over to my baby sister to keep her mind focused. "We are leaving, Shereene. Don't follow us, or Asia will kill you."

"That's not part of the deal. We all wait together until your ugly little bitch comes up with my money, and then you may go on your way."

"Shereene, watch your mouth! You nor anyone in this motherfucka are getting any of my and my family's money! You lost yo' fucking mind."

"But we are family. Asia, tell him, he can't do this to me. His big sister." Shereene was starting to play her little head games with Asia.

"Asia, don't listen to her. If you do, then you know what happens? We both end up back in that hellhole or dead. Neither of us wants that."

Asia looked up as Shereene cut on the light for the stairwell. "If I were really that important to you, he wouldn't have been raping me and you wouldn't have let him beat me or kidnap me. Fuck you!" Asia fired three rounds near Shereene.

We saw Shereene hit the floor. I had Jay Boogie unlock the front door so we could head to his car. I didn't notice anyone just sitting out front. Asia grabbed the keys, hitting the unlock button to see what car's lights flashed. After walking down both sides of the street twice, we finally came upon a cherry red Audi RS 3. Asia got into the driver's side just as I let my grip loose from Jay Boogie's neck. Grabbing the gun from Asia, I scurried to the passenger seat. As we drove past him standing there in the street hollering for help, I looked at him with a smile and fired every remaining bullet into his body.

"Let's get to our family," I said to Asia as she hit the gas, leaving Jay Boogie's body bleeding out onto the concrete.

Chapter 28

Nahima

Even though it hadn't been but a few days since Isaziah was taken from me, I felt as if my world was over. I refused to sit back and let him die without a chance. I had everyone we knew searching for the Gator Boys and anyone who may be associated with them. I hadn't slept or eaten since they came up missing, and I could feel my body crashing. We were riding on the highway back down to Tampa when I dozed off with the cool breeze hitting my face.

"Why are you always overworking your mind?"

"Isaziah?" I looked up and there was my fiancé, standing over me, looking as scrumptious as ever.

"Who else would I be? You cheating on me or something?" Isaziah teased me.

"Never in a million years. How did you get here?"

"Babe, we been home. I only left the room to grab the pizza from the delivery guy."

I sat up in our California king–size bed, pulling the all-white comforter over my naked body. The comforter smelled of his Gucci cologne with a mix of my Bombshell perfume.

"Why do you look so sad, baby? What's wrong?" Isaziah asked me, rubbing his hands through my hair.

"You were taken from me. I got to save you. I have to save you. I don't know how to live without you."

"No one took me from you. I'm right here. Even if they attempt to take me from you, I'll always make my way back to you. Thug love like ours never dies. You're my Hoodyonce and I'm your Jay-Z, remember?" Isaziah took me into his arms, lowering my body onto the sheets.

"I love you so much. Don't ever think I don't."

"Oh, I know, baby." Isaziah slid inside of my wet pussy, and with the first gasp of pleasure being released, my body jerked.

It was at that moment I realized I had been dreaming and Marcus had hit some animal on the road. I got aggravated with him, only because I wanted to finish my dream, and I missed my baby. The longer I sat in the car watching Marcus move the roadkill out of the road, the more aggravated I became. It took Marcus about fifteen minutes to move the deer out of our path. Marcus was approaching the car when his phone went off with an unknown caller.

"Who is that, boss lady?" Marcus asked, stepping back into the car.

"I don't know. Call them back. It may be a lead on how to find bae and Asia," I instructed, looking down at his phone.

Marcus put the car back in drive. As he drove, the phone rang again. This time, Marcus answered.

"Yo, what's the word?" His phone played through the car speakers.

"Marcus! Marcus! Bro, where are y'all at?" The voice on the other end of the phone shocked us both.

"Is this a joke or something? We're gonna find y'all bitch-ass niggas who took my brother and kill ya. Ya heard me?" Marcus screamed into the speaker.

"Mothafucka, it's me! It's Isaziah, nigga! Me and Asia were barely able to escape. But we need to get everyone together like now!" Isaziah was yelling back at him, breathing hard and sounding more nervous than he'd ever been.

"Whose phone are you calling me from?"

"I found it in the car. You know I'm good with numbers, and that's how I remembered yours. Where's Nahima?"

"I can hear you, baby. Are you okay? Where are you?" I shouted, full of all types of emotion.

"I'm not sure. We just drove until we saw a highway. We got about half a tank of gas. I'm just hittin' the gas until we run out."

"Are you able to see a restaurant, gas station, or something? That way you can grab the address and wait there. We can meet you," I asked Isaziah, trying to get a better grasp of his location and how far he may be from me.

"Where were y'all headed to?" Isaziah questioned.

"We were headed back home. We thought y'all were in Tampa," Marcus informed him.

"Well, I'm gonna get off at this next exit. There's some shit on this next exit. I'm gonna have to grab an address from a spot there. Stay by y'all phone. And, Nahima?"

"Yes, baby?" I answered gleefully.

"I love you. I'll see you soon." Isaziah hung up the phone.

Looking at Marcus, I instructed him to keep driving until we got to a rest stop. It was about twenty minutes later when we got a text with an address. After we received it, Marcus placed the address in the GPS. Isaziah was about forty-five minutes from our current location. Once we pinpointed the location, I shot him a text.

Me: Hey, babe. Stay where you are. We are on the way.

Isaziah: Okay. I'm right here.

Marcus spun out of the rest area. The crew was not that far behind us. We were going to meet my baby. My spirits were uplifted knowing that I was going to see him sooner than I thought.

Chapter 29

Shereene

My brother and little sister escaped. I was way beyond frustrated and furious with Jay Boogie. He was incompetent and weak as fuck. Things were set up where everything could've been over and I could finally rise to the top.

"Jay Boogie! Jay Boogie!" I shouted, running into the street.

His body was losing blood rapidly. He reached out, grabbing my hand as the blood spilled from his mouth. His words were barely able to form, but I could read his lips.

"I know that you been raping my sister since I brought her into this. I'm not stupid. But I needed you just like you needed me. Now you're going to die here alone with no one who loves you." I grabbed my pocketknife, stabbing him in his abdomen. "I'm going to take over your crew to accomplish what I need. Then, one by one, I'm going to get rid of them all. But this is for killing my mother and raping my sister. Rot in hell, you piece of shit."

I yanked the knife from his body before getting up from the ground. I closed the knife, then placed it back into my pocket. I went to walk away when my ankle was grabbed.

"You lying bitch. They're going to kill yo' ass too," he muttered out.

"Well, you first, my darling." I kicked him away from me and walked back toward the house.

The remaining members of the Gator Boys were sitting around with depressed looks on their faces. One of the youngest in the crew looked up at me when I walked in.

"Where is he, ma'am?" he asked politely.

"Jay Boogie is no longer with us. He has passed over all the commands to me and asked me to take over the Gator Boys."

"Well, Miss Lady, I don't mean no harm when I say this, but he didn't know you long enough to pass over anything. Nor any of us to be honest. So, I'm not taking no commands from you," this tall, broad-shouldered, dark-skinned fellow stated, getting up from the stairs.

I looked at him with a wince. "Hey, what was your name again?"

"It's Jeff," he responded with an attitude.

"Well, Jeff, I don't care if you know me or not. But you can either fall the fuck in line and respect my authority, or you can leave." With my hands on my hips, I stared at him, waiting for the reply.

"I'm going to take the second option. If y'all are smart, you'd be with me. If you stay, you're all gonna die."

Jeff and a few of the others stood up and headed for the door. I despised the thought of someone disobeying me now with all the power in my hands. I never led a group before, but I knew that Isaziah and I could run them and everyone better than any thug out of there in the streets.

"Jeff," I said, turning toward the door.

"What's up?" He turned his body slightly toward me, with one foot out the door.

I pulled a gun from behind my back and shot twice. His body fell to the ground. The other men with him ran, leaving him there to fend for himself. The youngest of the crew was still sitting in his same spot, frightened.

"Hey, you. What's your name?" I asked since I didn't know him or the others.

"My name is Rayshawn, ma'am."

"Well, Rayshawn, it seems that me and you have to do some rebuilding. Let the rest of them go and leave Jeff there to either die from bleeding out, or he'll come to his senses and get help from us. But follow me."

"Yes, ma'am." Rayshawn's voice was so shaky and nervous. He was terrified. I was sure he was thinking I was going to kill him next.

I had him follow me upstairs into the master bedroom. Motioning for him to sit on the bed, I undressed so I could wash all the bad vibes off of my body, plus some of Jay Boogie's blood. I was walking into the bathroom when I noticed his eyes were covered.

"Son, what the fuck you covering your eyes for? You never seen a naked woman before?" I teased.

"You're my boss. I can't see you like that. That's all. Trying to respect you, ma'am." Rayshawn was too country and polite for my liking.

"You don't have to call me 'ma'am' all the time. And if I didn't want you to look, I would have said so. To make things even, get naked. I want you undressed fully when I get out this shower. If you aren't, I'll think you're hiding something, and I will kill you right where you're sitting. Understand?"

"Yes, ma'am. I mean, yes."

"Good. I'll be back."

I stepped into the steaming hot shower and allowed the water to just run all over my body. Since I had taken my wig off earlier that day, I just let my natural hair enjoy the goodness from the water. I may have had nigga naps, but my little 'fro be cute sometimes. At least when it was tamed. I had a plan, and hopefully it would work this time. Rayshawn was going to be my pawn. He was so timid, and he seemed easy to manipulate. *Why not take him, promise him the world like these niggas be doing to us females, and drop this pussy on him once every blue moon? He'll be wrapped around my finger. I can just feel it.*

With all the devious thoughts and plans running through my brain, it made me excited and horny. I hadn't planned on fucking the little nigga right off the bat. But since Jay Boogie got himself killed earlier than expected, I needed a new toy, and Rayshawn was going to be my victim. I was sure my brother was trying to find his way to his precious Nahima. Little did he know I was going to have her killed, and she would be out of our lives forever. Isaziah just needed me by his side, not even the rest of our sisters, because their asses were always so scary. They barely would pull a trigger. If Asia had killed Nahima in the hotel room, we wouldn't even have been going through this madness right now. He didn't understand at first, but he would understand soon.

The shower was amazing. I stepped out of the shower smelling like warm vanilla from Bath & Body Works. Rayshawn was sitting on the bed naked, holding his dick.

"Why you covering yourself up?" I walked over, holding my towel.

"I just was doing as you wanted. I don't wanna die." Rayshawn was adorable in a weird way.

"I am not going to kill you. I'm going to make you my second-in-command. We are going to rebuild this organization, and everyone will have to answer to us. The only thing that I ask is that you make no decisions without me or my input first. Understood?"

"Yeah, I got you."

"Good. Now this is the only time you get an option." I dropped the towel and got on my knees in front of where he was sitting.

"What's that?" He looked down at me on my knees with a sly smile.

"Tell me if you don't want this." I removed his hands from covering his dick.

Without a second thought, I began sucking his dick. Rayshawn leaned back with a slight moan. I knew then he was going to be hooked. His legs trembled like he was having a seizure.

"Have you never gotten head before?" I asked while slowly jacking his dick.

"Yeah, but not like what you're doing. Do it some more please. Or can I fuck you? Please?" Rayshawn pleaded as he grabbed the back of my head, lowering it back onto his dick.

He must have been fucking with some ducks, I thought as I gave him another little sample. I can't lie, the more he moaned like a bitch in my ear, it turned me on. My pussy was purring, and I needed to feel something in a different part of my body. I jumped up from my knees, not thinking about a condom or anything, and straddled him, sliding his thick, medium-length dick inside of me.

Slowly, I rode his dick from behind. I wanted to feel him fill my pussy up until I couldn't take anymore. I could tell he was holding back. But I wanted to be fucked like I saw Isaziah fuck Nahima one night when I was at their house. I hollered for Rayshawn to fuck me like a slut. Soon, he unleashed. Rayshawn grabbed my wrist, pulling my body back some. It arched just a tad. That boy tossed that dick up in me like I never had before.

"You wanted me to fuck you right, bitch? Right?" Rayshawn uttered, pushing me onto the bed on my stomach.

As he spanked my ass, he positioned me into doggie-style. I was expecting him to take it easy on me, but he straight dogged my pussy. Both of his hands around my neck, he slowly stroked my pussy at first. Each stroke hit a different side of my pussy, and I was loving the young nigga's dick. Rayshawn sped up, getting rougher with me.

"Aye, bitch, come on my fuckin' dick, you hear me?" he shouted as I felt something enter my asshole while his dick still pounded my pussy.

I allowed Rayshawn to fuck me like he probably couldn't fuck the young girls he was messing with before. But the way he screamed when he busted his first nut inside of me, I knew my pussy alone was going to make him do as I said. My plan was about to become easier to execute with him around.

Chapter 30

Isaziah

I was so anxious just to get back to my wifey, my heart was pounding through my chest. Being without her for that amount of time alone was enough to make me understand I couldn't be without her period, unless it was in death. Even then, as a spirit, I would be right there. Asia seemed to be more quiet than normal while we waited for Nahima and everyone to arrive. I figured it had something to do with that nigga Jay Boogie raping her or her actually going through the process of having to shoot someone. Asia would need to speak to someone, outside of our sisters and Nahima, who could help her through this better than we could. There was no telling how long that had been taking place prior to my arrival.

Now I may not have been a victim of nothing else but a sick family betrayal, but Asia suffered so much more. We were waiting for Nahima and everyone to pull up on us when I noticed Asia passed out. She was twitching and mumbling the word no in her sleep. When she got louder, I tapped her so she could wake up. I had tapped her three times on her leg when she finally woke up startled and in a defensive mood.

"Damn, sis. I was just waking you up. Don't fight me," I joked with her.

"Fuck. You scared me, Isaziah, shit." Asia straightened her jacket, then rubbed the excess slobber from her cheek.

"What were you dreaming about? You kept shouting no." I wasn't trying to be nosy, but I was concerned.

"I wasn't dreaming about anything or talking in my sleep. You hearing shit. Maybe you need a nap." Asia turned on her side, then leaned her seat back to get comfortable.

"I'll sleep when we are away from all this bullshit. And when I can hold on to my baby again. I just wanted to make sure you were okay. Go ahead back to sleep. I'll wake you when they get here."

"Good. Until then, I'm going back to sleep, brother." Her eyes closed, and Asia said not one more word to me.

Time went by, and it seemed slower than ever before. All I wanted was to go lie up with my wife-to-be. Nahima was the peace every hood nigga deserved in their life. I was blessed to have such a powerful woman in my life. God knew what He was doing.

It was about twelve thirty when a black SUV pulled up beside us. Tapping Asia to alert her, I reached for the gun, cocking it and waiting to see who it was. Asia woke up, looking at me, startled again. I motioned for her to look outside, and when she noticed the car, she looked around as quietly as possible, hoping to find something to use as a weapon. We had no clue what type of time we were on.

Sinking down in the seat, I watched the car doors open but couldn't see who got out. The vibration from my phone scared me a bit. I forgot I had it on silent. I answered the phone in a whisper, hoping it was Marcus or Nahima.

"What's up?" I whispered.

"Fuck is you whispering for? I think we in the right spot," Marcus responded as he smacked in my ear.

"Nigga, I don't know where I am or who that was who pulled up beside us," I stated.

"Was it a black truck?"

"How the hell you know?"

"Nigga, that's us. I switched cars halfway here. Come on out, man. I'm gonna finish checking out. Y'all want anything?"

"I don't, but ask Asia." I tossed her the phone as I dashed out of the car.

Heading over to the black SUV, I opened the driver side door to find Nahima sitting there.

"Isaziah!" Nahima shouted as she unbuckled her seat belt to get out.

"Hey, baby. Get your ass over here to daddy." I knew my smile was all over my face.

Nahima crawled over the seats and rushed into my arms. I grabbed her, then tossed her body onto the hood of the car. "Words can't describe how happy I am to see you."

"You have no idea how glad I am just to feel you holding me." Nahima pulled my face closer to hers so she could kiss me.

"That was the best part of this whole day. Let's find a room or something. I just need to shower with you and lie beside you."

"Aye, man, y'all can't wait until we get somewhere to do all this extra-ass shit!" Marcus came from behind us, shouting.

"Man, what's up, fool?" I had to hug my brother. Marcus kept my wife safe and always had my back.

"I knew nobody was 'bout to kill my mans. Glad to see you, bro." Marcus dapped me up and leaned over to look inside of the car Asia and I were in.

"Asia, come on out! Everything is good." Marcus tapped on the window glass.

Asia came out of the car slowly, holding her hands around her waist. "Hey, y'all."

I could tell Nahima was feeling uncertain about Asia, wondering if she was a pawn or a part of the crew trying to out us. Her vacillations were felt by everyone.

"Glad to see you're okay, Asia." Nahima turned around and went back into the car.

"Nahima, please talk to me. I'm sorry for what I attempted to do, but it wasn't on purpose." Asia tried following Nahima to make amends.

"Listen, if you were trying to kill me then, I don't know if you won't try again and this time succeed. For now, you stay the fuck away from me until all this shit is over. Let's see whose side you're really on," I heard Nahima tell Asia before slamming the car door shut.

I turned to Marcus, asking him for the keys. I asked him how much money we still had and if we had made anything in between time. We still had about $25,000 in cash, and transactions were still coming in from the stores. That was good enough to grab us a little room in a ducked-off spot just so I could get everyone in order.

"I'm going to drive, but we're leaving this car here in case they attempt to trace the tags or anything. By the time anyone finds it or tows it, we'll be gone."

"So, where are we going then?" Asia asked me, still holding herself.

"We're going to hit as close to Tampa as possible. But we need to stay low-key. She may think that we're going home and is possibly putting some shit together to catch us."

"She? Who the fuck is she?" Nahima hollered through the car as she overheard me talking since the driver's door was still open.

"I'll explain tomorrow. Right now, I just wanna lie down." My other sisters and the rest of the crew were parked around the little gas station we were at. I waved at them just so I could get love from them.

Each one came over and cradled me and Asia with love and hugs. After we got our hugs and physical checks out of the way, I instructed that it was time for us to hit the road. Everyone got back into their respective places. I led the way onto the highway. When we got deep on the road, the phone I took from Jay Boogie I tossed out onto the highway. There could be no way for us to be tracked at that point if my ugly-ass sister tried. We didn't have a chance to double back to make sure Jay Boogie was dead. They both could be on the hunt for us now.

We drove out about forty more miles before a few signs showed some hotels and food spots near the upcoming exit. I noticed there was an extended stay hotel on the sign, and that was going to be our spot for the next few days. If Shereene remembered anything from all that time around me, she was probably headed back to Jacksonville. I couldn't hit the city in full force yet. We would have to come in little by little. I knew one thing: my family would find it hard to believe that Shereene was the one behind all this. That she would be the one who had to die for us to all be saved. That was the fucked-up shit.

Chapter 31

Nahima

It was great having Isaziah back where he belonged. But even with all the happiness he was showing, he still seemed bothered about something. I was going to find out one way or the other what was so heavy on his mind. But at that moment, I just wanted to be in his arms. The weight of the world seemed to be all over him, and I needed him to just relax. Once we got checked into the extended stay, Isaziah and I walked off to our room, leaving everyone to do their own thing.

We weren't in the room five minutes before Isaziah had stripped down and was running his water for his shower. The bathroom glass was becoming foggy as he dug through some of my luggage for his bathing products.

"You getting in with me. I don't know why you're clothes still on." Isaziah walked past me into the bathroom.

I never heard him come at me like that before, but it turned me on. Considering I hadn't had sex since he was taken from me, my pussy was long overdue. I stripped down, leaving my clothes on the hotel floor. I wrapped my weave into a high ponytail before grabbing my warm vanilla shower gel from Bath & Body Works and followed my man into the shower.

The water was almost scorching hot, but it was the perfect temperature. When I hopped inside the tub, he turned around with his dick in hand, the soap still lathered up over his body. There were some bruises from where I could tell he had been beaten. His eyes were full of sorrow and anger. Taking my right hand, I took his washcloth to finish cleaning him. When I touched certain areas, he would make a soft moan as if it was still sore. He whispered for me to stop, then leaned over to the edge of the tub to grab my shower gel. Isaziah took my soap and the other washcloth to wash my body. With every place he washed, it felt like a massage, his big hands washing and caressing every inch of me. I was enjoying every moment. When he got to my pussy, his fingers slipped inside of me.

I almost slipped on the water while spreading my legs for him to go farther inside of me. "It feels good, doesn't it, babe?"

"Yes, daddy," I moaned out, pushing his fingers deeper into me.

"That's enough." Isaziah pushed me back, removing his hand from my pussy.

"What are you doing? Don't stop, babe." I begged him to put his hand back, but Isaziah wasn't going for it.

"You won't cum this way." Isaziah grabbed me by my waist, taking me out of the shower straight to the king-size bed in the middle of the floor.

"Tell me what you want," Isaziah whispered in my ear while rubbing my clit vigorously.

"To make love to me. Please fill my pussy."

"I'm getting you pregnant tonight." Isaziah stood back and spat on my pussy before ramming his dick inside of me.

His hands wrapped around my neck, he leaned forward, stuffing his mouth with my left nipple while digging in my pussy. It felt so good. Isaziah's tempo went from fast to slow, moving his body in a circular motion, his dick hitting every wall I had. Isaziah leaned up, slowly stroking my pussy, moving his body like a snake. My pussy grabbed hold to his dick, pulsating on it as I released in ecstasy. Isaziah removed his grip from my neck, slowing, taking his dick out of me.

"Suck that cum off of my dick," Isaziah instructed as he kneeled on the bed.

As daddy commanded, I sat up and ate his dick like a good girl. The deeper his dick went down my throat, the more my eyes teared up. I loved choking his dick and the way Isaziah whispered out a subtle "fuck" as he watched me gobble up his dick in glee. It wasn't much longer before he pulled me up, kissing my lips as he sat me down onto his dick. My legs wrapped around his waist. I slowly ground my pussy on him as he kissed on my neck and his hands gripped my ass cheeks.

"This pussy missed daddy, didn't it?"

"You know it did, baby. You know it did."

"Then show me. Ride this mothafucka." Isaziah lay down, still holding my ass cheeks with his dick deep inside me.

I tossed my hair to the side as I threw my ass back on his dick slowly. Every time I bounced back, it felt as if he was reaching deeper inside of me. After a few slow strokes, Isaziah spanked my ass, then held my ass cheeks. Spreading them apart slightly, he then tossed his dick in me balls deep. His big, juicy balls were slapping my ass as he threw that dick. Before long, my pussy was squirting all over the both of us. But Isaziah didn't stop. If anything, it gave him ammunition to keep going.

We switched positions and went round after round until the sun met our naked bodies after our last nut. The sun had risen as we lay intertwined, catching our breath. Isaziah stroked my back softly with his fingertips.

"Now that we're semi caught up on all that, what's the issue at hand?" I turned over, facing him.

"Babe, let's take this moment, get some sleep, and just enjoy holding one another again."

"You're deflecting. Tell me. Something is troubling you and I want to know what it is. Did you find out who killed Shereene? Was it one of them? What happened while you were gone?"

Isaziah became restless. He wouldn't even look at me. His face frowned up with anguish. I wanted to know what troubled him so. *But if there's one thing I learned over the years, if you keep pushing in situations like this, he'll turn away before he'll open up.* Lightening the mood a bit, I kissed his chest softly.

"We can talk when you're ready. You're right though. Let's just be grateful that we have this moment. I honestly wasn't sure what our future held. I'm just glad you're right here. I love you so much."

Just as I grabbed the ugly hunter green blanket to cover our bodies, Isaziah stopped my hand and said to me, "Shereene is not dead. She's alive."

I sat up in complete shock, trying to grasp what he just told me. "Isaziah, what did you just say?"

"Nahima, Shereene . . . my sister is the one behind this. She staged her own death."

Just hearing those words come out of his mouth ran a piercing, cold chill through my body. Instead of reacting and going off like I wanted, I could see Isaziah bursting into tears. My only job and concern at that point was making sure he was okay. As I consoled him, my mind was running in circles. When he was ready, he would tell me everything, but until then, I was going to come up with a plan myself and call in my extra reinforcements.

As Mufasa said in *The Lion King*, "It is time."

Chapter 32

Isaziah

"Shereene! Shereene, you don't have to do this! Please!" I hollered and then the gun went off.

I woke up in a cold sweat. Nahima was still fast asleep, and I didn't want to wake her. To dream of my sister killing me was enough to fuck anyone up. I couldn't explain it, but I honestly just wanted to have it not come in my head again. Instead of waking up my queen, I decided to take a little walk through the hotel and see if maybe they had a gym or something. I was sliding out of the bed when Nahima lifted her head, questioning where I was going. I simply explained that I was going to the bathroom and told her to go back to sleep. With a yawn and a nod, she replied, "Okay," before turning over and going back to sleep.

Once I realized she was back asleep, I grabbed some sweats, a hoodie, and the car keys, then made my way out. Not looking back, I passed through the lobby where this older black woman was sweeping through the hotel lobby floor, humming an old song.

"Hey, ma'am. Sorry to bother you, but is there any breakfast or anything served here? Is there a gym?" I asked her with a slight tap on the shoulder.

"Well, no, there's no breakfast, but there is some freshly brewed coffee I just made. Would you like a cup?" The older woman stood straight, pushing her glasses back on her face, and smiled at me.

"That's okay. I'll go grab some food somewhere."

"You look troubled, son. Why don't you have a cup with me? You don't have to tell me your problems. But I will say this—your family will always be your strength and God removes people from your life for a reason. It may be hard sometimes, but keep God first and everything else will fall in place."

I looked at her, puzzled. Her little words of encouragement came out of nowhere. Curious about her thoughts and why she came at me that way, I decided to have that cup of coffee with her. I wanted to know more.

"I guess you're wondering how I was able to say that to you without really having a conversation?"

"Yeah, I am." I chuckled as I took the white Styrofoam cup from her hands.

"Well, with old age, you don't just get older, but you get wiser. When you add being faithful to God, you are able to let your spirit guide you. Most of the time, I can read a person just from the energy they give off. It can be a gift and a curse. You want some cream and sugar?"

"Yes, ma'am, that would be fine, thank you."

"Here you go, honey. I am not one to force religion on you or anyone. But do you mind if I just pray for you?"

"You know what, I could use a whole lot of prayer right about now." I leaned back toward the wall, releasing a heavy breath.

"Well, come on, son. Take my hand and bow your head." She took my hands into hers and began to pray.

"Lord, we come to you today to ask for grace, saving, peace of mind, and most of all, protection. There is something attacking this young man from every angle. Lord, we just come to you today to grasp strength for him to beat these devils. We know with you, Lord, we can conquer all things. If you just allow this man to touch the hem of your garment, Lord. Lord, let him touch it to gain all the power he needs to do what is needed and right in your eyes, oh, God. With you, he is the head and not the tail. The devil will be defeated! Jesus, you are our protector and our King. Continue to protect him and his family. In Jesus' name we pray. Amen."

"Amen."

She didn't just pray for me. She prayed for my family and friends. Just hearing her prayer made me cry one of those ugly cries. But a sense of calm hit my body as if I knew it would all be all right. I knew then that I could handle this and handle it in a way that could not just save me but everyone close to me.

"Thank you."

"Aww, son. Come here, give me a hug." She embraced me like a grandmother or mother would. In her arms, I felt safety and solitude. Something I hadn't felt since my mother passed away.

"Thank you for that, the prayer and the coffee. What was your name?"

"Everyone here calls me Momma Josie. As long as you're staying here, you can call me that too."

"It's nice to meet you, Momma Josie. I appreciate you. I should head back to check on my fiancée."

"Well, if she's up, bring her by. I'm sure she's beautiful inside and out."

"You have no idea. If she's up and you're still here, I'll bring her by."

"All right. If not, y'all have a great day and remember you are stronger than all of this!"

I smiled back at Momma Josie before walking back to the room. When I returned to the room, Nahima was lying in bed, flicking through the channels with the remote.

"Where you been, big daddy?" she asked, still looking at the television.

"I just went through the hotel looking for a gym or a pool. Sometimes a little workout is good for the mind. You know how I get."

"I assume the workout we had earlier wasn't enough. Do we need another round?" Nahima teased, tossing the remote on the bed.

"Not right now. First, I would like to talk to you about what I told you."

"Are you sure you're up for that?"

"I have to be. I don't want to just tell you. I want to tell everyone. Get everyone here in an hour. Let's order some food, and we'll get everyone in order. Asia is also a key and, like you feel, may be still a pawn. I'm not too sure. But she has a lot to tell."

"All right. I'll hit up Marcus, get everyone here, and order the food."

Nahima got on her phone making the arrangements to get everyone's food choices and give them the time for them to be at the room. I was ready to let it all out. I wanted to make sure that my thoughts and my plan came across clearly.

Chapter 33

Shereene

It'd been a good day or so since Isaziah and Asia escaped. I had minimal time to get a new team that I could trust. So, I decided to let my new boy toy gather up some of his friends. I needed a team of simple-minded niggas. You know, the kind who could take orders without talking back. If his friends were anything like him, it would be easy to control them all. I was sure if Isaziah had made it back to that bitch Nahima, then she and the whole crew knew I was alive. Maybe revealing myself so soon wasn't the smartest decision. I moved on instinct and figured it would be the best decision at that time.

When I awoke the following morning, Rayshawn was still sleeping on the floor. His snores reminded me of a large bear. Yeah, he was good enough to fuck, but I did not want him in my bed. Stepping over his naked body wrapped up in the white throw blanket like a caterpillar in a cocoon, I went to take a shower. I figured if I had the water hit my body, it would help me come up with a master plan. Lighting two of my lust-scented incense sticks, I turned on some wave sounds and ran a nice, hot shower.

The subtle tunes made me feel a sense of tranquility. It was like everything in my life in those few moments wasn't as crazy as the past few months. The water hit my body, and I began to think about how all of this started and if it would all be worth it in the end. I wanted Isaziah to be with me all the time, of course our sisters too. But Isaziah had so much of my heart that I couldn't take being serious with any other men. I knew they would never amount to the man my brother was. Why allow myself to get my feelings involved when all I would be was disappointed in the end?

When I first met Jay Boogie, I was out of town to do a pop-up shop in Orlando. I was staying at the Best Western downtown where he either was staying or seeing someone. I was making my way out of the hotel with all my props and my purse when a whole bag fell out of my hands and everything fell out. Jay Boogie just happened to be right there at the right time. He walked over in his freshly ironed white jeans and white tank top. His little muscles and his tattoos glimmered in the sunlight. Jay Boogie helped me gather my things, then escorted me to my rental car.

"Are you from here?" he asked, following me slowly.

"Nah, just here visiting. You?" I unlocked the car from the entrance of the parking garage.

"The same, pretty lady. Are you single?"

"Why? Why did you just call me pretty lady?"

"Because you pretty as hell. You act like you don't hear that a lot." Jay Boogie opened the trunk for me.

"Thanks. I appreciate your help and the compliment. I'm Shereene."

"Jay Boogie is what they know me by."

"Well, Jay Boogie, it was nice meeting you. If you aren't busy, you and your people should come out to the event I'm here for." I reached into my purse and passed him a flyer.

"Word up. When I finish my little business around here, I'll swing through." He flashed a cute smile, showing off his dimples.

"That's what's up." *I got into my car and watched him walk back toward the hotel.*

I was at the little pop-up event, slanging my custom mugs and shirts, when he walked in with a crew of guys all dressed in red shirts and black jeans. It was then that I knew he had to be in some of the same type of business as myself and my family. Jay Boogie came over to my table, buying $200 worth of merchandise from me. I was shocked to say the least, and prior to the event ending, he asked me out on a date. I'm sure you can guess the rest of that history.

It only took about six months to finally realize that Nahima was the key to Isaziah. With her gone, I could confess my feelings and take the throne beside my sexy black man. Months went by, and Jay Boogie's partner had lost about $100,000 in gambling. Jay Boogie needed a way to get out of owing their connect and having to reup. I offered to rob Isaziah and make it easy for them to take over most of the territory my brother was over if I got to call all the shots. But killing my mother wasn't a part of the plan.

The shower ran cold, taking me out of my deep thoughts. I reached for my towel as I stepped out of the shower. Rayshawn wasn't in the room when I came back. As I looked around, I could hear Future's "Transformer" song echoing from another room. Getting dressed quickly, I made my way toward the music. Six niggas sat in the living room area as Rayshawn was in the kitchen bagging up weed and frying some bacon on the stove.

"You finished your shower and stuff, babe? I mean, Shereene."

"Yeah, I did. What's going on out here?" I was curious about all the people sitting in the living room as if they were awaiting orders.

"You told me to come up with a team. I got some of my closest homies to come work for you. I told them you would let them know about how money would be given. Right now, I'm getting this weed ready to go out. I thought you may want to eat something before starting your day."

"Well, look at you on top of your job. I like that. Keep it up." I winked at Rayshawn before going back to the living room. "Fellas, thank you for coming. I'm Shereene. If you decide to work for me, you do as I say when I say. If you don't like that rule, or anything I ask of you, there's only one way out or in."

"You act like we're a gang. I'm not trying to be a part of no gang or take orders from some little girl who's probably just in this 'cause her old nigga made her mad," a light-skinned guy responded. He reminded me of Isaziah, just a little more scrawny, low fade, and gouges in his ears.

"What's your name?"

"You can call me daddy. But everyone knows me as Racoon."

I chuckled at the thought of calling him or any man at that point "daddy." Walking over to him from behind and grabbing my Swiss army knife off the coffee table, I opened it and quickly stabbed him in his left shoulder blade.

"I won't call you daddy. If anything, I'll call you my bitch. Now again, all of you have two choices. You can be in, or you can walk out of this house. If you work for me, you will respect me and do as I say when I say it. Understood?" I twisted the knife to the right as Racoon hollered in agony.

Everyone but two people agreed, and the other two walked out. Didn't matter much to me. I knew they weren't fitting for this. Racoon, on the other hand, currently at my mercy, shouted that he understood. Hearing it was like music to my ears.

"Great. Now remember, I won't be calling you daddy. But you will be calling me momma. One of you help that asshole take care of that stab wound. The rest of you prepare for your day with Rayshawn. He's in charge of the street crew. Bring me back sixty percent of what you make throughout your time out of there. I have other things to put in motion for us."

I left them to do as I instructed before going back into my bedroom. Now with a new team that was all in my control, I prepped for the major kill. I needed to meet with Isaziah and make him an offer he couldn't refuse.

Chapter 34

Isaziah

This meeting with the team was going to be harder than normal. Considering my team was made up of mostly my family, how would they or anyone want to hear that Shereene was the one responsible for our mother's death and our worlds turning upside down in a matter of moments? Nahima ordered a bunch of Chinese food, and I ran to the liquor store to grab a gallon of Patrón. By the time I got back, everyone was already in the room. The atmosphere was filled with laughter and conversations. The room was filled with positive energy. I hated that I was going to ruin it with the news I was going to drop.

I noticed Asia sitting on the bed, being more timid than usual. I set the liquor store bag on the counter near the kitchenette.

"Everyone's here, babe. Food will be here soon," Nahima greeted me with a warm smile.

"Good, let's just chill out until after the food comes." I took one of the paper cups and poured myself a shot.

The food arrived and everyone was licking their lips, ready for a bite. Nahima ordered a feast. From fried rice, chicken wings, lo mein, and more, we had enough to eat now and later. Once we all got our plates and began eating, it was time to start unveiling the truth.

"Asia, can you come sit by me and Nahima?" I patted the empty space between my fiancée and me. "Listen up, y'all. What me and Asia are about to share may be troubling to hear, but it's the only way we can end this sooner rather than later."

"What's up, bro?" my older sister Raye asked while she bit into her chicken wing.

"Isaziah, I don't want to do this," Asia whispered.

"Asia, they need to know. We all wanna go back to life as we know it. If we can't beat her as a team, more importantly a family, we will lose and possibly die." I took my sister's hand with a smile.

Asia just glanced at me as if she was ashamed of what happened to her. It only fueled me with more anger. Everyone around the room got silent, waiting for me to say or do anything.

"What Asia and I are about to disclose may be hard. But it will again make it easier for us to eliminate the target."

"So, it's just one person we're looking for?" Marcus questioned.

"We're going after Shereene," I said almost in a mumble.

"Wait, what?" Raye and my other sisters stopped eating and focused their attention on me.

"You all heard me correctly. Shereene is our only target. Asia can explain from what she knows up until when they took me."

"How can she explain? What are we missing here?" Raye seemed puzzled and alarmed.

Asia took a deep breath and released her truth to everyone. "Basically, I involuntarily became a piece of the plan from Shereene and the Gator Boys."

"Bitch!" Raye shouted toward Asia.

"Raye, please just let her finish. Asia, just let it all out. Don't stop telling anyone what happened." I gave her a little nudge while my eyes locked with Nahima, and she looked disgusted before Asia could finish.

"I was pulled in, but I wasn't ready for what they really had in store. Shereene had just told me it would be some extra easy money, but I couldn't tell anyone because she said you all would get jealous of us. It started with just moving little bits of weight here and there. Then once they felt I was trusted, I was in charge of spying on the family and the team. The more information I brought back to Shereene that she wasn't already aware of made me the best spy for the team. Then everything happened without me knowing until she told me she was going to kill Nahima. She partially convinced me that Nahima was trying to eliminate us, his sisters. That she was going to kill us all and that Isaziah wouldn't stop her. When Momma was killed, Shereene had asked me to step out of the house to meet her somewhere. While I was with her for those few moments, I got back and it was too late. It was too late and I couldn't save Momma."

"Asia, what the hell?"

"That's not it, Raye. She then left me at Jay Boogie's disposal. She wanted to take charge of the family. When she left me alone with Jay Boogie, he would rape me every time. No one would hear me screaming. I couldn't get any help, not even from her. Then when she set me up to kill Nahima in her hotel room after she got out of the hospital, I realized then it wasn't right. I was aware of her fake death. But I didn't think she was going to take it this far."

"You're trying to get us all killed?" Raye jumped up out of her chair onto Asia, slinging punches left and right.

"Man, y'all stop! Stop, Raye!" I shouted. They couldn't just jump on her like that.

"Nahima, help me!" I hollered.

I could tell she wasn't in the mood to. But at the same time, she loved my family like I did. We were finally able to get Raye off of Asia and kept them separated.

"Isaziah, I say we kill her. We can't trust anyone who betrays us regardless of what she says. You know how we do. If you can't be trusted, then we don't need them."

Asia ran behind Nahima for her to shield her. But my wife-to-be moved over slightly so she could still be seen.

"Asia, right now, just go back to your room. We will reconvene this meeting later. I think everyone needs time to cool off. Asia, go ahead. Once you're in your room, let me know, and then everyone can go."

"Okay." Asia scurried out of the room fast as hell.

I could see the way everyone looked at her as a traitor. But all I could see was my little sister who was scared. I wanted to save her. She needed help through everything. She was a victim. Asia texted me shortly after she left, letting me know her location. I told everyone to leave me and Nahima to ourselves.

"That didn't go the way I thought it would," I said, plopping down onto the bed.

"Babe, what did you think? I didn't even know that backstory. Did you?"

"I knew about the rape but not that other shit. She's gonna need therapy and shit after all this."

"I guess. But we can't treat her like a victim. As much as she says she didn't know what was going on, she had to have some kind of clue. Like, there may be more that she knows. But honestly, do you think she can be trusted?"

"I hope so, babe. I really hope so." I pulled her into my arms. "I was thinking . . . why don't we get up in the morning and get married? We can do the big, fancy wedding you want after this is done. But if I die before then, I wanna know that I died as your husband and not just your fiancé or boyfriend."

"I hear you, baby." Nahima kissed my forehead and dozed off shortly after with her hands on my chest.

Chapter 35

Nahima

My thoughts were rapid with everything Asia did decide to tell us. Asia did need to deal with being raped, but the rest of it, I couldn't tell you how I really felt about any of it. It was still early when I dozed off. I wanted to forget about all of it, but it was going to be hard to. Isaziah being back was everything, and he was the love of my life. He was the only man who'd ever truly been inside of me as well. I couldn't see my life with any man but him. But I was hesitant about whether I wanted to still marry into a family like this after everything that happened. *What am I going to do? Walk away or get married?*

Isaziah wasn't going to let Asia be treated disrespectfully by anyone. I could tell from the brief family meeting that he was going to do whatever was necessary to protect her. I just hoped it wouldn't get him killed in the process. After my quick nap, I awoke to find a big black box wrapped in a red ribbon on the bed next to a Nieman Marcus bag. The shower water was running, so I made my way into the bathroom. I could hear Isaziah singing "Pretty Brown Eyes" all off-key and a cappella at the top of his lungs.

My baby had a lot of talents, but singing wasn't one of them. I stood in the doorway listening to his croons. The shower stopped running, and as he reached for his towel, I walked in to hand it to him.

"Thanks, babe. Did you see the stuff on the bed?" Isaziah stepped out of the shower with a towel dangling from his dick.

"Umm . . . yeah, I saw it." I couldn't focus with his half-erect dick in my face.

"Did you open it? Or you too busy looking at this towel? I can drop it if it's easier."

I was sure he knew what I was thinking. There wasn't anything about any presents on my mind. That dick was poking out, and it was all fresh from the shower, too. I wanted to hop on my man. My mind was not on all the bullshit. It was on escaping it. Isaziah needed to release some of that pressure as well.

"Babe, stop looking at my dick and go open the stuff on the bed." Isaziah's towel dropped, and I was discombobulated.

He guided me toward the bed and waited for me to open everything. "Can I open them later? I have something else in mind I want to do," I stated with a sly grin.

"After." Isaziah handed me the black box first.

As I untied the red ribbon from the top, I slowly opened the box to reveal a beautiful rose-colored diamond necklace set with matching watch and earrings. My face lit up like a kid on Christmas. *I guess it pays to be the plug sometimes.* But we'd lost so much money on rental cars and hopping in and out of hotels for our safety, and we weren't making it back fast enough.

"Babe, I love it. But maybe you should return it until we get back all the way right."

"I bought that prior to everything going down. I made sure Marcus brought it with him, and I knew I would give it to you at the right time. I will say what's in that bag is what I did recently purchase while you were asleep."

"Well, I wasn't asleep that long."

"Long enough. Now open it, sexy." Isaziah pushed the Nieman Marcus bag in front of me, watching my every reaction.

Inside of the bag was a beautiful cream-colored dress that seemed to be form-fitting and a pair of matching Christian Louboutins. I had no idea what to say.

"I was serious when I said let's get married. I also made the call to the courthouse to get the marriage license done and set a time for us to get married tomorrow morning. I'm picking up the license in an hour."

"Isaziah, we have more important things to take care of first. We can wait to get married."

"Not anymore. I wasted time waiting all these years. I should've married you before. We are both married to this game, but I want to say 'I do' to you now. I have a will in place for before you become my wife and after. The way things are, I want to make sure that everything you are supposed to get, you do."

"Will? What will?" I never heard him discuss anything about a will to me before.

"I'll explain when the time is right."

"No, you need to explain now! I mean, right now."

"Nahima. Let's just get married and we will talk about it later."

"Isaziah, goddamn it! Listen to me. I'm not going anywhere and neither of us will be disappearing or leaving one another for a rave anytime soon. I know that you are nervous about your sister and everything. It's all going to work itself out."

"I created the first will because I wasn't sure if the beef with the TaynoSayes was going to pan out, and I wanted to make sure everything was covered. Then after the Gator Boys came for us, it ruined the night I was going to initially propose. But here we are, and I'm not letting anything or anyone take what we've earned. Now can we just get two witnesses and prepare for tomorrow?"

"Baby, I want nothing more than to marry you. But do you think your family is gonna be here for us getting married without all of them knowing? Secrets, whether good or bad, never end well. I wanna do everything the right way. Okay?"

I could sense the disappointment coming off of Isaziah, but he also understood. "You know what, that's why I love you."

"Why is that?"

"Because whenever I think or react on emotions, you bring me back down and help lead the way. What would I do without you?"

"Probably go insane or worse," I joked.

Isaziah was about to lay me back on the bed when I felt the vibration on the bed from my phone. I grabbed it as I allowed him to finish undressing me. It was an inbox message from a page without a name and a display picture. The message read:

You stupid little bitch. He may be there with you now, but he won't be for long. Count your days, Nahima. Soon everyone will be singing sad songs and bringing flowers to your grave. Watch your ass, bitch!

I showed the notification to Isaziah as I sat up on the bed.

"Who the fuck sent you this shit?" Isaziah shouted.

"I don't know, probably your crazy-ass sister."

"Nahima!"

"Isaziah, it's true! That bitch has been trying to kill me and has hated me from the start! You can't just sit your ass here like you don't know this already! I've been nice and I've tried to let you handle her. I almost kissed her ass just for the sake of everything, and what the hell did she do?"

"Nahima, I get what you're saying, but Shereene may be just going through something. And if I can get her to just talk to me, maybe we can end this peacefully."

"There's no more peace when she attempted to kill me, killed our unborn baby by stabbing me, then helped kidnap you and Asia. There is no more peace when it comes to that psychotic bitch! If you don't wanna make the plan to kill her, then I will. But I have to know you won't stand in the way."

I was overly irritated with the way Isaziah was still defending that bitch! I pulled my tights back on, grabbed the car keys, and stormed out of the room, leaving Isaziah where he stood. *He may feel like Shereene is worth saving, but I know for a fact me and Raye think differently.* Shereene was sending out threats, but I was going to deliver mine in person.

Chapter 36

Shereene

It was going to be so easy to tear the two love birds apart. I just had to give that ho Nahima a reason not to trust him. Or I had to make them argue over something or someone. I was sure that once she knew I was alive, she would want my blood. I created a fake Facebook page so I could see if I could watch their locations and any status updates. To my surprise, no one had posted anything since Momma's funeral. Now a piece of me hated the feeling of being the one to possibly ruin our family for my own personal reasons. But the other 95 percent of me was excited to see what the future held for Isaziah and me.

I watched Nahima's page night and day, but there were never any updates. I was watching *Criminal Minds* when I decided to slide in her DMs. I wasn't sure how I was going to write the message. I just allowed my fingers to do the talking. Once I sent the message, the phone stayed on my lap as I waited to see if she would respond. Disappointment set in quickly when hours passed by and I got nothing back. I needed to speed up the process of things. I was growing tired of these stupid little boys around my house, and Rayshawn had become clingier than I would have liked him to be.

I needed to make Rayshawn become less focused on me and more focused on the business. The crew he picked out wasn't good for anything. They were moving the weight too slowly. They would bring me back no more than $200 a day. That wasn't the money they all expected to get paid. If you couldn't bring me back a stack or more, how could they expect any type of money from me? I knew Isaziah didn't do that shit when he first started. My brother would bring home at least $5,000 on a slow day. I had to be able to make that myself before becoming his number one.

Rayshawn was out watching my new little soldiers when I got a visit from Racoon. He came in through the back door abruptly and full of anger.

"Aye, you announce yourself when you come into my space. Why are you here instead of at your post?"

"Rayshawn said he wanted me to come back here because I almost got caught by the cops fighting a junkie."

I couldn't help but laugh. "You were fighting a junkie instead of serving him?"

"He didn't wanna pay for the product. He told me to give him one off of GP and that he would bring me the money later. I said no nicely the first time, but he wasn't taking that for an answer. When he got aggressive, I shoved him onto the ground. Then it just went left. Rayshawn pulled up on me right as the cops were slowing down watching the scene."

"Well, he did his job. If you got locked up, they could've come looking for me. I don't need that shit."

"Bitch, I don't give a fuck what you need. You don't pay nobody anyway. Where's all the money you get from us, huh? You don't do shit but sit in here while all of us do all the dirty work."

"You need to watch your tone."

"You can suck my dick, stupid-ass bitch. I didn't trust you in the beginning and I don't trust you now."

Normally, I would've just killed that nigga for his disrespect because I could do so. But his frustration and the way he was talking to me turned me on more than a little bit.

"I think that's what you want. You want me to suck your dick, don't you?"

"Man, what the fuck is wrong with you?"

I grabbed my semi-automatic from my chair cushions, stood up, and walked over to Racoon. "We can do this two ways. Drop your pants and them drawers and fuck my pussy like you wanted to keep beating that junkie up. Or I can shoot your ass right here for disrespecting me."

"That's rape, what you're trying to do."

"Your dick print is showing, and that doesn't look to me like it's rape." I lowered the gun long enough to get my shirt and leggings off, revealing my body in nothing but a bra.

Racoon stood there with a look of conflict on his face. I knew he wanted to fuck me. I could feel it. I wanted some new dick because Rayshawn wasn't doing it enough for me. Placing the gun on the TV stand to the right of me, I dropped to my knees and waited for his next move.

"You won't tell Rayshawn? He really likes you, and that's like my brother."

"My organization. My house. He's just a soldier, and a loyal one. He is not my man. Nothing to worry about." I motioned for him to come closer as I caressed my body slowly.

"I'm gonna give you what you want then." Racoon got naked where he stood and rushed over to me, forcing my mouth open and sliding his dark chocolate dick in my mouth.

His moan escaped loudly as he called me a bitch while fucking my throat. His hands gripped my hair tightly like a set of fresh box braids. "Yeah, I'm not nutting in your mouth yet, bitch. Get up and bend over. I don't wanna see your face when I fuck you."

He yanked his dick from my mouth, and I was forced on all fours. I didn't know if this nigga had a condom, but I surely wanted to see what that stroke was like. Racoon grabbed me by the throat as he slid his dick inside of my wetness. His strokes came hard and rapid.

"You take this fuckin' dick, bitch! Cum on my fuckin' dick! Oooouuu yes, bitch, you gonna come on this dick and call me daddy!" Racoon was talking all that shit when his stroke was okay.

I could feel it but not feel it, if that makes sense. He was doing a whole lot of nothing, and my pussy wasn't enjoying the beat-down like we should have been. I could hear a car pulling onto the gravel while he was still moaning louder than me. I knew it was only Rayshawn, and I figured this would be the time to give a perfect performance.

"Shit, someone's at the door." Racoon stopped fucking me and was about to pull out of me when I shouted for him to keep going.

Racoon was loving the pussy so much, he listened and continued fucking me. He beat my pussy, and I moaned out louder than I did before. With a quick glance at the door, I saw Rayshawn standing in the doorway watching his best friend fuck me. I threw my ass back on his dick, forcing myself to cum as I looked right into Rayshawn's puppy-dog eyes. He seemed shocked and was stuck in that moment. I gave him a huge smile as I yelled for Racoon to nut in my pussy.

"How could y'all?" Rayshawn pulled out his pistol, shooting in our direction.

I knew he wouldn't shoot me, but Racoon was a dead man. Rayshawn followed him into the back kitchen area. I heard one last shot, and the sound of a loud thud hit the floor. After putting my clothes back on, I went to see if Racoon was dead or just severely injured.

"Fuck! See what you made me do? You made me kill my best friend!" Rayshawn pouted.

"Baby, listen, I told you not to get so caught up with feelings and things. If you weren't so wrapped up in your emotions, this wouldn't have happened."

"No, if you didn't fuck him, this wouldn't have happened. I'll be back later. I need some space and shit."

"That's fine, honey, I understand. I'll have someone come get rid of the body and your gun. Just go cool off."

Rayshawn threw his gun on the kitchen table and stormed out of the house. Either my plan worked and I killed two birds with one stone, or I just gained another enemy who could potentially run to my brother and help him with sealing whatever fate he chose for me.

Chapter 37

Isaziah

I wanted to chase after Nahima, but it would have been hopeless. Maybe she was right and I needed to be sterner with the idea of killing off one of my siblings. I just couldn't see Shereene doing all of this because of me or her. There had to be more to the story we didn't know. I figured maybe Asia knew more than what she told us as well. While my fiancée was out doing whatever she felt to blow off her steam, I decided to have Asia come hang out with me for a while. I took the elevator up to room 334. When I approached her hotel room, I could hear her arguing with someone over the phone. With my ear pressed up against the door, I tried to eavesdrop just to see if I could hear anything.

"Listen, this is all your fault! If you had never done any of this, we would still be a happy family!" Asia was going off and blaming someone. "You need to listen. I am not your pawn, your friend, your sister, or anything anymore! I'm done and so is this family. I suggest you find a place to hide before our brother or, worse, Nahima gets to you. Don't ever call or reach out to me again. For what you let happen to Momma, I hope they all kill you. Rot in hell!" It sounded like Asia had thrown her phone or something against the door when I heard the bang against the opposite side of the door.

I waited a few minutes before knocking. I didn't want to seem obvious that I was there and overheard any parts of the conversation. But I wanted to know who she was talking to and why. My gut said it was Shereene, but I wanted to make sure before I started having doubtful thoughts about my little sister.

Knock. Knock. Knock.

"Asia, it's me. Open the door, sis."

"Okay, hold on, I just got out of the shower. Let me grab some clothes really quick."

"Okay." I leaned against the wall, pulling out my new iPhone 11 Max to text Nahima.

Me: Babe, listen, I understand that you're upset, but I think I just overheard Asia talking to Shereene.

A few moments went by before she finally texted me back.

Nahima: Talking to who? Talking to who? You got to be kidding me. She has to die too or something.

Me: We will talk when you get back. I'm about to go meet up with her.

Nahima: Fine, see you later.

Me: I love you, beautiful.

Nahima: I love you too.

Asia cracked her hotel room door open, checking out the surroundings. "Hey, bro, come on in. Sorry about that."

"You good, what's going on?" I asked as I walked into her room.

I could sense she had been nervous about something. Asia sat toward the back of the king-size bed, being really fidgety.

"What brings you by?"

"I wanted to just see how you were doing from the altercation with Raye earlier. You know how she can be sometimes."

"Yeah, I'm fine. I'm glad that you came to check on me. I didn't expect Raye to act like that."

"You know I didn't either. I was astonished to say the least."

"Astonished?" Asia burst into laughter. "Nigga, who are you, T.I.?"

"Nah, I don't think I'm nobody. But who do you think you are?"

Asia stopped laughing and looked at me suspiciously. "What you talkin' about?"

"I'm only going to ask you once. Please don't make this harder for me than what it already is."

"Isaziah, what's your issue? What are you talking about?"

I hated the thought that Asia was truly an accomplice and not a victim. Would I have to do the unthinkable to two of my siblings? It was hard enough trying to fathom Shereene being this evil.

"Who were you yelling at on the phone before I knocked on the door?"

"What? What are you talking about?"

"Don't play stupid with me. I heard you arguing with someone, but I don't know who. So, tell me right now."

"I don't have to tell you anything!"

I threw the TV remote against the wall, infuriated. "Goddammit, Asia! I am the only one trying to save you at this point. Nahima would be on your side, but after you tried to kill her, she barely trusts you. Do us both a favor and tell me who the fuck you were talking to. Not now but right motherfucking now!"

Asia stared at me, her eyes filled with fear of what I may or could do. Grabbing her by her arms tightly, I shook her as I yelled over and over for her to tell me until she hollered she would.

"It was Shereene. I called her on Facebook when she inboxed me, asking me to tell her my location and asking all these questions."

"What did you tell her?"

"I told her nothing. I promise! I didn't tell her where I was. That's why I was yelling. I want you to know I won't betray you."

I loosened my grip from her arms, and then her phone rang.

"Who is it?" I asked, hoping it wasn't who I thought it was.

Asia grabbed the phone and tried to hide the phone from me. Before she could toss it under the pillow, I yanked it from her hand. It was Shereene calling Asia for the third time. The notifications on her phone showed three missed Facebook video calls from Shereene's actual page.

"I propose you reach out to your big sister for help since you care for her conversations so much after she tried to kill you. Oh, and let's not forget letting her boyfriend rape you. I mean, that's if he really raped you at this point. Who fucking knows with all your lies and bullshit? But from now on, if you stay here, your trust has to be earned. You have to protect yourself." I got up from the bed, leaving Asia there alone.

I was beyond disappointed in her choice to deal with Shereene on any level. Raye and Nahima were right. At that point, Asia couldn't be trusted. Without knowing whose side she was truly on, she had to be watched closely. *Asia could be our downfall.*

Chapter 38

Nahima

Two days had gone by, and Isaziah was more distant than normal after one of our little spats. Normally he wouldn't just be so quiet. Something was off. Whenever I asked him about Asia or Shereene, he would just dismiss the conversation. Something wasn't right, and I was determined to figure out what exactly was the issue. I knew things were not going the way he wanted, but he couldn't be a brat about it forever.

Isaziah was out with Marcus when I took it upon myself to have a little girls' day. I wanted to just spend time with all of his sisters and try to live life like we used to. Most of his sisters were down with the idea except Asia. I was sure it was because she was afraid that either Raye or I would beat her ass and leave her stranded. I wouldn't harm her without Isaziah knowing or his permission. That would end our relationship or change it drastically.

Raye was one of the first ones at my hotel room. I let her inside, and she smelled like a pound of weed.

"Damn, bitch, did you smoke all of it or did you leave us some?" I teased, closing the door behind her.

"Man, you know how I do. I'm 'bout to roll up right now before we leave."

"I bet your ass is. Fucking pothead."

The television was on HBO as they played *Aquaman* for the fifteenth time. "Girl, I cannot wait to get home. I can't wait for all this shit to be over."

"Man, who you telling! I ain't had no good pussy since we fucking left."

"You sound like a straight nigga just now. You need some pussy? Why don't you just look for a little fling out here?"

"Now you know you don't just put your mouth on anyone."

"That's true. But shit, I haven't really been with anyone like that but your brother."

"Bitch, wait a fucking minute!"

"See, don't start your shit, Raye."

"You mean to tell me you never slept with anyone outside of Isaziah?"

"I've had a nigga play in my pussy, but that's about it."

"Yeah, bitch, you fucked up out here. Now you gon' be with the same dick the rest of your life." Raye couldn't help herself.

She teased me left and right. I got the point that I should have experimented more in my life, but I was content being with Isaziah. Shit, what if he did allow me a chance to experience some new dick and it was horrible? It would be a waste. Raye finally stopped joking about my inexperienced sex life and started asking questions about Asia.

I could tell she was still pretty disturbed about the information Asia relayed to us the other day. Was Raye right about not being able to trust Asia? *That's the real question.* Before Raye could go in depth with her feelings, the rest of the gang arrived.

"Aye, so what are we gonna do today? 'Cause a bitch is tired of just seeing the damn walls of a hotel room and shit," Mary, Isaziah's twin, asked.

"Shit, what y'all wanna do? I was thinking we could just get some food and some drinks. We need to just unwind."

"Is Asia coming?" Tanya, the second-youngest sister, asked.

"She wouldn't answer my calls or any text messages from me. I did attempt to invite her."

"What the fuck for? She's a traitor," Raye murmured while finishing rolling her second blunt.

"Because she is still our sister. She was raped and manipulated. We should be giving her nothing but love right now. Not treating her like she is the enemy. Right, Nahima?" Tanya looked at me, waiting for confirmation.

"To be honest, I believe both of you have a point, and I just say we play it by ear. But if we all go together to her and make her feel that shit hasn't changed, maybe she won't be so reluctant to be around any of us. Especially you, Raye," I said, standing in the middle of the hotel room floor.

"I ain't do shit but what needs to be done. This ho kidnapped Isaziah, tried to kill you, and helped Shereene kill Momma. I don't know if she was helping them escape because she wanted to be free or if she was doing that as part of a plan. She could be playing both sides, and that's not cool."

I hated to say it, but Raye was right. If she was playing both sides, Asia would be playing a dangerous game that could possibly end up with her getting seriously hurt or, worse, dead. I wanted Asia to be taught a lesson, but I couldn't fathom killing her at that moment. Maybe if she was just scared a bit, she would realize where her trust should be placed.

"Listen, I'm going to go personally invite her. We are supposed to be family, good or bad. To be honest, maybe she was the victim in this whole situation. But we never will know the whole truth if we just jump down her throat every chance we get," I declared as I tossed a pair of black Vans on.

To be honest, I really didn't want to have her around, but I needed to feel out the energy for myself. Energy was one thing that would never lie. To her hotel room I went, my stomach bubbling the whole ride up the elevator. I knew it wasn't that I had to shit, but it was my nerves. All I could do was pray that the outcome would be just right. As I approached her room door, I could hear more than one voice in the room. I knew it wasn't any one of the sisters. Maybe it was just her watching the television or something on her phone that was louder than what it needed to be.

Knock, knock, knock. There was no answer. I knocked again a bit harder. Asia finally came to the door, and before she could open it all the way, I heard a familiar voice say, "Well, it's not as nice to see you. I thought you were Isaziah. Asia, push the door open so she can see."

There, sitting on Asia's hotel bedroom floor, was none other than Shereene. Before anything else could transpire, I ran back toward the elevator, searching for my phone, only to realize I left it inside the room. I could hear Shereene yelling for Asia to follow me. Hopefully, I could make it back to the room. The elevator opened just as Asia caught up to me. I scurried onto the elevator, pushing the button to get the doors to close before she could hop on.

I got back to my floor, out of breath and watching behind me as I made it down the hallway. Raye and everyone were still inside, as was Isaziah. I locked the door behind me immediately, which alarmed everyone.

"Shereene is here. In Asia's room. Right now." I breathed heavily, leaning back against the door.

Chapter 39

Shereene

The surprise effect worked perfectly. To see that shocked look on Nahima's face was priceless. Asia was feeling exiled, and she finally called me back. To say the least, she needed someone, and I gave her what she needed. To be quite frank, Asia was just a pawn, and she was going to lead me in the right direction. I knew Nahima was about to run and tell Isaziah about seeing me, but by that time, I planned to be gone.

Asia came back to the room out of breath. "I couldn't catch her."

"It's cool. We will get her another day. The goal, my darling little sister, isn't to kill anyone, but to make them fear us so much that they have no choice but to do what we want them to do. I have a plan, and I know it's all going to work out."

"Shereene, maybe it was wrong telling you where I was. I wasn't trying to start anything with them, but I thought we could all just talk it out."

"There's not much to talk about, Asia."

"There is. Like why would you want to kill Momma? Or have her killed?"

"It wasn't my choice. They forced me to do it. I wasn't sure she was going to be home."

"Shereene, I think that's truly a lie. You told me to leave. You didn't say anything to me during that call about where Momma was. It's almost like you wanted her to die."

Asia started that wimp shit, and I hated that. She needed to grow up. Life wasn't fair, and she needed to know that in the game of love and war, there were casualties. Granted, my mother was the first, but she was never truly loyal to me. I remembered the first time I knew she loved every one of my siblings, especially Isaziah, more than me.

It was Christmas of 2009. We were all home dealing with the bittersweetness of Christmas. That year, our great-grandmother had passed just two weeks before, and she was a vibrant light in each of our lives. To my mother, it felt like her world was over. No grandma, no mother, no husband—she didn't have much to lose.

I was happy to see her at first, smiling and singing along with us when we belted out Christmas carols. But that evening, something switched up. My mother wasn't a heavy drinker, but that particular day she was. I watched my mother down four bottles of wine, some vodka, and some Crown Royal. Her happiness slowly faded drink by drink, and her depression started to show. Isaziah went to her as she sat on the brown velvet rocking chair beside the television.

"Isaziah, you are the best child a mother could ask for. You're always here for me," I overheard her tell him as he grabbed the empty wineglass and bottles from the floor.

"Momma, all of us are your best kids," Isaziah rebutted.

"Some of y'all are. I will say Shereene's been different without y'all daddy around for years. It made her cold. Sometimes I feel as if she faults me."

"We know it wasn't your fault, Ma. She doesn't fault you, and none of us do."

Isaziah had stood up beside her, and she tapped his right cheek. "I love you, my son."

"I love you too, Momma."

I stood there feeling unsettled. So, I approached her after Isaziah left. I didn't care if she was drunk. She was going to hear me.

"Momma?"

"Hey, my beautiful little girl."

"I'm not your little girl. I'm grown as hell. You need to get off yo' drunk ass and sober up. You still have to raise Asia. Who's gonna take care of her if you kill yourself like this?"

"Shereene, you watch how you talk to me."

"If I don't?"

"Child, go 'head now. You not too grown to get your ass beat. You know better."

"Nah, Mommy, I am too old to get my ass beat. You wouldn't talk to Raye, Reecey, Isaziah—"

"I will talk to any of my children how I see fit. What the hell is wrong with you?"

"I can tell you what's wrong. Daddy left because of you. When I got locked up a few months ago, instead of helping me get home and being there with me, you left me alone in jail. You wouldn't accept any of my calls. Like, you hated me."

"I did not hate you. You needed to learn your lesson. If you wanted to be out of there following behind some stupid-ass nigga and get locked up, that's on you. I warned you several times and you never listened. Never!" My mother rose up out of her chair so she could face me.

"That was your way of making me learn? By making me feel alone?"

"You were never alone. You were there for only a week. The only good thing that boy did for you was letting you get off free. But you are still so naive and stupid!"

"Just because I was with him doesn't mean I had parts to anything. You never wanted to hear my side of the story!"

"I don't need to hear your side. Shereene, you almost lost your life to the fucking jail. I did not come here with everything I had for you to drop out of school and chase behind a piece of dick!"

"He chased me, Momma. Difference!" I got in my mother's face as if she were a random girl off the street picking a fight.

"Rayeshawnna! Raye! Come get your sister right now before I kick her ass!" my mother hollered to my sister.

Before Raye showed her face, I had slapped my mother across the face as hard as I could. My hand stung from the slap, and my mother's face was red like a burning fire.

"I'll kill you!" My mother tackled me, grabbing me by the throat and banging my head onto the wooden floor in the den area.

By the time my siblings realized there was something serious going on, I got the upper hand, and I was caught shoving Momma into the bottom corner of the wall.

"Shereene! Stop it!" Asia screamed out.

When I looked around and saw the look of disappointment and disgust on everyone's face, I scooted away from her back toward the entrance of the den.

"Get out of my house! You are to never come back until you learn how to respect and talk to your mother. Ya understand me?"

"Fuck you! Fuck all of you!" I ran out of the house so fast, grabbing my little black clutch bag and sweater.

I sat outside on the steps crying my eyes out for a while. No one reached out to me. No one checked on me but Isaziah. He came out of the house about thirty minutes later.

"I don't know what that was about. I hope you are okay though. But you gotta go."

"Why should I go?"

"Because Asia called the police on you. Just go now. I'll call you later. I love you."

"Thanks. Love you more than you know." I blew Isaziah a kiss and ran off down the street to my car.

I never trusted or liked my own baby sister after that. When the Gator Boys positioned themselves into my life the way they did, it was my way of getting my revenge for that bullshit that happened. I pretended to forgive, but I never forgot any of it. I knew about Jay Boogie raping Asia. I suggested that he make her his bitch while she stayed and helped us complete our plan. But my plan was never the same as the Gator Boys'. I planned a different outcome. The time was nearing, I just prayed that little pop-up did not ruin it too much. Soon, everyone but Isaziah was going to be held accountable for the way they treated me.

Chapter 40

Isaziah

Hearing that Asia allowed Shereene the satisfaction of knowing not just the city we were in, but our actual location, had me furious to say the least. Nahima was filled with rage. She wasn't prepared to deal with Shereene, but Marcus and I stayed ready. I instructed Raye and Marcus to come with me to Asia's room to deal with both of them. I figured this was our moment to end it all. By the time we got to Asia's room, her door was cracked, and she was sitting there with this dumb look on her face.

"Where the hell is she?' I shouted, not caring who heard me.

"Isaziah, she's gone. Listen to me please." Asia stood up, approaching me slowly.

Raye came from behind me, gun in hand, pointed at Asia's chest. "Stop moving toward my brother or I'll shoot you where you stand!"

"Raye, put the gun down for now. Asia, you have five seconds to tell me where the fuck Shereene is before Raye busts a cap in yo' ass with no hesitation."

Asia was scared. It was all over her face. There was a need for her to fear now. The betrayal had been set in stone. The more we tried to forgive her and treat her like the victim, the more it seemed as if she was a coconspirator.

"Isaziah, please just hear me out. I didn't want to say anything. I wanted it to be a surprise so that way we could all talk. I just want us all to be a family again. She agreed to meet with all of us to talk and work things out."

"You fucking crazy? She ain't trying to make shit right! She wants to kill us! I cannot believe you are that fucking stupid!"

"I'm not stupid! Don't talk to me like that!"

"Listen, bitch, you're gonna get dealt with like the random hoes on the street from here on out. Don't come near me, and don't come near this family. You are not a part of us. You are never allowed around any of us again. You a piece of shit."

I walked out of the room, not looking back.

Asia was calling out for me, and it fell on deaf ears. My emotions were on a roller coaster. At first, I was done. But the closer I got to the elevator, and she still called out for us, I wanted to turn around and make it better. My best friend and my second oldest sibling beside me, I went back down to the first floor. Back in the room, I could hear everyone through the door talking loudly.

When I walked back into the room, Nahima looked at me, eyes wide open. "Well, what happened?" she asked, her hands clenching the sheets of the bed.

"Nahima, let's talk about it later."

"No, Isaziah, we are going to talk about it now! Isaziah, she allowed that ho into our hideout location without a thought or anything. So, where are they?"

"Asia is not the enemy! She is our family. Right now, she feels alone, and I probably made that worse."

"What's that supposed to mean?" Nahima's voice had more bass in it than before.

"Shereene wasn't there when we got to the room. Asia was though. My brother let her go with a warning," Raye informed the room as she looked at me with disgust.

"You let who go? Asia? So, she's out there somewhere with Shereene, plotting on how to kill us all?"

"She was still in the room when we left. I'm sure she's still there! She claimed she wanted us all to talk. Shereene wants to talk."

"No one wants to really talk, Isaziah! But I am going to find out now." Nahima jumped up from the bed and gathered herself to head out the door.

"Where the hell are you going?" I asked, grabbing her. She snatched her arm away from me.

"I'm going to figure out why either of them are still living. Raye, Nay, and Shayna, y'all with me."

My sisters looked around the room at her then back at him. Guns cocked and loaded, they followed my fiancée out the door. Marcus looked at me nonchalantly, and I found myself getting aggravated with the entire situation at hand.

"Man, she's right and you know it. It's time to just get rid of all the dead weight. We're losing more money than we making. Just dead this shit so we can get back to living life and making money."

"Marcus, no one in my family should die behind this," I said solemnly.

"You have to realize what you told Asia is true. There is no family right now. We are at war for our lives. Either we can be some pussies and let your sisters kill all of us, or you gon' man up and go help your future wife take control of this shit?"

With my back leaned against the wall, I began to think of all the worst scenarios. What if Asia set us up and Shereene was waiting to kill Nahima? What if Asia was going to kill them and leave Shereene for me? What if Asia and Shereene were plotting against me since I started making more money? They were the problem. Marcus was right. At this point, I was being a bitch. I had to be sterner and treat them like I would do every enemy who ever came my way.

"Grab your shit. Let's go," I instructed Marcus, grabbing my gun and an extra chamber.

By the time we made it back to Asia's room, the door was open, but no one was inside. There were little specks of blood on the walls and the carpet. My mind immediately thought the worst.

"Isaziah?" Marcus whispered my name as we looked around the room.

"Go see if anyone heard anything. I'm going to call them now. Either they have Asia or they have them."

Marcus went out of the room and did his part of investigating. I grabbed my phone out of my back pocket and attempted to call Nahima and Raye but got no answer. I just prayed for a response from them soon.

Chapter 41

Nahima

It was hard as hell for me to get Isaziah to see the truth. I wanted nothing but to believe Asia wasn't a part of the problem, even with the past situation in the hotel. Sometimes people have to do things when they don't want to due to a life being on the line. But Asia proved me wrong with Shereene in her room, and I refused to keep some type of snake like that in our circle. Family or not, she had to go. I knew Isaziah wasn't here for helping us, but these bitches had to be eliminated one by one.

Inside of Asia's hotel room, when we got there, she was packing her bags. Raye had kicked in her door, giving us access. Asia jumped, shook at what was happening.

"I'm glad you're packing. Follow us and don't think of making a scene." I walked up, grabbing Asia by her arm forcefully.

"I'm not going nowhere with any of you! Help! Someone, help!" Asia shouted, trying to grab the attention of anyone walking nearby.

I tried telling her to shut up, but she kept getting louder. When Asia wouldn't stop, Raye took the barrel of her gun and shoved it down her throat. "Now shut the fuck up and do exactly what Nahima tells you, or I won't hesitate to blow your fucking brains out right here."

Asia started to whimper but quietly shut her mouth. Taking her down the hall, we took her past the lobby and into one of the rental cars. We weren't that familiar with the area, but we drove until we could find a secure, low-key location. My intent was to keep her locked away and secluded until we got to Shereene.

We drove for at least thirty minutes or so before we located a quiet little bando in the middle of this hood. There were a few people out but not that many. Across from the gray and white wooden house, there was a brick two-sided home with a gang of niggas sitting on the porch. Raye decided she would be the one to talk to them and see what information she could get out of them. I told her to go to the trunk first and grab a couple of bands. We could use those niggas if need be and make them our guard dogs.

Raye, being who she was, stepped out of the car and did exactly what I told her to. I watched her walk up to the guys at the house while Nayshaya, aka Nay, sat in the back with Asia, holding a gun to her stomach, advising her to stay calm and quiet. Raye was over there with the guys for a while until she turned back around, giving me a nod, letting me know everything was good.

"Listen, we are going to go in this house. You are to get out and not make a sound, try to run, or do anything stupid. If you try, Raye will kill you with or without my command. That, I don't want. Do you understand me? I'd rather have you alive and away from us than dead."

Asia nodded her head and followed Nay out of the car. Raye ran back across the street to us as the guys across the street watched. The house smelled like piss, the floors were squeaky, and the walls had spots of mold. That house had to have been abandoned for years, and the bums had taken complete advantage of it.

I found a broken wooden chair with one leg missing, and the seat had pieces of wood split up. Raye tossed Asia into the chair with every bit of force she had. Asia looked at the three of us with remorse written over her face.

"What are y'all going to do with me?" she asked as her eyes wandered around the room.

"Nay or Raye, someone find something useful to keep her tied up to the chair. We can't leave her like this when we dip out."

"She wouldn't risk leaving, now would you?" Raye walked up to Asia, putting the gun barrel to her chin, lifting her head up.

"Y'all have to believe me. I didn't call Shereene to harm anyone. I just wanted us to be a family again."

I was so over Asia's desperate attempt at trying to get through to us with her lies. "Find something to gag her with, too."

I was not here to hear any more of Asia's bullshit. While Raye took the task to gather things to keep Asia sustained and quiet, my phone began to ring. My phone was in my back pocket, and when I grabbed it out, Marcus was calling me. I was sure he was with Isaziah and wondering where we were.

When I went to answer, Asia jumped from the chair and tackled me. I was able to knee her in the stomach, making her fall on her back. With one good swing, I punched Asia in her jaw before climbing on top of her. As I was on top of Asia, I wrapped my hands around her neck. I caught Nay out of the corner of my eye as her left foot kicked the left side of Asia's abdomen three times. Each kick seemed to gain more and more force.

"Now you can get back in this chair or I can kill you right here! I told you I wanted to keep you alive, but I won't be attacked by you or anyone. Remember who I am." I banged Asia's head against the wooden floor a few more times before letting up off of her.

Raye came rushing inside with some rope and tape. She said she got the rope from the trunk of the car and the tape came from across the street. I had Raye and Nay hold Asia in the chair as I took the duct tape and wrapped it around her mouth.

"Now you stay here. We will be back later. I may feed you when we get back. Don't misbehave 'cause if you think Jay Boogie hurt you, think what those strong black throwed-off niggas across from this house will do." I tapped her on the cheek and gave her a wink before heading out the door.

Asia was on borrowed time. Until I talked to Isaziah or found Shereene, Asia's fate with me was uncertain.

Chapter 42

Isaziah

Marcus attempted to call Nahima several times and got no response. After going through every room on the floor of Asia's room, we found that no one claimed to have seen or heard anything. The only way I knew I would reach Nahima and them at this point was just waiting for her to feel like it was right to talk to me. Maybe she would call or maybe they would all emerge when I least expected it. Marcus and I drove around the city for an hour with hopeful thoughts of the three of them doing the right thing.

It was about 6:30 that evening when I finally got a call from Nahima.

"Hello?" I answered the phone on the first ring.

"Hey, babe. Listen, I'm going to give you an address. Meet me there. I have something to show you."

"Where's Asia? Can I talk to her?"

"Nah, but you can when I see you. I'll be waiting to hear from you." Nahima hung up the phone. No "I love you." No type of small talk. Just simple and straight to the point with a nigga. Her tone was even stern and straight business.

I was sure she thought I was going to cuss her out or something, so she didn't hesitate to see if that was going to be the case. Sometimes, as the man, we forget that our woman can lead. When we don't support their decisions or follow their lead, it blinds us to what they'd already seen. Nahima doesn't have to say it, but her actions spoke loudly with everything she did or touched. I fucked up by not taking her lead or her advice when dealing with Asia. If I had handled Asia differently from the start of knowing her involvement until now, maybe we would have been ahead of Shereene's game if not done with this whole situation.

I received a text message, and it was Raye sending me an address. I showed the address to Marcus, and he placed it into the GPS. It stated it would take us about twenty minutes to get there. I told Marcus to hit the gas and get there, in the words of T.I., expeditiously. With little traffic on the route it took us, we got there in almost half the time. I called Nahima, letting her know we were pulling into a neighborhood, and she said they would be standing outside when we got there.

Lo and behold, Nahima, Raye, and Nay were standing out front of this ugly-ass, abandoned house. We parked right behind them and noticed a few guys standing on a porch watching us. Raye announced to them that we were good and that Marcus and I were with them. When I got out of the car, I attempted to hug my fiancée, but she gave me the cold shoulder.

"Follow me," Nahima said, turning her back against me.

"Nahima, can we please talk before we go in this house?"

"No, we can talk after. Business before personal at this point."

Nahima walked up the steps, leading Marcus and me into the house as my sisters trailed behind us. I prepared myself to see a dead body inside, but to my surprise, I walked in to see Asia alive and tied up to a chair. The house reeked of piss and it was hard to stomach.

"Asia, are you all right?" I asked, standing in front of her.

"Now I allowed y'all to come here because we're supposed to be a team. Asia will be cooperating with us to help get Shereene. This isn't a request I made, but a demand. Either she complies or dies." Nahima cut her eyes at me before walking toward the back of Asia's chair.

"How can she tell us anything if her mouth is closed up?" Marcus asked sarcastically.

"Are we a team or not? I don't have time for this shit. Aren't y'all tired of being away from home, living from hotel to hotel, not making no money? This little bitch right here is the key. I don't know about y'all, but I'm ready to get back to a normal life. Isaziah, I understand she is your sister, but two of your family members have crossed the line, got your mother killed, our unborn seed killed, tried to kill me, and kidnapped you! If you aren't pissed off, then you have become their bitch. Right now, I need to know if you're all in. I can't have my fiancé and partner second-guessing me or risking all of our lives, including his own. So, what is it going to be?"

The pressure that was applied to me at the moment was undeniable. Nahima wasn't wrong for the choices she made within those past hours or what she would do in the moments to come. I watched everyone waiting for my reaction and answer. Flashbacks started to run through my mind. My mother's dead body, rushing Nahima to the hospital, seeing Shereene stand beside that little nigga Jay Boogie after kidnapping Asia and me. I was more than pissed. I was way beyond that point of anger. That anger was going to get me through this.

"I'm all in, babe. We are a team always, even when we don't see eye-to-eye at first."

"Then prove it," Raye whispered in my ear before passing me an army pocketknife. "Don't kill her yet. But prove you're all in."

Asia's eyes pleaded for help, but her help was no longer available through me or anyone in our family. In one quick motion, I stabbed her right hand, leaving the knife in her as her screams were mumbled by the duct tape.

"Do as my wife says, and I'll try to convince her to let you live." Tears ran down Asia's face as she attempted to let out a scream over and over again.

Nahima removed the knife with a plastic bag, then passed it back to Raye. "Let's go eat 'cause I'm starving. We can deal with this ho tomorrow."

No one looked back. No one gave Asia any comforting words. We all just left her there in the wooden chair with a hole in her hand. There was no coming back from where we were going to go.

Chapter 43

Shereene

It had been a few days and I hadn't heard from Asia. My sisterly intuition was telling me something was off. Maybe she decided she wanted to be on Isaziah's side after all and we would connect during our final brawl, which I knew was going to happen sooner rather than later. Or maybe my sister needed me. I went back and forth to that hotel for the last few days. I either sat in the parking lot or the lobby. I didn't see anyone come in or out. I was confused as to whether my times were fucked up with theirs or if they were just good at hiding.

It was that following Saturday when I decided to take matters into my own hands to see if I could get any information from the desk clerk. The way my life was set up at that time, I wasn't sure how good my luck was going to be. I arrived at the hotel around noon, and I couldn't recognize any of the cars in the parking lot. I walked into the hotel and noticed no one was at the front desk or in the main lobby area. I waited for about five minutes when no one still came. After checking my surroundings, I thought it would be a good idea to just take it into my own hands.

The computer screen was locked with a password. I was usually good at cracking codes, so I tried a few before the computer locked me out. Pissed off at the timeout screen in front of me, I let out a slight scream in aggravation when I saw an older woman walking toward the lobby.

"Hey there. Can I help you with something? You aren't supposed to be back there, you know." The older lady was approaching me at tortoise speed.

"My Chapstick fell out of my bag and rolled behind your counter. I just was picking it up." The lie came out so smoothly, she had to believe me.

"Well, I'm glad you were able to get it. Young lady, what can I do for you?" She finally made it back to the counter, and I prayed she didn't notice the screen being locked.

"I was trying to see if my brother and sister-in-law were still here. We were traveling together, and I decided to stay at a different hotel. I have been trying to reach them all day but couldn't get an answer on any of their cells. I just remembered dropping them off here. I don't even remember what room they told me they were in the other day," I responded with a smile as I closed my little pocketbook I had hung over my shoulder.

"Well, I cannot give out room information, especially since I've never seen you before. I can tell you to just give them a call again. Maybe you'll catch them this time."

"I wouldn't ask if it weren't an emergency, and I understand you have a policy to follow. But I really need to find them."

"It's an emergency?"

"Yes, ma'am. Our little sister has gone missing, and we need to get back home to help our mother find her."

I could tell that pulled on the old lady's heart strings a bit. "Well, I really want to help. Let me just look and see, okay? Just don't tell anyone."

She went to the computer and tried to log in, but from her facial expression, I could see that she was still locked out.

"I'm sorry, but you may just have to come back in a little while. This stupid old computer won't let me in." She kept her eyes on the keyboard, and I could hear the clicks of the keys over and over.

"Well, thank you for trying. I'll try back in a few and try to call them again. I appreciate your time." I walked out of that hotel feeling unaccomplished.

Things were going to have be done differently in this case. I had to find a way to get their location. Either no one was coming out of their rooms, or they had moved on and I was stuck trying to figure out where. Once back in the car, I released my frustrations out on the steering wheel. After punching and yelling in the car for a few moments, I was able to regain some of my composure.

I checked around me and noticed no other cars near me or people in the parking lot. I needed to clear my mind to think of my next move. The one thing that always seemed to help was a blunt and masturbation. I leaned my seat back to pull my pants down and get in a better position. My glove compartment kept not only my gun but one of my vibrators in it for emergencies like this. I grabbed my purple jackrabbit and searched through some saved videos on my phone until I came across the one I made of Isaziah and Nahima a few months ago.

I propped my phone up on the dashboard as I spread my legs. I watched how he bent her over and stroked her body deep and hard. Her moans made my pussy wet, but I got pissed off at the same time. I fucked myself fast and as rough as I could. I could hear the ass cheeks smacking against Isaziah as I closed my eyes and was beginning to reach my peak.

Nahima's moans were so loud. She really was getting dicked down by my brother. I needed a good pounding in my life. I was cumming before I knew it from the vibrations against my clit. I started moaning out Isaziah's name as I envisioned him sucking on my pussy. After releasing the frustration, I moved my seat back to its proper position before exiting the parking lot.

    The one thing I needed to accomplish that day, I couldn't. Maybe I missed them and they were already headed back to Tampa. That was my next destination, but I wasn't going alone. My new little henchmen were going to come with me to help take everything that belonged to me, especially Isaziah.

Chapter 44

Isaziah

Three Days Later

We took shifts watching Asia and waiting for Shereene to hit her line. Nahima wouldn't allow Asia to even get up to piss. Her clothes were soiled and her hair mangled. She needed to shower and get something to eat. Nahima's instructions were to let her eat only once a day. I didn't agree, and after three days, I just wanted to make things better. My sister needed a hero, and I was there, but not with the S on my chest. I was Lex Luthor to her at that moment. How could I turn this around? I contemplated trying to have a conversation with Nahima, but that could cause some type of problems.

With us just barely speaking to one another, I had no clue how a conversation about Asia would go at that moment. I still had to try though. I arrived back at the house where Asia was being held after running down the street to a local McDonald's and grabbing everyone something to eat.

"Everything good?" I asked, noticing Asia's chair and Nahima were missing.

"Yeah, your wifey's just having a moment with your sister." Marcus looked up slightly before digging into one of the bags and grabbing out a large fry.

"Where?" I asked, looking around before I heard a sound of a thud like someone fell or someone got hit.

Marcus pointed toward the back of the house. I never went behind the house the past few days. I took a deep breath and went to the back. I didn't make it to the back door before I saw Nahima beating the shit out of Asia.

"Nahima!" I shouted, running into the backyard. "What the hell are you doing?"

"I'm just trying to get some answers. Since she won't tell me, I thought I would just get it out a different way. You are more than welcome to help." Nahima kept her back turned toward me as she stood with the baseball bat.

"Nahima, don't!" I shouted just as I watched her swing the bat into Asia's right leg.

I was too late. Nahima swung so hard I knew I saw her knee pop out of place. Running behind Nahima, I snatched the bat away before she swung again. Nahima's eyes pierced through my soul, and I was stuck waiting for her next move.

"Let me talk to you right now!" she yelled, turning to walk back toward the house.

We got to the back door, and then Nahima went off on me. "What type of fuck shit is this? You trusted me all these years to get the job done, but now because it's your sister, it's supposed to be different?"

"Nahima, there has to be another way to get this done. You don't have to torture her like this! Yes, she and Shereene are both my sisters. But we don't know where Asia's loyalty is as of right now. The more you fuck with her, the more you turn her against us."

"She told your wack-job-ass sister Shereene where we were! If I didn't know better, I would think that they are after me and you're in it too! What, you want me dead, Isaziah? Is that what you want?"

"What the fuck is wrong with you? Why would you even say something like that? I would never want to have you down that way. That's some bullshit and you fucking know it! You are my life, and I wouldn't be able to live without you!"

"Then fucking act like it! Right now, you are going to allow them to really kill me this time. And you standing here saying we don't know whose side she's on says a lot. You still have some type of hope in Asia when you probably shouldn't! Make your choice. Since you want to be Captain Save-a-bitch, take care of your sister. Get her to tell us something useful that I don't know. Shit is not working. I ain't buying it."

Nahima walked back inside, slamming the door behind her. Standing there with my mind in turmoil, I was stuck with running behind my love or trying to help my baby sister. I chose Asia. She needed me more than Nahima at that moment. With my hand up against the door, I took a deep breath, then went back to tend to my sister.

Kneeling down in front of my baby sister, I took my shirt off to help clean some of the excess blood off her face. "Asia, I'm sorry. I'm not sure what's gotten into everyone."

Asia spat out some blood on the ground next to her. The way she leaned over to the left, eyes barely open, I feared that Nahima killed her before we could accomplish anything.

"Asia, I brought you some food. I know you're hungry, right?" She nodded her head slightly before keeping it to the side. "Asia! Asia! Goddamn it, Asia, don't die on me, don't die on us, okay?"

I heard a dull whisper escape Asia's lips. She was still alive for that moment. I yelled out for Marcus to come help me get her back inside the house. Within the house, Marcus filled the bathtub until it was at the brim.

"Asia, listen to me. Marcus and I are going to get you better. But I need you to stay with me, all right? Marcus, go get whatever supplies you can find now!"

Untying her from the chair, I lowered her body into the water like she was getting baptized.

"Isaziah, what the hell?" Nahima shouted from behind me.

"We all need Asia alive. You ain't gonna get shit out of a corpse. So, either help me or get the fuck out of the way!"

That was enough of everyone's shit. I continued to hold Asia under the water when I noticed a familiar body shape in the corner of my eye.

Chapter 45

Nahima

I was discombobulated after the way Isaziah yelled at me. I missed hearing him boss up and yell at mothafuckas with that deep-ass voice. I was so turned on. I just wanted to do what my baby was telling me. Even with everything that had transpired, I had not once taken into consideration how it made this man feel. It was my fault that we got to this point. With a throbbing pussy, I kneeled down beside my man, following his orders with helping to nurse Asia back to a decent state.

"We should take her out now. We've always had new clothes for her in the car. Let me and Raye take it from here. Tell Nay to grab the clothes out of the trunk, and we will take it from here."

"How do I know I can trust you not to kill her?"

"I could've killed her and come back to you days, damn near a week, ago. I could have killed her and not said a word. We have to trust one another. I haven't been the easiest to deal with and I'm sorry. But one thing at a time."

Isaziah departed from the bathroom after we took Asia out of the tub. I could hear him call Nay to the bathroom to help me. She stood there in confusion.

"I know. But as angry as we are, we still have to keep her alive for now. She's not going to tell us anything if we keep treating her like shit."

"Then what's the plan now?"

"We let her eat, change clothes, and rest in one of these nasty-ass beds. Take the rope from the chair and then tie her to the rails there. She'll still be in one spot."

"For how long?"

"Until she gives up y'all big sis. Once Shereene's out of the way, we will handle Asia after." Nay held up the left side of Asia's body as I held up the right.

We took her to the bedroom adjacent from us. The room was disgusting. I could smell wasted alcohol, also as if someone took a deep-ass shit in there. The room was unsanitary to say the least. As much as I would have rather tied her up in that room, I wouldn't sit there on my worst day. I advised Nay that we should take her back into the kitchen area and tie her to one of those chairs after dressing her.

Isaziah came into the kitchen with the remainder of the food in the McDonald's bag. I grabbed the food from the mister that he informed me belonged to Asia. Piece by piece, I fed her as if she were an infant.

"Why are you being nice to me now?" Asia uttered in between chews.

"I'm not being nice. It's being civil. I loved you like my own sister, but you have given me several reasons not to trust you or love you anymore. Yet I still have love for you. However, betrayal is unforgivable, and a lesson has to be taught."

"This is my lesson?"

"Partially. Your eyes won't be swollen forever. Finish eating for now. But later, you will tell all of us how we can find your sister and what she has planned. Because if anyone knows, you do."

"I don't know anything. I do know that you're gonna die by her hand. I wanted to stop it. But now, I hope she does kill you." Asia tried to chuckle but stopped suddenly when my hand was wrapped around her throat.

"Asia, mark my words, you'll be dead way before me. You stupid little bitch." I released my grasp and left Asia sitting there without the rest of her food.

I was annoyed and aggravated at that point. I just wanted to put a bullet in between her thick-ass eyebrows. Without a second thought, I went over and grabbed Isaziah's arm, interrupting the conversation he was having with Marcus.

"What's your problem?" he asked as I grabbed hold of him roughly.

"Your sister just told me I was going to die! Die, Isaziah! Talk to her before I kill her right now myself with or without consideration. Make a choice right now. Her or me! The next time, you won't have to make a choice." I stormed off out the front door, leaving Isaziah where he stood.

I went across the street to the guys who were helping keep watch on the house. I needed to just breathe and relax for a moment. I noticed that they were rolling a blunt and had a fresh twelve-pack of Coronas.

"Aye, fellas, what's good?" I greeted them with a smile.

"What's up, sis? Y'all good over there? Need anything?" said the taller one to the left of the porch with his long Rick Ross beard and beer belly.

"Yeah, everything's all good. Can I hit that?" I pointed at the blunt that was being sparked by the stud standing adjacent to me.

"Here, shorty." The stud passed me the blunt and went into the house.

I stood on the porch smoking with their crew, not thinking about anything going on across the street. As I watched these niggas, my mind started thinking. Ideas formulated in my head, and I was ready to make Asia eat her words.

"How much would y'all need to help me deal with a little problem?" I leaned on the wooden rail on the porch as I inhaled and exhaled one last time. "I could use your help. . . ."

Chapter 46

Shereene

There was still no word or sign of my sister or the rest of the family. I decided to meet up with my henchmen to see if they could be useful in some kind of way. Especially since they couldn't even make over a stack a day if that with selling the weed. I got back to our current trap house, and only Racoon was there. I walked in, and everyone had this depressed look on their faces as if they lost their best friend. I spoke to everyone, and they just nodded their heads. Rayshawn was the only one missing out of everyone. We all sat in silence for a few minutes. I observed the atmosphere and the body language of everyone. Since no one wanted to acknowledge my presence fully or have a conversation, I was going to break the ice. Someone was going to talk.

"I been gone a few days and the only thing y'all can do is just sit here and nod y'all heads. Whose gonna tell me what the hell is going on?"

Racoon looked up at me from his hunter green lawn chair, eyes filled with dolor. "Rayshawn got hemmed up by the police yesterday. I was on the phone with him when they pulled him over."

"Where is he? Is he still locked up? Like, why you beating around the bush? Tell me what's up." I walked in front of Racoon, arms folded, waiting to hear the rest of the story.

"I was on the phone the whole time. He was arguing with the cop and wouldn't get out of the car when he was asked to. I ain't sure what triggered the cop yelling 'stop' at him, but next thing I heard was shots ringing off. Rayshawn never responded to me. Everything went silent, and then the phone hung up."

Startled by the news provided to me, I was dumbfounded. You see these things happen on the news every day. That shit hit close to home, and I wasn't sure how to react. I knew he still had some family where he was from, but I didn't know much. I was concerned that no one was contacted who could help his family. There was a bit of money left in my stash account, and I wanted to help with anything I could.

"Has anyone talked to his family? Where's his body? What are we going to do to help them?"

"That's the thing. His body and his car are both missing. I'm not sure what we can do."

"Your stupid ass should have been to the police station this morning when you didn't see that nigga! Why didn't you call me immediately?"

"You gave us orders not to call unless it was an emergency. I wasn't sure what transpired. I still am hoping my friend walks through these doors or calls me. You ain't give two shits about him or any one of us. If Joe blow on the corner had shot him, you wouldn't be this fucking concerned. You're a fuckin' narcissist!"

"Listen here, little boy, you don't know me. I keep telling you that. You have no clue who my family is. If you did, you would watch your mouth!"

"Bitch, I can give two fucks about you or your family. They probably ditched your retarded ass and that's why you here with us!"

"My family never left me! But you keep talking, and your family will be burying you real soon."

"I do not take threats lightly. I been real easy 'cause my people fuck with you. We move because of him. Without him, me and these niggas to the right and left of me ain't doing shit else for you. Either dead us all right here or leave us the fuck alone."

"If you walk away from me, how y'all gon' make any money? How you gon' have the freedom you have now?'

"Bitch, ain't no freedom! We ain't making no money, you are! How about you go hit them blocks and make that money for all of us? Stupid-ass ho. You wanna care now? Maybe go find him instead of chasing after some dick that don't want your ugly dike-looking ass." Racoon calling me anything less than beautiful was crazy. I may not have been a Nia Long–looking ho, but I was all woman. Five eight in height, size-D cup breasts complemented my nice, round booty, and my deep chocolate skin was the icing on the cake. I only dressed baggy at times because it was comfortable. I'd never been called ugly, so I knew he was just mad.

Racoon had me fucked up if he thought I was going to take that bullshit he said so easily. There was a time and a place for everything. The thought that Rayshawn's body could be somewhere rotting without his family being aware was fucked up. I couldn't find his body alone. Pride to the side, I needed Racoon and the rest of the guys to help find him.

"Listen! Stop right there!" I shouted right as Racoon was going to open the door.

"We out. Ain't shit else to talk about."

"I want to find his body. But we all need to help find him. You may not think I care, but I do. Help me find him, and then you all can go about your way."

Racoon turned back toward me slowly. "I'll help you find him dead or alive, and then we all walk away. Don't look for us or contact any of us to do anything. That bullshit-ass money you were giving out didn't mean a thing. Let's go find my homie."

Racoon then opened up the door, leading the way outside. Even though my targets were not in range and I needed to get to Isaziah and Nahima as soon as possible, the situation with Rayshawn had my spirit unsettled. He was now my focus. I prayed for the sake of everyone who could be affected by this that the outcome would be different than the other countless dead black men at the hands of police. My biggest fear was if they ratted us out—hell, ratted me out—then the whole operation would die. Them fools didn't owe me any loyalty. If it came down to it, they would choose their own asses over me any day.

Chapter 47

Nahima

I planned everything out perfectly. I may have been sweet at times, but I was not here to be played with. One thing Asia and Shereene should have always remembered was that coming for me started a war all on its own. Isaziah had been blowing up my phone trying to find my location, but I was busy putting my own things in place. That little trick was about to eat those words she said to me. I examined the house from across the street, waiting for the right moment to implement my plan.

"Aye, Miss Lady, what time you tryin'a have us make that move? I got some possible clients to meet up with," the youngest one of the crew, Rock, asked me.

"Rock, I don't want you a part of the first portion. I'll inform you when it's time to link to do the rest."

"Man, what you mean? I'm grown. I can handle anything."

"What I have planned at first is something I know you don't have in your heart to do. I could tell by the way you looked during the meeting we had about it."

"But you paid me to."

"I did, and that you can keep. I'm not changing your pay 'cause you're squeamish. Your brothers and I can handle everything else until I need you. Just be ready to play your position."

Rock looked at me with those dark brown eyes, and I could sense something was on his chest that he wanted to tell me.

"Your energy is off. I know I don't know you that well, but I can sense you have something on your mind."

"This, what you're doing to your sister-in-law, is it the right thing to do?"

"If you loved someone and they betrayed you, attempted to murder you several times out of greed and whatever other emotions they were feeling at the time, what would you do?" I took a glance at him, then returned my focus to the house.

"I guess I would be put in the same position as you."

"Exactly. You never know how far you will go until you're put in situations that cause you to dig deep down and pull that shit out of you. Like I stated before, you still have some kind of heart, so you wait for my text and go from there."

"Yes, ma'am, if that's what you want."

"That's what you need. Now go and handle your business."

Rock sprinted back into the house without saying another word.

I grabbed a wine wood-tip Black & Mild out of the box on the porch and sat on the black lawn chair to keep watch. I knew Isaziah would be leaving soon to go grab food. I had only informed Raye of the plan. I knew that she would be the only one to help me. Raye had sent me a text while I was smoking with the fellas across the street earlier that day.

Raye: Yo, this bitch Asia tripping. She just bit Isaziah's finger when he tried to finish feeding her.

Me: What the fuck? Are you serious? I got something for that ho.

Raye: You know Isaziah ain't going for that. Even now, he holding his hand, trying to withhold his temper.

Me: Bitch, this isn't his call anymore! He fucked up by being nice to that ho. Family or not, it's time for her to go.

Raye: Well, what's the plan then? I'm fuckin' with you, sis.

Me: That's what I like to hear. I'll send you the deets in a few. Just solidifying some things on my end.

Raye: Bet, Nahi, keep me posted.

Since Raye would have my back regardless, I decided I would rock with her on my little mission. The sun had set, and my phone was vibrating from all types of notifications, texts, and calls from the hubby. No matter how we disagreed when it came to business, family, or our relationship, I loved Isaziah. Whatever I did was to only help the both of us. While I sat outside, a car pulled up blasting The Box.

"Aye, nigga, that's my shit. Turn that shit up!" I hollered from the porch.

"Mine too, shawty," the dude in the driver seat yelled.

I couldn't tell who it was, but I knew, according to the guy named Jarod, that he had a connect who could help us with disposal and shit effortlessly. Asia was going to die tonight, and I was ready. One less person to deal with. Even though Asia could lead us to Shereene possibly, she was disrespectful and a silent threat. Her intentions weren't clear at first, but that last few hours provided more proof.

The driver of the car came out to meet me. "You must be the lady with the plan and the money."

"You must be the man who makes anything or anyone disappear." I extended my hand to shake his.

"You got that. I hope your husband knows what kind of wife he has on his team. 'Cause a nigga like me could use a queen like you."

"Well, I appreciate the compliment. I will let him know that he has some competition out here." I chuckled, releasing my hand from his.

"I'm Rog. You gon' tell me your name, pretty lady?"

"You can call me Nahi. Let's go inside and talk." We went inside the house where everyone was preparing their weapons.

Rog walked in behind me. I could feel his smile on his face and his eyes on my ass. I walked over to the counter where Rock was standing, leaned my back against the counter, and waited for everyone to turn their attention toward me. Rog went over to everyone, showing them love.

"All right, folks, so what's the plan?" Rog asked, grabbing one of the dining room chairs to sit in it backward.

"I have a major problem within my organization I need taken out. But I don't want it swift. I want it as painful and long-lasting as possible. The target is currently strapped to a chair across the street. I want her to believe that someone named Shereene is behind all of it. But I want to be the one to give her the final blow to cause her death. I don't do well with betrayal, lies, or disrespect. If you're gonna be a part of my team, understand that trust is earned, not given immediately."

The room was quiet to the point where I could hear a pin drop. Rog stood up, pushing the chair back into the middle of the floor. "Well, the same way the trust from these guys and myself has to be earned, so does yours."

"That's true. Let's see how tonight goes, and from there, we will see how we can all trust one another. Everyone but you, Rog, has been paid. Here is your payment, sir."

Rog took the golden envelope and opened it, checking the money count. "All right. Everything good here on my end."

"Good, now let's get to work."

Chapter 48

Isaziah

The night was young, and I wondered how I could make things right with Nahima as I attended to my frustration with my sister, Asia. She seemed to be more devious than I could have imagined. Asia played me. I assumed she was the one being manipulated, but it was all of us the whole time.

After Nahima stormed off, I went to have a conversation with my baby sister. I just wanted things to be better. But Asia was a conniving, stupid little bitch. I hated to call her that, but after the things she said, plus her biting my hand, I was over her and helping her in any way. I went back into the kitchen to ask Asia what she said to Nahima and why. I grabbed the chair to the left of me, sitting diagonally across from Asia's chair.

"What exactly did you say to her?" I asked while grabbing the bag of food off of the table.

"What needed to be said. Isaziah, you don't need her or anyone outside of Shereene and me. The rest of these fools are only here for money. Shereene made me understand after a time that we were the only people around you who truly love you. This is what we're trying to get you to see! Nahima tied me up and tried to kill me until you stopped her!"

"I stopped her because I didn't want to see you die like that! But you sound crazy as hell right now! Do you even hear yourself?"

"Do you hear yourself? Isaziah, I hear myself loud and fucking clear. Nahima, Marcus, and the rest of our siblings are going to die. You won't be able to save any of them. Just untie me and help me get to Shereene so we can finally end all of this madness."

"The only thing that I want to see Shereene for is to kill her myself for all the pain and trauma she has caused all of us! I hate both of you! Obviously, neither of you care. Asia, you're dumber than I thought!"

"The only dumb person is you! If you weren't so damn blind to everything, you wouldn't be in this position now. Don't you think Shereene trying to kill Nahima not once but twice was a sign?"

"So, the whole victim role you played was all a lie? Did that man even rape you?"

"He was a part of the plan. We knew you would do anything to protect us. Jay Boogie was just a young, dumb, country bumpkin who was a casualty."

"You're a stupid, young, dumb-ass ho! Whatever karma serves you, you deserve!"

I went to smash the remainder of her fries in her face when Asia took a big bite out of my hand, piercing my flesh. I screamed in agony, and Raye was the one to help Asia let go of my hand by punching her on the left side of her face.

Asia was just as much at fault for all the bullshit as Shereene. I didn't want to know any extra details as to what made her get to that point, but I was over it and her. As Marcus and I drove around the city, I attempted to reach my fiancée to not only find out her whereabouts, but to also inform her about my hand.

I wondered if this whole situation was going to tear us apart before making us stronger. Nahima always had my back, and sometimes I knew she felt as if I didn't have hers. Nahima was not answering the phone no matter how much I called or texted. That was the bullshit that pissed me off. Knowing that anything could happen to any of us at any moment, I seemed to be more of one of her enemies every day.

I made the decision to call her one last time. That time, whether she answered or not, I was going to make sure she knew how I felt. The phone rang and rang until it went to voicemail. Just hearing her voice through the other end of the phone would have made me more at peace than anything else in the world at any given day or moment.

"Hey, you know who you reached. Leave a message after the tone." Beep!

"Baby, it's me. I know you're upset, probably a little bit more than upset. I just want you to know that I love you. I know lately we haven't been on the same page, but you have to know that I'm always gonna ride with you like you ride for me. Whatever you up to, just make sure you come on home. Please, I miss you, and I need you. Love you." I disconnected the call and tossed my head back on to the seat in anguish.

Marcus turned the volume down on the radio. "Aye, man, you know Nahima better than the rest of us. You know she will not only come home but has probably got us twenty steps ahead."

"Yeah, I hope you're right. I just know that I partially fucked a lot of this up."

"That's the only way to do that thing called growth, my brother."

Nahima

After I received confirmation that Isaziah had departed the house with Marcus by his side, I was free to move in and execute my plan. Everyone was in position. The goal was to make it look like a break-in. The fellas from across the street came out, Glock .40s in their waist, black ski masks on, and black gloves. Once the signal was given, everyone moved in. We had the two thicker men break in from the back, and the rest of us took the front. The sun had just set, the moon and dark gray clouds filled the sky, and I didn't know if it was going to rain, but either way shit was going to get done.

Asia awoke from her sleep frantically, looking around and screaming for help.

"Aye, bitch, shut the fuck up! Ain't no one gon' help you. We already took out anyone else around."

"You fuck-ass bitch! You wouldn't kill half of the people in my family! My brother will kill you!"

Rog stood beside me, winked, then moved closer to Asia. Before I could blink, he had slapped her across the face with his pistol.

"I don't give a fuck about you or your brother."

He slapped her so hard I could see her mouth had started bleeding. To keep her from knowing I was there, I held a voice changer on my throat. "We are here on your sister Shereene's orders. Shut up and follow our directions or die. Understand?"

"Oh, okay, I get it. I get it now. She always said we did what we had to."

Asia went from frantic to calm with the mention of Shereene's name. She really believed that Shereene would come to rescue her in this way. We were able to get her out of the house quietly. Once she was in the trunk of Travis's car, I took my mask off and met Raye in the back of the house. Raye and Nay were sitting in the backyard, waiting for my direction. I instructed them to follow us. I was going to ride with Rog to Asia's final destination.

For thirty minutes, we drove and drove until we got to this quiet area. Nothing but train tracks and empty lots were around the area. Asia was taken out of the trunk, hands still tied up and mouth gagged.

"Put her on her knees." I didn't want to torture her. I wanted everything to be quick.

"What you wanna do, boss?"

"I want her to see me. Take the blindfold off." I was surrounded by all my new employees, if you want to call them that, Raye, and Nay. I was going to end this ho just as quickly as her mother said it took for her to enter the world.

"Remember you said I would die before you? Guess not." Those were the last words I said to Asia. Before she could respond, everyone opened fire on her. I was sure she was dead, but to seal the deal, I walked over to her, putting two bullets in her skull.

"See you in hell, bitch." I walked off with Raye and Nay beside me.

"What about her body?" Raye asked. "It's only going to cause attention."

"Don't worry. That's why I paid Rog. He'll take care of that. The message will still get to Shereene. I'm sure she's somewhere lurking and waiting."

Chapter 49

Shereene

After searching and searching for two days for Rayshawn, we had no luck. But surprisingly, the officer Racoon heard on the other end of the phone that day magically reappeared. We were sitting at the hideout when the four o'clock news came on. There he was about to hold a press conference. His name was Officer Walter D. Thompson. With a name like Walter, he had to be black somewhere. Lo and behold, I was right. This high-yellow, coon, Uncle Tom–looking man stood on my television screen. He seemed to be about five foot eight, his lips were redder than a cherry, and he had a shaved head and a little goatee. His face had some bruises as if he had gotten into a scuffle. And his right arm was in a sling because he apparently broke his arm during the scuffle with a suspect.

"Hello, ladies and gentlemen. Thank you all for your time today. My name is Officer Walter D. Thompson. I'm a native of our great city here in Orange Park. Three days ago, I was attacked by a young male of color after stopping him for speeding and a broken taillight. The young man was very confrontational from the start. It was only when I asked him to step out of the vehicle that things took a turn for the worse." The officer drew Racoon's attention from his phone to the television screen.

"Yo, that sound like the fuck-ass pig who stopped Rayshawn the other day when I was on the phone," Racoon stated, keeping his eyes glued to the TV.

"Are you sure?" I asked.

"I think so. I know I was smoking, but I remember it all. That sounds just like his punk ass!"

Racoon was adamant that this was the officer. But before our own justice could be rendered, I had to make sure. Then this fool told on himself. They posted a picture of Rayshawn on the screen taken from what was left of his vest cam.

"This is the man who attacked me. I barely was able to get away. If you see him, please contact us immediately as he may be armed and dangerous." The officer continued to spew his lies, and I couldn't stomach hearing any more.

"Turn that shit off!" I walked away from the television, biting my nails.

"That gives us no lead. We don't know if he's alive or dead. For all we know, he could be tied up in some damn barn or something!" Racoon hollered.

"We go to the officer's house late tonight. One of y'all can be smart enough to grab all the info we need to know so we can move in on him as soon as it's bedtime. Check to see if there are any children, wife, husband, anyone else who could possibly be in the house. We are not killing anyone innocent in this unless we have to. Understood?"

"You want to kill him? How does that get my brother home?"

"He's gonna die regardless of the information he gives or doesn't give."

"Me and the fellas will ride out and see what we can dig up. What you gon' do?"

"Don't worry about me. Y'all go do that. After we find Rayshawn, we are all done. Cool?"

"Perfect."

Racoon and the other guys made their way out of the house.

With my thoughts starting to spiral, I realized it was harder to be in charge and know everything at once. I didn't understand how my brother kept up with everyone for so long. Not only did I have to find Rayshawn or his body, but I also needed to find a way to get through to my siblings. I paced the floor in a circle. Thinking about calling Asia, taking another drive back to Isaziah's last known location for a chance to see him, and the thought of finally getting rid of Nahima was way too much going on in my head.

I felt obligated to help Rayshawn and his family in any way. But there were other pressing matters that I had to attend to. The realization of me not knowing whether Asia betrayed me was the hardest pill to swallow. The only way I would find out was if I tried getting through to her once more.

I called her phone three times before I finally got an answer. When the call connected, it automatically switched to a FaceTime call.

"Asia? What in the entire fuck? Why haven't you been answering my calls?"

But when the light turned on, it wasn't Asia I was FaceTiming.

Isaziah

Nahima finally reached out to me hours after disappearing. Her call was short and cutthroat. She provided an address to me but advised that I go back to the bando first to gather anything that may belong to Asia that we took there and to also check for Asia's phone. She didn't have to say much. When that was mentioned, I knew

Asia was either already dead or about to be. I was sure that Nahima wouldn't kill Asia without talking to me first or at least allowing me to be there for a final goodbye. Puzzled by the cryptic message, my mind was racing with all kinds of thoughts. But no matter the betrayal, Asia was still my sister, and I was responsible for her. I never could think of losing her, especially this way.

It hurt to say I needed my little sister killed, but there are some people who become casualties and some who get their karma. I hated to say it, but everyone at this point had gotten tired of Asia. Her karma was about to be served. Following Nahima's instructions, we went back to the hotel and the house we kept Asia tied up in to gather anything that may belong to her. The location we received was about thirty minutes or so out of the way. Marcus and I said barely anything to one another during our drive. I was anxious to see what I would be walking into.

"At least we know Nahima isn't going to kill you," Marcus joked as he parked the car.

"Was that a joke?" I was not in the mood for the satire he spat out.

"Just tryin'a lighten up the air. Shit. There's been too much heavy, negative energy these past weeks. Shit, a nigga needs to laugh." Marcus slammed his car door behind him. "Where do we go?"

"Toward the train tracks, she said. I'll send her our location. Maybe she can help guide us. It's dark as hell out here."

We walked for what seemed to be forever when I heard someone approaching us from the front.

"'Bout time the two of y'all showed up. Hurry up so we can get through with this." It was Raye's voice echoing in the dark.

"Raye, it's too fucking dark out here. Where's the fucking flashlight or something?" Marcus belted out.

"Use your phone, dummy, or just follow my voice and footsteps. Stop being a bitch." The spark of Raye's lighter allowed us to catch a glimpse of our area as she lit her Jazz-flavored Black & Mild. We were out in what seemed to be the woods. Nothing but trees, some broken glass on the tracks, along with some pieces of wood.

Soon we approached my fiancée and a group of men surrounding someone or something. Nahima nodded before she walked over to me. We seemed to be at a little wooden cottage off the tracks. A small candlelight lamp sat on top of a black painted wooden lamp table that was by the door. The door was painted a deep cherry red with a brass doorknob. Nahima's touch was what I had been missing, and feeling her embrace meant the world to me. I knew by the way she hugged me that she was still in love with me.

"This was the only way, especially after having my life threatened. I have had enough of all this fuck shit with your family! Now all I ask, especially if you truly love me, is to not disagree with me right now, but support this choice that had to be made."

"I don't know if you listened to my voicemail, but I love you so much. I have been so wrong with the way I handled everything, to the point where I feel like I'm losing you. I can't lose you ever. Asia threatened me and bit me. I'm not sure what you've done, but I know I cannot be upset at you or anyone for providing justice to our family."

"I'm glad to hear you say that. I needed to hear those words from you finally. I know none of this is easy for you. But you have to always know that at the end of the day, I will always do what's right for you, our family, and our business."

Nahima had always held me down, and the one time she needed me to, I didn't. I made a promise to myself to never do that to her again. Nahima took my hand and guided me toward the circle.

"Take a deep breath, then look," Nahima advised, clenching my hand tighter.

Everyone moved back, and there she lay. Asia's blood seeped out of her body onto the ground. I kneeled down beside her, feeling her lifeless body. The world was meant to be easier for us. Not once did I think the day would come when I had to see my sisters and mother laid to rest.

"What are we going to do with her body?"

"That's why I'm here. I'm Rog. I get paid to dispose of problems discreetly or however my client wants it. Your wife has made it clear how she wanted to have things handled. There will be nothing left behind to tie any of us to her death."

"You're sure about that?"

"Never had a fucked-up moment. Trust me, it's all going to be handled." Rog assured me over and over that everything would be fine, but it still wasn't over.

Nahima pulled me from Asia's body and into her arms. I belted out my cries. I was heartbroken and pissed. I didn't understand why we couldn't handle this a different way. I failed my family, I failed Asia, and I failed Nahima. My baby sister was gone. I went completely numb as my heart hit the pit of my stomach. Nahima then asked me if I was able to retrieve Asia's cell. I motioned for Marcus to come to us, since he was able to gather some of her things. He rambled through the pockets of his sweatshirt when he grabbed the cell phone Asia had.

"It has her thumbprint on there. We can't just unlock it."

"Nigga, give me the phone." Raye snatched the phone from Marcus's hand and went over to Asia's body, grabbing her left hand to unlock the phone.

"Why do we need her phone?" I asked, wondering what part of the plan this was.

"Shereene had to have been trying to get in contact with her. Hopefully, we will be able to reach her and stir a fire. If Asia had just cooperated, this would not have happened to her," Nahima uttered, watching Raye unlock the phone.

"Here, sis. So, what do we need to do now?"

"Let's go through her contacts, locate Shereene, and let's give her a nice little call. First, take a picture of Asia's body. We'll need that. She won't believe that she's dead."

Raye went and took the picture before handing Nahima back the phone. I watched Nahima take control and handle everything with none of my direction. It turned me on so much I wanted to fuck the shit out of her right where she stood. I was sure others probably wouldn't think like that. But me, shit, I loved a woman who took control and could handle her own.

"Hey, babe! Let's deal with Shereene tomorrow. Let's just go home for the night."

"Rog, you got it from here? Or do you need any of our assistance?" Nahima questioned, walking toward this Rog guy.

"Yes, ma'am. I got it. I'll call you after."

"That's a bet. I'll be touching base with everyone tomor--row." Nahima and I walked off into the darkness, hand in hand.

Chapter 50

Nahima

Isaziah and I had arrived at the hotel about an hour after leaving Asia's body in the hands of Rog. By the time we checked into the hotel, I received confirmation that Asia's body was disposed of without a trace. Knowing that piece alone was a quick breath of fresh air. Before we could lock the hotel room door, Isaziah's body was pressed up against mine.

"You are so fucking sexy, and smart, and such a bad motherfuckin' ass," Isaziah whispered into my right ear as I could feel my pussy pulsating.

It had been a while since I allowed my man into my vessel. Especially when we were used to fucking several times a day. Feeling his breath against my neck had my body weak.

"You don't hate me?" I asked in between breaths as his hands made their way toward my thighs.

"How could I ever hate you?" Isaziah kissed me and my hands freed, dropping all my bags on the floor.

"Fuck me please," I whispered as his lips went from my lips to my neck.

The way Isaziah grabbed my body and tossed me on the bed, I knew I was going to be fucked like I deserved to be fucked. He tore off my clothing from my black shirt to my black leggings, leaving me with just my bra barely hanging on as he popped one of the straps.

"I'm sorry. I should have done better."

"Don't apologize anymore. I'm right here. I'm not leaving you. Just don't ever forget who I am and how much I love you ever again." I shoved his head in between my thighs.

I didn't need to hear any more words. The feeling of his tongue against my clit was amazing. Isaziah reached up, grabbing my neck, choking me slightly. I ground my hips to match his pace as my moans escaped loudly. The harder he sucked on my clit, the tighter his grasp got around my neck. I was ready for dick at that point. He was eating me so good I was begging for the dick.

Isaziah slid the rest of his clothing off onto the floor before tossing my legs back to my head. I felt Isaziah stretch my tight pussy with every inch of his dick slowly entering me. The way he slowly ground in my pussy was heaven. I felt him hitting every wall I knew I had and then some. Isaziah took my right foot, sucking on my toes as he pumped my body. My moans escaped slightly as I took every stroke. Isaziah was trying to make love to me, but I wanted to fuck. I wanted it harder and rougher. Lowering my leg, I clenched up so he could slide out.

"I want you to fuck me! Don't make love to me. Just make me take the fucking dick," I stated before I arched my back, sticking my ass up in the air and taking his thick dick into my mouth.

Isaziah groaned as I took every inch into my mouth, relaxing my throat, allowing him to go as far down my throat as he could before I gagged. His dick exited my mouth, and he yanked my body in position. My hands touching the floor, my booty up in the air, and his finger in my booty, I felt his dick stretch me out.

His strokes were hard and steady. Each pump rocked my body, and I couldn't do anything but scream out in pleasure. Daddy was killing this pussy, and I was cumming intensely from it. He was hitting my pussy so hard I almost fell off the bed at one point. After switching positions and having Isaziah fill my garden with his seeds after the first two rounds, we decided to take a break.

All that fucking and no food or hydration wouldn't be good for anyone. We lay out on the bed naked and covered with sweat and one another's juices. We lay cuddled up, catching our breath.

"Where's Asia's phone?" I asked, tracing my fingertips along his chest.

"Somewhere on the floor," Isaziah responded.

"I think now is the time to make a call." I figured since 90 percent of my aggravation and stress was somewhat gone, it was time to stir the bee's nest.

"Who do you want to call? I know you aren't trying to fuck up our current mood. Bae, I just wanna chill and enjoy our vibe." Isaziah sat up from the bed, looking at the mess we left on the floor.

"Isaziah, we need to get her stirring. If we capitalize off the situation, it will cause her to fuck up and make it easier for us to get to her."

"Nahima, I don't know. What if she's planned for that?"

"No, that dummy ain't that smart or think that far ahead. You know Shereene better than anyone. If we call her or send her the picture, you know how she'll react and where she'll go." I insisted on getting him to see my side of things.

"Fine, but if this doesn't work, then we need to come up with a different plan to draw her out. Understood?"

"Yes, daddy." I blew a kiss at him as I watched Isaziah get up from the bed naked with his dick slanging from side to side as he walked.

When he grabbed Asia's phone off the floor, I looked at him and smiled. I was going to be the bearer of bad news to Shereene with her brother beside me, and I couldn't be any happier.

Chapter 51

Shereene

"Why the hell are you calling me from my sister's phone? Put Asia on the phone," I demanded, seeing the sinister look on Nahima's face.

"That's gonna be a no-go. She doesn't have anything else to say to you or anyone," Nahima responded.

"Is that Isaziah? Isaziah, speak up! Where is Asia?" I tried to see around the room, but Nahima wasn't moving the phone too much.

"Baby, you wanna talk to your crazy, evil, stupid sister?"

"Bitch, watch your mouth! Isaziah, you gon' let her talk to me like that?"

"This is my mouth! I will talk to you any way I like! You can't deny that you're a fucking lunatic! There's something seriously wrong with you and your little sister."

"Nahima, say something else, I will be the one to put the bullet straight to your head. I fucking hate you and always have! Isaziah, you aren't going to say anything?"

Isaziah took the phone from Nahima. His face was full of disappointment. "What's up, traitor?"

"Isaziah, don't talk to me like that. We are so much better than that."

"Are we, Shereene? You were my sister. But after this, all I know is who you used to be."

"Isaziah, please, you have to understand that I'm doing everything for us. Tell me where you are. I can get rid of Nahima for good. We can go back to it just being us."

"Nahima ain't going nowhere. If you even attempt to harm her again, I'll kill you! It will be a long, painful death." Isaziah's words cut me deeply.

"She's brainwashed you. You are not the same Isaziah I love, but I know he's still in there."

Nahima placed her head on his shoulder and smiled at me before she said, "You're going to die a painful death either way. Whether it's from me, your other siblings, or Isaziah himself. You know we don't make empty threats."

"Bitch, you could never replace me in my family! Or in my brother's life!"

"I am not trying to replace you. How do you think your family felt hearing Asia tell them how you plotted to kill your mother? How you plotted to get rid of all of us to take over our empire that we built? You destroyed your family! Not me or my relationship with your brother. You!" Nahima disconnected the FaceTime, leaving me stuck.

I let out a loud, agitated moan just when my notifications went off. I received two text messages from Asia's phone. I was nervous to open them, but curiosity got the best of me. The first picture I saw was Asia tied up, beaten, and gagged. The next was what I assumed to be Asia's dead body laid out on the ground. Since the body was turned over, I couldn't see her face, but the body mirrored Asia's body shape and density perfectly.

Me: Y'all are gonna die if my sister doesn't call me in ten minutes. This is a sick-ass joke, even for your bum ass.

Asia's phone: Lol. Bitch, you're funny! Asia won't be calling you or anyone else for that matter. Do what you wanna do.

Me: Bitch, I am only gonna say this one more time. I want to talk to my sister. Right now!

As I was sending texts back and forth, Racoon and the remainder of the crew walked into our little trap house.

"We were able to find an address. He has a wife but no kids. The chick is pregnant." Racoon kept sucking his teeth as if there was food stuck in his tooth.

"Can you stop making that annoying-ass sound? Give me the address. We move in on that coward at midnight. We do not harm the wife unless we need some help with making him talk."

"Man, whatever. We gon' move however it is needed."

"No, you do what the fuck I say! You move how I tell you to move! Understood?"

"A'ight, bitch. Last time. We'll meet you at the spot at midnight." Racoon bucked up his chest at me but didn't say a word. On his command, they all left the house.

My mind was no longer focusing on Rayshawn or the possibility he was still alive. My baby sister was gone. I knew it was my fault. If they killed Asia, I had done the worst thing any big sister could do. I left her in the lion's den and didn't protect her.

Chapter 52

Isaziah

I was in shock that Nahima had really reached out to Shereene. Two days had passed, and we got no reaction or any more responses from her. I could tell it was bothering Nahima. She assumed Shereene would have reacted immediately, but to her dissatisfaction, she did not. We went from Nahima being excited to be on the verge of ending everything and gloating about how she got under Shereene's skin, to her being agitated and disgruntled for not getting a quicker response.

I watched Nahima constantly check Asia's phone for anything, but every time the phone did not receive any notifications, it pissed her off more. Instead of constantly sitting and waiting, I decided that we would take a moment for ourselves. I left Nahima in the room to meet up with Marcus and Raye to come up with a little surprise for her. I knew it would be what we both needed.

I had the two of them meet me at the Denny's restaurant that was about twenty minutes from the hotel we were staying at. We all sat in a booth in the back corner near the restrooms.

"We couldn't get a table closer to the front? We should be able to see our surroundings completely. Then on top of that, it smells over here. Like, what the fuck?" Raye's face scrunched up as the women's bathroom door swung open.

Marcus chuckled before agreeing with her. "Sis got a point. Shit, it smells like shit over here."

They were both right, and none of us could take the stench that flowed out of the bathroom every time the door opened. It smelt of old blood and like someone took a mean-ass shit. It wasn't decent enough to withstand to even eat or just have a conversation. Our waitress came over to the table with a huge grin. She seemed to be about our age, early twenties, fair brown complexion, tattoos covering her right arm, and her weave was pulled back into a sleek ponytail but was very nappy.

"Hey, you all! My name is Rachel. I will be your server for today. What can I start you off with?" She was very friendly, and her energy was great.

"We would be so much better if we could be moved to a different table. I wouldn't be able to eat a piece of bread over here the way it smells," Raye stated sarcastically.

"Yeah, there's other seats. Let me take your menus, and you all follow me." The waitress didn't hesitate to move us, especially after she got a whiff of what we smelled during our brief stay in that seat.

She moved us to a new booth closer to the front of the restaurant. After we were seated, we all provided our drink orders, then went over the menu one last time. While we waited for our drinks, I laid out a piece of the plan that was major in their role of helping me execute it perfectly.

"How do you suggest we get Nahima to even go with either of us anywhere? Her mind is focused, and she's not going to leave the room just to hang out at this point."

"I'm sure you and Raye can come up with something. I will be providing the different locations to take her to throughout the day tomorrow. You two will be taking turns. Raye, you will be bringing her to her final destination. Marcus, you will start her day off."

As we were going back and forth about how Nahima would react or if she would come with anyone, the waitress returned with our drinks and was ready to take our orders. After we ordered, we sat and I laid the plan out again so everyone could be in accord. I had to make this as perfect as possible. While we were sitting, a guy walked into Denny's whose face seemed familiar to me. Raye noticed me eyeballing the fellow in his Tampa Bay jersey and black sweats.

"Who's that, big bro? You eyeing him kind of hard." Raye asked, trying to connect the dots.

"I'm not sure, to be honest. He just seems familiar." I kept my eyes on the guy. He wasn't seated but went up to the counter. I assumed he had a to-go order.

I decided I would make a trip to the restroom to get a better look at the brother. He had to be someone I knew as a foe or a friend. I was determined to find out. When I got closer to his direction, the man looked up at me, squinting his eyes.

"Hey, excuse me. Do I know you from somewhere?"

"I'm not sure, do you?" I stood and looked at the young man, not giving him any emotion.

"Hey, I saw you when I was working with Jay Boogie," the guy responded to me.

"Is that right?" I looked behind me at my sister and my best friend and bodyguard.

"Yeah, man. That bitch he was working with was crazy. After he got killed, I dipped out. I have some information for you if you're with it. We can talk after this. I'll give you my number. Your rules, we can meet up, and I can talk to you."

"How do I know it's not a setup? You were there when they had me kidnapped and shit. So, why shouldn't I kill you right here?"

"You have every right to feel that way. But I promise you, I just want to help. I know it won't be easy trusting me, but please, that bitch got to go. Here, man, take my number."

I was hesitant, but his grudge toward Shereene intrigued my senses. If he was truly against her, he had information that could possibly be useful. I handed him my phone for him to input his contact info. I expressed that I would be giving him a call soon. By the time we wrapped up our conversation, his food came from the back, and I went on to the bathroom.

Once I was back at the table, Marcus and Raye were curious about the conversation I had.

"Who was he?" Raye questioned.

"He used to work for Shereene and Jay Boogie. He claims he has info on Shereene and wants to help us get rid of her."

"Do you really trust that? I wouldn't. She could be using his ass too and today was his lucky day."

"Well, he won't get so far. We are all going to meet with him, locked and loaded. Prepared for anything if he is on some fuck shit."

"Isaziah, what about this whole thing for Nahima?" Marcus probed.

"That is still happening. I will tell Nahima about the meeting after everything else is done. Not a word until then."

"Okay," Raye replied.

"You got it, man. But we better head back soon 'cause your fiancée has called me three times and sent a text asking about my whereabouts," Marcus responded.

"Let me grab her a to-go order, and then we can head out."

The waitress returned with our check, and I ordered my wife-to-be a meal to go. I was sure she hadn't eaten, so I needed to make sure she was straight before anything else. Once we departed from Denny's, I reiterated the plan all the way back to the hotel.

"Remember, first thing in the morning, we start. After I take care of Nahima, we will have this meeting. I'll set it up later this evening. Marcus, I need you to find me a discreet location. Just in case gunfire has to be let loose, no one would be in harm's way except for the intended target. Understand?"

Marcus nodded his head yes while Raye tossed up a thumbs-up. I was going to have a moment of peace in the midst of this madness we were currently entrapped in.

Chapter 53

Nahima

It was three days without any response or lead on Shereene's trifling ass. I was way too anxious to get my hands on her. But when I did, it was going to be a wrap for her narcissistic, evil, dumb ass. When I awoke that morning, Isaziah was gone. I assumed he went out to the gym or to grab breakfast. I was heading to get in the shower when there was a knock on my hotel door. It was 9:48 a.m., too early for room service. I just hoped it wasn't anyone with some bullshit. I grabbed my all-black Fashion Nova Lotus robe and walked over to see who it could be.
"Raye, what the hell do you want this early where you couldn't call me?" I opened the door, letting her in while holding my robe tightly.
"Isaziah told me to come meet with you. I thought he told you before I came down here. My bad, sis." I noticed Raye was dressed a little more classy than normal.
"What's up with this outfit?" I pondered.
"I just wanted to try a different look. Might meet my future wife out here." Raye giggled. "What's wrong, sis? You don't like it?"
"No, I think you look cute, sis. I promise. I would never steer you wrong. Know that. I guess I'll be your wing woman once we go meet hubby."

"Call me when you finish getting dressed. Oh, and Isaziah said to look in a black bag by the window for your clothes for today." Raye exited my room quickly, leaving me to get dressed.

Black bag? What the hell does Isaziah have going on?

I didn't remember discussing us doing anything crazy today. Maybe he got some info and he was ready to bust a move. I went searching for a black bag but didn't see it at first. I then noticed a medium-sized black gift bag sitting near the window in the corner. I took the bag and dumped the contents out of the bag. There was a pair of round-cut stud canary yellow diamond earrings, an all-white strapless dress, a faux mink, cropped jacket, and a note. The note read:

> *Dear my beautiful fiancée,*
> *I have mapped everything out for today. Wear this and go where Raye and Marcus take you. I know how hard you go for everyone and everything we do. Today is just about you. We will meet up later for some business. I love you always.*

That man was something else. I could use a day without that bitch Shereene on my mind. I was going hard on that ho and probably looking extra crazy. I took my shower, wondering what all he made Raye and Marcus do to accompany me that particular day. I dolled myself up for the first time since we'd been living on the run. It felt good just to get really cute, even if it was for nothing.

Raye was back at my door, ready to take me to wherever I was being taken. She escorted me to an SUV that was parked in front of the hotel. We were taken to a beauty salon named Precious Hair. There, they took care of my hair and makeup. Then I was taken to get my nails and feet done. By two o'clock, I was looking better than your favorite model. After Raye took me to do all these girly things, Marcus met us, and I switched vehicles. Marcus took me to a Masonry lodge. I was escorted into a waiting room area. No one was in there at first. Then, every minute, I received a knock on the door. My best friend, Jasmine, Isaziah's sisters, and two of my younger cousins popped up on me.

"What the hell are all of you doing here?" I was pleasantly surprised.

"Isaziah said you were out on vacation and you started tweaking out. He flew us in last night so we could be here with you. Help ease some of the stress, even if it's just for a brief moment." Jasmine wrapped her little, thick arms around me.

"Well, why are we in this room?" I let go of my best friend and tried to head to the door when my cousins, Tericka and Ericka, embraced me.

"Cuz, we missed you. You need to make some time to come back up top. You been missed. Especially by us."

"Aww, y'all know I'm coming to visit after I finish some things me and bae got going on. I may even move back. If I convince Isaziah to move out there."

I hadn't seen my two little cousins in possibly three years. Even though we talked or FaceTimed every day almost, life always got the best of me. I was always so close to my family. But the deeper Isaziah and I got into the streets, the less time I had to go back and forth to New York. It wasn't always like that. I used to go home for three weeks at a time after college just to have a taste of home every now and then. And I had been horrible about seeing or talking to family lately. I felt like shit about it before, but talking to them made it worse.

"Excuse me, everyone. We are ready for you. Nahima, let everyone go ahead first. There's someone who wants to see you," Marcus instructed as everyone walked out of the room.

After everyone was gone, my big brother walked in. "Patrick? The infamous PT, my big brother, came to see me?" I jumped into my brother's arms.

"Well, your fiancé called and filled me in on all the craziness, then told me how you been stuck in one spot and came up with this plan. I'll do anything to see my favorite sister."

"Nigga, I'm your only sister." I laughed out loud. "But I'm glad to see you. I love you so much!"

"I love you more, sis. Come on, I got you." PT took me by the hand, walking me toward the main guest hall.

When the doors opened for us, "Perfect" by Ed Sheeran and Beyoncé echoed through the speakers. Isaziah and our close family and friends were all around. Isaziah stood toward the end of the room in a crisp all-white tux. My brother interlocked his arm with mine, then smiled at me.

"What the hell is going on?"

"I always knew I would walk you down the aisle one day."

PT started guiding me down the aisle. The room was filled with white and gold decorations. White rose petals covered the aisle with a trail leading straight to Isaziah. It hit me as we walked toward him slowly that this nigga planned a wedding for us, literally in a day it seemed, without me knowing. I had no clue how that happened. But at that moment, it didn't matter. I realized that it was my wedding day.

Chapter 54

Isaziah

"Hey there, beautiful," I whispered as Nahima approached me at the end of the aisle. She looked so stunning. The white dress fit her body perfectly. The beautician had Nahima's hair curled and back to life.

"I'm going to get you. You do know that, right?" Nahima laughed while trying to dry her eyes slightly without messing up her makeup.

The minister came from around the corner toward us with his Bible in hand. "Isaziah, Nahima, such a beautiful couple. Who gives this beautiful bride away?"

"I do," PT responded.

"Patrick!" Nahima hugged her brother tightly, and I could hear her say to him, "I wish Mom were here for this."

"Me too. Now go get married." PT walked away with joyful tears in his eyes.

The minister did his thing, and the whole time, Nahima held on to my hands, both of us teary-eyed. It was a moment we had both waited for and deserved. The minister said his introduction, then allowed us to say our own vows. I was up all night trying to perfect what I was going to say, but being there at that moment, I went in from the heart.

"I will go first. I created this special day on a whim and a prayer. No matter what happens later tonight, tomorrow, three days from now, Lord willing a year from now, I will know that I was able to marry the most beautiful woman in the world. From her soul to her outer body, she is so beautiful. You not only complement me, but every day that we spend together you make me a better man. I couldn't continue going through anything without you legally as my wife. I vow to always protect, cherish, love, and elevate you forever. I promise to give you this good-ass dick—I mean, sex—every day, even on your pink sleep week." Everyone around started laughing with us.

"Nahima, when we first met in Times Square, I knew then that you were meant to be my wife. These past few years, you have brought me nothing but joy. I promise to always love, protect, honor, cherish, and so much more. You deserve the world. I know I may not be perfect, but I will do my best to make sure I do whatever it takes. There won't be no divorce. It will legit just be me and you, shawty, until God chooses to take me away from you. I love you so much. More than words can express. Thank you for choosing me to be your husband." I was a thug, you know, and thugs don't cry. But between the hell we'd been through the past few months, the thought of possibly losing her either in death or by a break-up, then being here holding her hand, seeing how beautiful she was, I couldn't control my own tears.

As I cried, Nahima grabbed my face, pulling it toward hers and landing a sloppy kiss on me. The minister then joked, "Nahima, we are waiting for you. We will get to that part in a second."

The crowd joined together in laughter at us, but it was a beautiful moment. Nahima looked around then back at me before she cleared her throat. If I wasn't a mess before, I knew hearing whatever she was going to say was going to make it worse.

"Hey, y'all," she started out. The crowd said "hey" back with chuckles in the midst. "So, first of all, it takes a man who truly loves you to put a wedding together in a day's time. Isaziah, you never cease to amaze me. When you came to meet my brother back in the day, I thought, he looks different. He's a little skinny, but he's a little cute. Why not? I thought we were going to be a little college fling. But I was so wrong. You became my amazing lover, my best friend, my boyfriend, the man in my life who I knew would love and hold on to me as I would do for him. I have never thought about being in love truly. I wasn't sure if I knew or understood what loved was, but you showed me. You have embraced every piece of me. Every day for me isn't great. My attitude sucks. When I'm pissed off, I don't want to cook. I can be a downright bitch and not care. But you never run. You learned how to handle the mood swings, the high days, and the low days without making me feel like shit. This had to be a lot to do, and I can't thank you enough for even giving me the chance to be a part of your world. I love you more than you know."

Nahima and I were back holding hands. It was time for the presentation of the rings. Her best friend, Jasmine, came up with the rings on a yellow and gold pillow. When she saw her wedding ring, Nahima almost passed out. I was able to find a 3.25 radiant-cut canary yellow diamond ring to match the studs I gave her with the dress. By the time the minister told me to kiss the bride, she was already in my arms.

Even though I wanted to do a whole reception, I had a meeting planned for us that would help put Nahima's anxiety about my big sister at ease a bit. Everyone, except her brother, Marcus, and my sisters, left to go to their hotels.

"Babe, we will finish celebrating later tonight. But first, we have some business to attend to."

"On my—I mean, on our—wedding day?" Nahima looked up at me with a smirk.

"I know, but it's a part of our wedding present. Your brother has been brought up to speed with everything. He's agreed to stick around so that he can help us."

"What's the move, big daddy?"

"We have a possible connection to Shereene. I met a guy the other day who used to work for Jay Boogie. However, she crossed him, and he wants her head on a platter supposedly. I picked the location, time, rules, and everything for the meeting. Everything we need is in the two SUVs parked out front. I say we change clothes and finish writing this chapter so us married folk can move on."

"I'm with it, babe. But just we're going?"

"No, everyone still in this room."

Nay walked back into the main hall with a Nike gym bag of clothes, black gloves, and ski masks. After we changed clothes, we headed to meet with Jay Boogie's ex-partner. He had two options: keep his word and give me insight on how to find Shereene, or try to play us and end up dead. After everyone changed their clothing, we said a prayer, and we all dipped out in the two SUVs that were parked out front waiting for us.

Shereene

The hour struck, and it was time to deal with the cop and find Rayshawn. Even though my mind was elsewhere, I still had one last thing to accomplish before setting fire to Nahima's body. I met up with Racoon and the other guys at the cop's house. All the lights were off in the house, so Racoon and I took the back. The rest of the guys were going to wait for our signal.

We noticed in the backyard a toolshed where music was playing softly enough for whoever was inside to hear, and there was a light flickering. Racoon and I decided to start there. Something in me told me that either the pig or Rayshawn was inside.

"Get the others to come here. We will go in after you, Racoon."

"Why me? You're supposed to be the leader, right?"

"This ain't the time for your shit. Just do as I say, goddamn!" I uttered with full attitude.

Everyone was in position just as we heard the music cut off.

"On the count of three. Everybody ready?" I whispered.

Everyone nodded in agreement. I counted up with my fingers. By the time I got to three, Racoon kicked the door open, only to find Officer Thompson standing in the middle of the floor, hands covered in blood. A body lay on the ground face down, and there was a chainsaw and a few nails on the ground adjacent to the body.

"Don't make any sudden moves or I will shoot you!" I shouted as my gun was aimed at his chest. Officer Thompson stood there like I was speaking French. I repeated myself one more time, but he still just stood there looking at me like a deer in headlights.

"Before you do anything, take this." Officer Thompson reached onto his tool table, grabbing an old-school recorder. "It has everything on there. You can take me down, but I don't have any more money. Please tell him that if I have more time . . ."

"Nigga, what the hell are you talking about? We want our brother who disappeared after you pulled him over!"

"That piece of shit? I killed him, then took the drugs and the little bit of money he had on him. Please listen. I needed to pay off some really bad people or they would kill me."

"Nah, you're gonna die right here. But first, what's on the recorder?"

"The recorder has my confession about all the money and things I have stolen from busts over the years, plus where your friend's body is located."

"Well, then, I hope you told your family goodbye." I nodded and we all let out four shots apiece. I watched Officer Thompson grab hold of his abdomen area, falling to his knees. With him bleeding out and howling a prayer as if it was going to save him, I let out one last shot toward his head, but I missed unfortunately. I was going to end his misery early, but considering everything that I had been through, that would have been too kind. I kicked him over, and he lay on his back, bleeding out.

The recorder was placed inside of a plastic bag I found in the drawer he pulled the recorder from. I provided instructions to everyone. We left his body there, and then Racoon took the recorder and parted ways with me.

Leaving Officer Thompson's home, my final destination was back to Jacksonville. That was where I started everything, and that was where I was going to finish it, once and for all.

Chapter 55

Nahima

I had no idea who we were going to meet, but Isaziah felt that he would be an asset. I had to trust my husband to lead us like I always had. We arrived at a parking lot where only one car was parked with their lights on. The parking lot was deserted, and I wondered how Isaziah found what seemed to be a truck rest area. Isaziah had Marcus flash his lights to make it known it was safe for him to approach the car.

The dark, medium-height figure walked slowly toward our car. I looked around and everyone had their guns on their laps, off of safety, waiting for anything to go left. Marcus rolled down the window and asked the mysterious figure if he was alone. When he replied he was as promised, he informed him to get in. Our backup was in another SUV on the other side of the parking lot, scoping for anything suspect. Isaziah received a green light, stating we were good to exit the parking lot, and we checked out the car to make sure he was alone. Using the flashlight on the phone, we looked inside and found nothing but clothes.

My brother, PT, took our new passenger in the last seat in the back to search him.

"He's clean. We're good," PT confirmed.

"Good. Well, now to our real destination." Isaziah looked back, holding my hand.

We drove back into the city, which took another thirty minutes. I was ready to get things over with for the night and finish celebrating my wedding the right way. Lots of dick and no guns. I wanted to have filthy, disgusting sex with my husband. To my surprise, we were back at the same bando where we held Asia.

"Is this the spot?" I asked, making sure I wasn't tripping.

"Yes. I already have your new people on payroll, in line for anything. Trust me, baby."

"Always. Let's get this over with."

We all jumped out of the SUVs, and PT led our mystery guy into the house. Once everyone was inside, we sat him in the same chair we tied Asia up to.

"Now we aren't going to do anything to you unless we are provoked. There's nothing to be afraid of. If you can prove yourself useful, we may be able to keep you around. Help you make some real money." Isaziah went on with his little speech, trying to keep the guy calm 'cause he seemed to be having second thoughts after seeing all of us huddled around and strapped up.

"Go ahead, tell us what you got for us." Isaziah stood beside me and waited for him to talk.

He leaned back in the chair, and then he let it all out. "My name is Dacario. I was working with Jay Boogie and his brother until Shereene convinced Jay Boogie that his brother was trying to overtake him and lied on that man. She had a plan to kill his brother and make it look like self-defense. I overheard her talking about it to a girl who looked like her."

"Go on," I said, waiting for something more intriguing.

"She had four people in with her on everything. Her, a girl name Asia I think, and a guy she kept calling daddy. Well, they all called him daddy, and there was one other girl. I don't recall if they said the other bitch's name though," Decario stated, looking at us.

I noticed that Nay was moving a little too much. She was very fidgety.

"Nay, what's wrong with you? Why you keep moving around like that?" I asked, turning to face her a little more.

"I don't know what you or he are talking about," Nay nervously spat out.

"No one said anything about him or what he said. I asked why the hell you so nervous and fidgety. You rocking back and forth like a crackhead waiting on their next fix."

"Nahima, what is wrong with you?" Isaziah asked me.

"Ask your sister. She's the one over there looking and acting weird." I refocused, but I could sense something was off. "Decario, can you tell us anything else about her plan or the people she was working with?"

"Not really. After Jay Boogie got killed and I saw how she was acting, I walked away. I wanted no part of the bullshit she was scheming up. Sometimes she would fuck in front of us and call out the name Isaziah while Jay Boogie and her did their thing. It was disturbing to say the least."

I was boggled. *Am I hearing everything correctly? What in the freaky fuck was going on?* I turned, looking at Isaziah and the rest of his siblings.

"Anyone care to help me make sense of what he's saying?" I asked as I looked around the room.

Boom! Boom! Two shots went off. We looked around and no one was hurt, but Nay stood there with her gun in hand smoking from the released shots.

"Damn, I thought I was good here." Decario tilted over and fell to the ground.

"Nay, what the fuck?" Isaziah shouted.

"He was talking too much. I had to. I had to. I promise I had to." Nay's hands were shaking, and she kept repeating that she had to over and over.

Raye took the gun from her hand, then went to hold Nay in her arms.

"Raye, let her go! He wasn't talking too much. He was telling the missing pieces to this story. You're going to finish telling it or you will end up like Asia." I moved Raye so I could be close to Nay.

"You heard Nahima. Tell us what you did and what you know. Now!" Isaziah shouted.

Nay fell back into a corner. Her anxiety was piercing through her body language. "Listen, I didn't think it would go this far. Shereene has been secretly in love with you since we were kids. I found out when I caught her recording you and Nahima fucking. She had some dirt on me from when I stole twenty thousand from you. She found our real father and brought him in. He said it was your fault we were left behind. I resented you for it, but I didn't know she was going to do all this. I promised Asia not to tell, and things went left. We both wanted out with Shereene, but it didn't work. I should've said something before. I'm sorry." Nay turned the gun on herself, shooting herself in the head with the barrel under her chin.

I tried to stop her before she pulled the trigger, but it happened so fast. I knew we could have avoided this. I just felt like there was so much more Nay knew and could tell. Her regret was what really killed her, but if we could've forgiven her, maybe I wouldn't have had her blood spattered over me.

Chapter 56

Shereene

I arrived back in Jacksonville around five in the morning. Since we hadn't done anything to our mother's home, I traveled there. I needed to rest and have a stable mind to construct the perfect plan. The house was so cold and empty. Within every hall was a memory. Looking at all the family pictures, I remembered when we had good times, more laughs than deaths. We had grown so much within these walls. But these walls also kept our secrets.

I went up the stairwell where all our bedrooms were. There it was, just how he left it all those years ago.

"Hey there, baby girl. Took you long enough," a deep male voice echoed from the shadows of the hall.

"Who is there?" I asked, walking slowly backward into the doorway of Isaziah's old room.

"Well, you didn't forget Daddy, did you? Not after you tried to leave me in that hellhole of a trap house."

"Hey, Daddy. I had no clue what happened. I promise it wasn't on purpose."

"Well, how do you fix it?" my stepfather said, stepping in front of me with his thick seven-inch dick in front of me in his hand.

"I promised to always please you." I dropped to my knees and tossed my shirt to the floor.

My mother had two marriages. The one to my biological father and one to my stepfather. When our biological father was gone, my mother met Franklin. For him to be knocking on the door of 60, he was still very handsome. When he came into our lives, I had to be about 6. My mother was pregnant with Isaziah right before she announced that they were married to Nay, myself, Raye, and our sister Jasmine. Jasmine was the only one of us who left Florida. We barely saw her after she moved away. She thought she was so much better than us, primarily me, because she had a better hair texture, and she stole my crush from me. I was happy she left.

As we got older, things between the two of them faded. He left us. That's when Isaziah stepped in. He took over the household and was the man in the house. That made me see him in a different way. Granted, we may have had half of the same blood, but it didn't make it bad that I fell in love with him. I fell in love with a boy who was a man long before he knew what it was to be a grown man. My stepfather came into play because I learned that he was left as a beneficiary on my mother's life insurance. I just couldn't let that happen. I tracked him down and sold him a bullshit-ass plan. This sweet pussy of mine sold the deal.

He knew I planned on killing my mother, and about the insurance policy. He didn't know that, at the time of his death, everything would then be split among all of her children and Nahima. The fewer people, the more money. So, everyone would have to go who I felt wasn't worth being here. My stepfather stood in front of me, waiting for me to take him into my mouth. I wanted to stab him right in his balls, but I had not one knife or blade on me.

"Come on, Daddy, teach me a lesson." I figured I'd get a nut and play out his fantasy one last time.

Franklin grabbed me by my throat, pushing my back against the wall. He pushed his dick inside of me, and I gasped in pure pleasure. It wasn't huge in length, but the thickness had a bitch shook. What I liked about fucking dear old stepdad was I could catch a fast nut and not even think twice because he was done right after. Six strokes in, I forced out an orgasm as he blasted his nut all over my thigh. Franklin lowered me onto the floor.

"See, you're such a good girl. Go run Daddy his shower. We'll talk about the mess you made and the money when I finish," Franklin instructed.

"Yes, sir."

I did as he desired, but I had a plan for him. It was so early I had to take the necessary precautions that wouldn't cause any scenes. Last thing I needed was the police showing up asking questions. When I had the water hot, I informed him it was ready and said I was going to make some coffee. As I heard him in the shower singing old-school Luther, I walked into the kitchen and quietly searched for anything that could be used as a weapon. All the appliances were put away and unplugged. By the time any electricity built up in the circuits, he would be out of the shower. That wouldn't work, so I needed another plan. I wanted to keep it as little bloody as possible.

"Think, Shereene. Think, bitch. Shit." I was ready to get him out of the way. I dragged things out with him for too long. I noticed the knives were still in their holder by the kitchen sink. I grabbed the eight-inch chef's knife. The water was turning off as I crept back up the stairs. I had no clue how this would play out. But I knew either way, I was coming out on top.

His wet footprints trailed into my mother's bedroom. He sat on her bed, towel wrapped around his waist. I knocked on the door, leaning on the left side of my body.

"You said you wanted to talk?" I asked in the most seductive, lighthearted tone I could think of.

"Yes, honey. Things seem to be a mess. Isaziah is very much alive and apparently has no clue about the will. I haven't been able to reach your other little sister, Nay. She and Asia were keeping me informed. Nay said you went crazy and started trying to kill everyone just for the hell of it. Want to explain what the hell you were thinking?" Franklin sounded disappointed in my way of handling things.

I slid the knife under my shirt and in the band of my Victoria's Secret Pink boy shorts. I had to make sure I didn't stab my ass cheeks while trying to hide everything discreetly. I made my way in front of him and down on my knees as if I was going to bless him with some fellatio. When Franklin lay back on the bed, that was my opportunity. I placed the tip of my lips on the head of his dick, and he was stretched out and ready.

"Go ahead, and Daddy will explain what we should do next," Franklin groaned.

"Yes, what shall we do, Daddy?" I eased my mouth a little wider, not to throw him off. Before Franklin could ease another word out, I slid the chef knife directly into his right ball sack slowly.

"Bitch, what the fuck!" he shouted as I inched the blade deeper into his balls.

"Daddy, you have helped me so much. But just like before, there is no need to be here. That's what you told my momma when you left us. This time, you won't be able to come back."

Yanking the blade from his balls, Franklin hollered for mercy. But the anguish, pain, and worry that flushed his face made it so much more enjoyable. With a smile on my face, I crawled on top of him. I took the chef's knife and carved the word "rapist" in his chest. In case his body was found, they would search for his possible victims, then who may have killed him.

"Daddy, you know what else gets me off? Shit like this!" With one slash, I slit his throat. As his blood trickled down his chest, I lay across him as his last few moments of life disappeared.

When he took his last breath, I got up and cleaned the excess blood off of the knife on his arm. I walked back downstairs to grab my purse so I could make the call to Isaziah.

The phone rang and went to voicemail at least three times. Even though I wanted an answer right then, patience is a virtue. I decided to take a smoke break and ease my mind. With the blunt in my mouth, I left the phone on the kitchen counter. It was about an hour later when I heard a notification go off simultaneously as my phone's ringtone went off.

It was a FaceTime call from Asia's number. "Hello?" I said with a twisted smile.

"Whatever sick game you're playing, it's ending today. We are all tired of you and all the toxicity you have brought in our lives."

"Nahima, I've been waiting on you or my handsome brother to get back to me. You should know where I am. Isaziah, I see you back there. Come meet me. I'll be home, like you wish our mother would be."

"You went inside our mother's house?" Isaziah seemed so upset. "Shereene, I promise you, the last time you will see me is when I'm strangling every piece of life out of you."

"I guess we will see if you can do that once we talk. Hurry up and get here. I miss you, brother." I hung up the phone and finished my blunt with a smile. I couldn't wait to see my Isaziah.

Chapter 57

Isaziah

I couldn't believe how calm Shereene was on the phone with us. I assumed she would have been a bit more hysterical, but she was in such a peace. Maybe it was an act. The nerve of her to even be inside of our mother's home after having her killed was downright disrespectful. We weren't off the phone with Shereene five minutes before I caught Nahima packing up the rest of our shit and doing a weapons check.

"Babe, what are you doing?" I asked, grabbing her from behind.

"Isaziah, we know where she is, and she won't be leaving anytime soon. We need to leave now. If she thinks we'll wait and come tomorrow or next week, it'll give us an advantage."

"Nahima, we get one shot at this."

"Exactly, one shot, babe. We are strong and our team is solid. We can do this. Get everyone up. It's time for us to go home." Nahima had a point. Our team was strong, and everyone would be needed to make this right.

"You think the new additions to the crew would want to tag along?" I figured since they'd been helpful these past two times, we could use them again.

"I'll make the call while you get everyone together." Nahima grabbed her phone and went to work as I did the same.

By three o'clock, we were all packed and ready to go. According to Nahima, Rog took care of everyone and made sure there were no trails or evidence left behind. By four thirty, we hit the highway back home. It was bittersweet. We were going home, but one more person in my family was going to die. It wasn't what I wanted, but by this time, there was no other way around it.

After a few quick stops for food and gas breaks, we hit Tampa late that evening. It was around ten that evening when we got there. The plan was for everyone to return to their apartments, make sure everything was the way they left it, and we would reconvene at midnight. A plan had to be formulated, and not knowing Shereene's current mental state could put us all at risk if we didn't prepare. Nahima and I got to our condo parking garage with Rog and his crew following behind us. We walked through the parking garage to the main elevators as Rog joked about us going to the strip club after we killed Shereene.

The light in the hallway to our floor was out, and we couldn't see a thing. "Everybody got their strap?" I asked, trying to catch everyone's voice as they responded.

"Our door is the sixth one to the left. Move quietly and quickly just in case," Nahima stated as she cocked her gun.

We reached our door, and it was locked. Thank goodness for that. I had Nahima use the flashlight on her phone so I could see the keyhole to let us inside. Our little home was just like we left it. Our lights turned on automatically when we walked inside.

"Shit, can't be too careful," Nahima said as she chuckled.

"You're absolutely right. Can't be too careful." Shereene emerged from the shadowed corner near our bedroom.

"How the hell did—"

"Did I get in, Nahima? You forgot all of us were given spare keys for emergencies," Shereene interrupted Nahima.

"Man, let's just shoot this bitch!" Rog shouted as he reached for his gun.

"If you kill me, my people won't know not to kill our other siblings." Shereene flashed her phone and winced at us.

"What the fuck do you want? Is everything you done worth it? Look at how many lives were lost in the process of your madness!"

"But I did it all for us! Isaziah, just listen to me. Nahima doesn't love you. If you were to die in these streets, do you think she'll be mourning for you like me? You did all of this the moment you decided to get serious, telling us you wanted to marry her before you proposed. I thought Momma dying would wake you up and make you leave her dusty ass."

"I'll show you dusty, bitch!" Nahima charged toward Shereene, but I was able to grab her by the waist to stop her.

"Nahima, until we know everyone is safe outside of these walls, we have to play her at her own game," I whispered in Nahima's ear.

Things were going to get messy before they got better. I let Nahima go and had her stand beside me. Hand in hand, I held on to my wife.

"Isaziah, let go of her hand right now!" Shereene shouted.

Even though I didn't want to let her go, I did, only to patronize Shereene for the moment, but when I noticed her reaching, I grabbed back hold of Nahima's hand.

"Isaziah, this is where you belong. Say goodbye." Shereene fired two shots at Nahima. I watched Nahima fall to the floor. My heart sank into the deep parts of my gut. Shereene had killed my wife. Shereene had killed or attempted to kill more people than I had all these years

I'd been on the streets. Rog was left with Nahima. That way she wouldn't be alone.

"Isaziah, come with me into the bedroom. The rest of you make sure her blood doesn't stain his floor." Shereene grabbed my arm and dragged me to the bedroom. I looked back, and Rog nodded at me.

I was completely at Shereene's mercy. It wasn't how things were supposed to go in our plan. Pitiful, I sat there, releasing every tear in my body.

"Oh, honey, don't cry. It's just us now. How it's supposed to be. Don't worry, I'll explain it all."

"Well, talk, because you killed my mother, Nay, and now Nahima! You better start making sense. And making sense now."

Shereene began tugging on my shirt, trying to bring me in closer to her, but I wanted nothing to do with her. The love of my life was dead, Shereene had lost her mind, and I wanted to strangle her but couldn't gather the strength to do so.

"Isaziah, the truth is, I needed to do all of this to make you see. You had to learn things the hard way. If I had just said it, you would not have believed me. Sometimes it takes extreme measures to make things understood."

"Well, I still don't understand."

"I love you, and not like family, but more than that. I have forever. I love you, Isaziah. We are meant to be. You're my soulmate. Don't you understand?"

"You sick as fuck! Do you hear what the fuck you just said?" I wanted to slap my sister. Shereene had truly lost every decent strand that made up her brain.

"No, I'm not! You sound like Momma when I told her! Isaziah, if you just kiss me, make love to me, you'll feel what I feel too."

"Fuck no!"

"Make love to me like you would Nahima, or I will have Raye and all our other siblings killed." Shereene held out her phone, unlocking it as if she was going to make a phone call.

"All right! All right! Just put the phone down." I agreed to do as she wanted, even with all the disgust in my body. Whatever it took to keep my family alive, I would do.

Nahima

I awoke on the floor, my chest hurting from the bullets that pierced my bulletproof vest. Isaziah thought Shereene would be at their mother's house waiting on us to pop up. I was sure that was her initial thought. But if someone is out to get you and can gain access to you by everyone knowing that they are siblings, it would be easy for her to get to us. I realized Shereene's focus wasn't on everyone. It was on me and Isaziah. After piecing together everything Nay told us before she shot herself, and everything that had transpired, I put a plan in motion just in case. On our last restroom stop, I took that as a chance to put the vest on. Rog and them were fully aware I had on a vest. Raye had the remainder of their siblings go to a hotel downtown until one of us called them to make sure things were good.

I figured if Shereene popped up at my house, I would be prepared. I knew she would attempt to kill me before she would harm Isaziah. Now Shereene was in my bedroom, begging her brother to fuck her, even when he said no. Little did she know, they were not in the bedroom alone.

"How the hell did you get here?" I heard Shereene yell.

I had Rog and the crew follow my lead. When I peeked into the room, Raye had Shereene in a chokehold she could not break from.

"Where should I take her?"

"Take her phone, Rog. Isaziah, take these. You get her hands, and I'll get her legs," I told Isaziah.

"I thought I lost you." His voice was weak and shaky.

"It's gonna take more than her to get rid of me." I winked at my husband as I finished tightening the zip ties.

"Isaziah, please don't let them harm me," Shereene pleaded.

Regardless of what she'd done, I understood that was still his sister. No matter what, he would still love her. With a kiss to my forehead, my husband whispered to me, "Do what is needed. I never want us to deal with her or any of this shit again."

"You got it, daddy," I responded right before he walked out of the bedroom, closing the door behind him.

Isaziah turned the volume up on our Bluetooth speaker where if the neighbors wanted to call about noise, they could.

"Look at that, it's just us. I know you been craving a good nut, so I thought I would help you out." I looked over at Rog. "Restrain her for me. This may be a little to kinky for her."

"What the hell you think you about to do? Isaziah! Isaziah!" Shereene shouted.

It made my day to see how scared Shereene was. I debated on how to start my process. I wanted to kill her slowly and as painfully as possible. Rog first shot Shereene up with a medicine that paralyzed her, but she would still be able to feel everything done to her.

"We're going to give it about five minutes to kick in. I think Raye should have the first go." I looked at Raye, and she was rolling up her sleeves, ready to get messy.

"Anything you say, sis." Raye smiled like she was the Kool-Aid Man.

We gave the medicine time to build up in her system. When we did a check to see what her body could do, Shereene was as stiff as a piece of cardboard.

"Now, sis, this won't hurt a bit. Well, maybe a little." Raye pulled out a cleaver. She started laughing like Harley Quinn when she was about to do something evil and badass. Shereene's shirt was lifted, and Raye yanked her boobs out of her bra. Titty by titty, Raye chopped Shereene's nipples off.

"Oh, don't shed a tear just yet. That was just the foreplay." I took the wooden handle from our pine-oak broom and shoved it in her pussy. "Oh no, don't try to run. I thought you liked it rough, bitch!"

I stroked the wooden handle inside of her deeper and deeper until I could see blood leaking from her vagina. Yanking the handle back out, I had Rog flip her body over.

"I know you probably like it from the back, too, huh, bitch?" I took the broom handle, no lubricant, and shoved it up her asshole. You could tell she wanted to scream or try to move, but the drugs wouldn't let her.

With the broom handle still in her ass, I straddled her from behind and leaned over, grabbing her neck.

"Now who's the last one laughing, stupid bitch? You will never hurt my husband or our family again. Burn in hell!" I took the cleaver and chopped down on her neck until her head was barely attached to her body.

Raye and I were covered in blood, but my sheets were full. Isaziah opened the door to check to see if we were done. He looked around the room and then came into my arms.

"I think we're going to need a new bed." He tried to make light of the situation.

"No, we can always find another house. We have an extra apartment, remember? And I know none of this was easy, but we will move forward every day, one second at a time."

"I love you."

"I love you more. Now let's go."

Rog was there to make sure Shereene's body was taken care of and not just found by anyone. We made a 911 call about someone breaking into my mother-in-law's house, only to find Isaziah's father Franklin's dead body there.

For months we were on the run, our lives and love tested. But here we stood with that book coming to an end, and we were still standing. I was still making love to my dope boy every night, and I was still the apple of his eye, running the streets of Tampa. I prayed soon we would add to our family a child of our own to take over what we built in our empire.

The End